From the reviews of *Clear*:

'Nicola Barker's linguistic exuberance got me hooked ... Like an angel dancing on the head of a pin, she takes a brief event in the crowded capital and uses it to whoop and whirl ... impressive, smart, funny, fast'   *Observer*

'Dazzling'   *The Times*

'A tour-de-force ... the writing is impeccable ... Nicola Barker has a way of making you think about things you thought you had shut the door on'   *Scotsman*

'Insanely inventive ... fired by a comic energy that dances on the edge of self-combustion. Barker knows how to manufacture an arresting image ... she is such a brilliant and original writer'   *Guardian*

'A hilarious mish-mash of urban stereotypes ... The prose is rhythmi▆▆▆▆▆ ▆ ▆ ▆ ▆ ▆▆▆   *Time Out*

'A sharp idea, carried off with great brightness and energy … It's the sort of book to take on holiday and down in one'   *Literary Review*

'In *Clear*, Barker's most purely enjoyable novel to date, the depths of everyday madness are dazzlingly illuminated'
                                                                              TLS

'Here is a highly intelligent writer. Here also is an undoubtedly innovative and talented one'   *Spectator*

'***** amazing'   *Heat*

'This novel is a box of magic'   *Sunday Herald*

BY THE SAME AUTHOR

Love Your Enemies
Reversed Forecast
Small Holdings
Heading Inland
Wide Open
Five Miles From Outer Hope
Behindlings

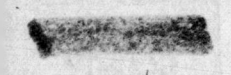

Clear

A Transparent Novel

NICOLA BARKER

HARPER PERENNIAL
London, New York, Toronto and Sydney

Harper Perennial
An imprint of HarperCollins*Publishers*
77–85 Fulham Palace Road
Hammersmith
London W6 8JB

www.harperperennial.co.uk

This edition published by Harper Perennial 2005

1

First published by Fourth Estate 2004

A catalogue record for this book
is available from the British Library

ISBN 0 00 719361 0

Set in Trump Mediaeval by
Palimpsest Book Production Limited, Polmont, Stirlingshire

Printed and bound in Great Britain by Clays Ltd, St Ives plc

For my Dad, Derek Royston Barker,
For Ben Thompson's Dad, the Right Revd Jim,
and for Tina Miller's Dad, Dick, who stood helplessly
by, as a boy, and watched an illusionist die.

One

I couldn't even begin to tell you why, exactly, but my head was suddenly buzzing with the opening few lines of Jack Schaefer's *Shane* (his 'Classic Novel of the American West'. Remember?). I was thinking how incredibly *precise* those first lines were, and yet how crazily effortless they seemed; Schaefer's style (his – *ahem* – 'voice'), so enviably understated, his artistic (if I may be so bold as to use this word, and so early in our acquaintance) 'vision' so totally (and I mean *totally*) unflinching.

'I have huge balls.'

That's what the text's shouting:

'I have *huge* balls, d'ya hear me? I have *huge* fucking *balls*, and I *love* them, and I have *nothing else* to prove here.'

The rest – as they say – is all gravy.

Because let's face it, when you've got balls that size, you automatically develop a strange kind of moral authority, a *gung-ho*-ness (for want of a better word), a special intellectual *certainty*, which is very, very seductive to all those tight-arsed and covetous Princess-Tiny-Meats out there (the Little-Balls, and the No-Balls – Good *God*, let's not forget about them, eh?).

I don't make the rules, okay? I'm just a dispassionate observer of the Human Animal. If you feel the urge to argue this point (you're at *perfect* liberty to do so), then why not write a detailed letter to Ms Germaine Greer? (That's it, love, you run off and fetch your nice, green biro ... *Yeah*. And I'm sure she'd just love to read it, once she's finally finished rimming that *gorgeous* teenager ...)

Schaefer (to get back to my point), as a *writer*, simply jumps, feet-first, straight into the guts of the thing.

If I might just ... *uh* ... quote something, to try and illustrate (and this is entirely from memory, so bear with me) ...

'*He rode into our Valley in the summer of '89. I was just a kid back then, barely as tall as our perimeter fence ...*'

Yes. So that's a really (*Ouch*, no ... I mean a *really*) rough approximation of the original (I can't find my copy. And don't sue me, Jack, if you're still alive and misquotation is the one thing that keeps you up at night. Or – worse still – if you're some crusty bastard working in the copyright department of some big-ass publishers in Swindon who just *loves* to get his rocks off prose-cuting over this kind of harmless, well-meaning shite: it's meant to be a *tribute* to the man, so will you maybe just cut me a little slack here?).

It's a *rough* approximation (as I believe I already empha-sised), but I'm sure you get the gist of the thing ...

Let's cut it right back to the bone then, shall we?

He. Yeah? The first word: He. That's *him*. That's *Shane*: The Man.

Just a single, short breath into the narrative, and already he's *here*. He's arrived. It's *Shane*. He's standing right in front of us: completely (quite *astonishingly*) dimensional.

And in the *second* breath? (If you can just *try* and suppress your excitement for a minute.) In that second breath he's . . . Oh. My. God. He's coming *even closer*.

WAH!

He's almost on top of you now (Smell the warm leather of his chaps – the sweat on his horse – the grease in his gun-holster).

Uh, let's rewind for a moment: the second word (*second* word, right?) is 'rode'. He rode . . . He *rode* . . . (just in case some of you weren't keeping up).

'He rode into our valley . . .'

He *rode* . . .

And there you have it. In just two, short, superficially insignificant words, A Hero Is Born.

God.

It's so fucking *humbling*.

Please (pretty please) don't let me harp on too long about all of this (because I will harp. Harping's my trademark) but what absolutely *immaculate* styling, eh?

(Give the man credit for it why don't you?

Schaefer?

Stand up and take a bow!

Schaefer . . ?

Wow. He's certainly getting *on* a little now, isn't he?

And . . . *uh* . . . he's kind of wobbly on his . . .

Whoops!

Can he . . ?

Would you mind . . ?

Oh.

Is that his *secretary*, just next to him there?

3

Could she maybe . . ? Yeah?

Well that's . . . that's *good*. Great . . . *Uh* . . .

Hup!

Wowsa.

Phew!

Steady. *Steady* . . .

Aw.

Just *look* at the old dog – *look* at him! – lapping it all up.

And the audience?

On their feet. Waving their *bic* lighters, singeing their thumbnails. Stamping their feet. In a state of complete bloody *ecstasy*, and all because of just *two simple words*. That's two. *Count* 'em.)

You can't learn that stuff. No way. It's *born* (I'm serious. I should know). And you can call me naive (if you like. I'm man enough to take it), but I'm not seeing Schaefer (in my mind's eye), his head tilted on one side, his mouth gently gaping, his pencil cocked, taking detailed notes on 'structure' or 'the use of metaphor' at some cruddy creative writing seminar in some embarrassing further education college in the American Mid-West circa 1947. (Fuck *off*!)

Because this is no-frills writing at its *very best*. This is 'am-it', 'lived-it' stuff. Shane (yeah, remember him? *He* . . ? He *rode*?) is the first person Schaefer mentions in the book; the first *syllable*, no less. And if I've got this right (and I'm fairly sure that I have . . . Okay, *bollocks*, I *know* I have), then he's also the last. He's the *last* syllable.

(Cue music for *The Twilight Zone*.)

It can't be an accident! It just *can't*.

The novel ends on his name (this time, though, Shane

is leaving, not arriving). The whole narrative essentially *resounds* to the rhythm of his name:

Shhhh-aaay-yne (Yeah. I think that works better phonetically, for some reason).

Please note – the secret poets among you, especially – that perfect *hush* in the first part of the word – *Shhhh*! Be *quiet*! Someone *important* owns this name! Pay attention! *Shhhh*!

(Okay, so maybe I'm starting to over-egg this thing a little.)

But the name definitely chimes. It's almost as though the book (that heavy weight in your left hand – the pages read – and no weight at *all* in your right, because it's over: the journey is travelled, it's done) is just this great, big, old grandfather clock, striking for all it's worth. This huge, sonorous bell:

'And he was *Shane*.'

(That's the last line.)

Boinggg!

I mean *Ka-fucking-Pow* or *what*?!

I'm actually laughing out loud. I swear to God (sad bastard? *Me*? Won't bother denying it). Because I am putty – literally *putty* – in Schaefer's hands. And I *love* his hands (Calm down. There's nothing even remotely unmanly about it). I just love this feeling. I do. To be manipulated, to be led, to be *played*, and so artfully. It's just . . . I'm just . . . I'm very, very happy to be a part of that process. Because you can't beat that sensation (so you might as well join it, eh?).

Bottom line: Schaefer's just *owning* that shit.
(Man, you've got to own your shit. *Fact*.)

So maybe I think about *Shane* a little too much, sometimes. And maybe I'm prone to overanalysing everything, but then 'life is in the details', as they say ('they' in this particular instance being the Special Features Writer in a copy of *Elle Decoration*, which I paged idly through at the Sexually Transmitted Diseases Clinic in Bow last Tuesday, who was holding forth – and so passionately – about leather-look wallpaper. It's the coming thing).

It was his first book, actually. *Shane*. It was Schaefer's first. I read his other big one – can't remember the title (*fuck* it. That's so . . . *uh* . .).

Company of Cowards!

Ting-ting!

Yeah. It just wasn't so good.

But then lightning rarely strikes, etc.

Hmmn.

Are you . .? Am *I* . .?

Let's press *rwnd* for a moment, shall we?

Slow it *right* down . . .

Then just . . . *uh* . . .

. . . *HOLD*!

Good.

Freeze it for a second...
Yes...
Uh...
Oh. *No*.
Okay...
Just a couple of frames more...
Just a couple...
STOP!!!
That's *it*!
That's *me*. I'm just...
I'm very *small* right now. Okay? Bottom left-hand side of the picture...
If you could maybe...?
Bingo!
So we're jumping around a little – the focus is all shot – the sound's terrible. But I think if you look closely you can just about see me, hanging around, unobtrusively, almost lost in the background...

I'm sitting, slightly hunched over (my habitual posture – I have a clinical condition known as 'Masturbator's Back'), my free hand jammed deep inside my trouser pocket and my headset blasting (ODB, *eff*-ing and blinding for all he's worth – which is quite a lot), and I'm thinking about *Shane* while I munch on my sandwich (it's lunchtime). I happen to be straddling this gonad-freezing marble wall by the mother of all rivers (No. *Not* the Nile. You want Agatha Christie? Then look under C).

The River Thames:
Tah-dah!
In all her sweet autumnal glory. Tower Bridge is quite literally towering behind me – her huge, turquoise ramparts (okay, so I'm no whizz on architecture) flying

7

out from between my two puny shoulder blades like a couple of crazy *bat*-wings (this image so very nearly works that I'm tempted to leave it in. Yes, it *is* a tad far-fetched – especially when you consider the angles and everything – but I think Jack would've approved. I think Jack would say, 'You're doin' real good work here, kid; but just remember the story. Keep your mind focused on the *narrative*, because that's what truly counts in this business. That's what really *matters* here.'

Is this guy some kind of *saint*, or what?).

We're in only the second week of Master Illusionist David Blaine's spectacular Public Starvation Pageant, *Above the Below* (so how the fuck does he go about translating *that* into plain English, without sounding a complete twat?).

It's day 8 or day 9 – I forget which (can't quite read it on that handy 44-day digital clock of his from where I'm currently sitting) – but it already feels like it's been going on for ever (we've had the golf balls, the eggs, the girls baring their breasts, we've had the paint gun, the fences raised, the security doubled and Shiraz Azam with his all-nite bhangra drum . . .).

Don't think (for a moment) that it's just some lucky accident that I'm perched here (right in the *hub*, you might say), because I work (as a clerical assistant, much against my will, my instinct, my inclinations) in the only building directly adjacent to this psychotic happening (you might've seen us – in all the design magazines – early last year): a huge, grey-green-glass Alessi milk-jug of a structure (a tipsy fat penguin): the Greater London Authority Building (we were the centre of the world till they went and built that stupid gherkin near Aldgate. Now we're just last night's chip paper. Modernity's like a badly trained dog: try and make it heel, even for a moment, and it turns and bites the hand that fed it. *Snap*).

I'm sitting a little way along from all of the kerfuffle. The press are still very much in attendance, having their field day, 'making' all their pictures, 'writing' all their commentaries (*uh*, is it just me, or don't they actually realise that this slightly chubby, very famous 30-year-old illusionist *isn't really going anywhere*? Don't panic, lads, you have about 36 more days to sort out your copy. Sit back, *relax*. Just do as the magician does).

It's a tragic fact, but Blaine is definitely bringing out the worst in we Brits. I don't know if this is what he wants (if it's all part of the buzz for this American Christo-like) or if it's what he expected, but he's headlining it in most of the tabloids today. They're calling him a fake, a cheat, a freak, a liar. They're up in bloody *arms*, basically. And it's a *moral* issue, apparently. Because it's in Very Bad Taste to starve yourself if you have the option not to – *yeah*, so why not go and tell all those fucked-up, deviant *Anorexics* that? – especially (*especially*) if you're calling it Art (and pocketing a – purely coincidental – 5 mill. pay-out).

Cynical? *Moi*?

Look, I'm just sitting on this damn wall and watching all the colour unfold around me. I don't quite know if I'm loving it or loathing it (you'll find me on the fence. I'm the kind of guy who used to actively enjoy leaning on his bike's crossbar as a kid). But who (*who*?) can deny that it's a big story? It's a big *setting* – I mean *Mary Mother of Jesus*, how the hell did the council give *permission* for all this crap? Right here, on their doorstep? In the middle of everything?

It's just a wild guess, but I'm definitely getting the impression that some poor bastard has currently got his nuts in a vice over this whole farrago.

'*Uh...*' he's stuttering, 'I thought it might attract the *tourists*, Mr Mayor. I thought it might be a nice ... an impressive *culmination* to some of the other cultural events we've been staging in the park throughout the summer. I mean the kids *loved* the visit from the local city-farm, didn't they? All the goats and *hens* and everything? And then there was that *cookery* demonstration in the striped marquee. That went swimmingly ...'

The cleaners (let's get down to brass tacks) are absolutely fucking *livid* (I'm not certain if they have the mayoral ear, but if they do, then that fall guy's nuts are definitely for the high jump).

I'm actually on nodding terms with Georgi (Gee-or-gi. Twenty-two. Toothless. Romanian. Angriest man in the world right now).

Georgi already deals with a lot of shit (he sells me dope, the occasional E), because the life of a cleaner on this part of the river is not an easy one. The whole area's paved – and enclosed – for one thing. And it's a huge tourist draw, a landmark (the whole world feels like it already owns this view, and in some ways – if affection begets possession – it does).

It needs to look good – at *all* times – and because of the tons of dodgy marble and smooth cement and dramatic architecture, any stray detritus just – kind of – *sits* there. It stands out. It looks *bad*. It needs to be dealt with, and quickly (So fuckin' jump to it, lad), else all we proud Londoners (okay I've lived here 10 years, so I think I qualify) start to look shoddy.

And we don't like that.

10

But with the advent of Blaine's box, things have started to go crazy. Is it Blaine himself? The excitement? The fury? The awe? Whatever the root cause, people suddenly seem to feel the powerful need to generate mess. It's Goo-ville. It's Crap-town. There's old fruit, rotten eggs (British poultry farmers are just *loving* this situation. Fuck Sky, man. We really need to start seeing the colour of *their* sponsorship money), and worst of all, there's the 'human' element.

Now don't get me (or Georgi) wrong: people have *always* pissed in corners (a bridge – any bridge – almost demands as much from any man with a working penis), but the way things are currently, it's like the embankment is a toilet and Blaine is just the scented rim-block dangling in his disposable plastic container from the bowl at the top. It's getting completely *degenerate*. People are shitting *everywhere*. Man, it's *Shit-o-fucking-rama* down here. Huge steaming *piles* of the stuff, in every alcove, every crevice, every corner. And then there's poor Georgi – with his broom, his weak hose, his little shovel – being expected to clean all this crap – *your* crap – up.

But here's the best part: He doesn't blame *you*.

Uh-uh.

Not at all.

He blames the hungry (and decidedly shitless) bugger in the *box*.

Blaine.

'Is *him*,' Georgi gesticulates irately towards the pallid New Yorker with his broom, 'tha' stupid, crazy, dirty-fucky-bastar' *Jew*.'

Yeah. So where the *hell* am I supposed to stash my sandwich wrapper?

I have an agenda. You really need to know that. I mean all this isn't just *arbitrary*.

Uh-*uh*.

I *have* an agenda.

So my dad's name – for the record (and this *is* pertinent; it's the *core* of the thing, the *nub*) – is Douglas Sinclair MacKenny, and all things being equal, he's a pretty run-of-the mill kind of guy. He enjoys gardening, *Inspector Morse*, steam trains and Rugby League. He's into trad-jazz, Michael Crichton, elasticated waists, Joanna Lumley and lychees. When he was nineteen years old he swam the English Channel. But he doesn't swim much any more.

He runs a sub-post office in north Herefordshire (where I was born, 28 long, hard years ago – not on the *counter*, obviously, let's not be *that* literal, eh? – his lone progeny: Adair Graham MacKenny). He's happily (well, within *reason*) married to my mum (Miriam), and he's fundamentally a very genial, affable, easy-going creature.

(*Fundamentally* – so he doesn't like black people or queers, but which underachieving 55-year-old, small-minded, Caucasian, Tory-voting cunt does? *Huh*? Name me one.)

Nothing bugs him (not even the long and inexorable queue of pensioners at closing). *Nothing* winds him up.

Well... *okay*, then. So there's this *one* thing... it's a really *tiny* thing... and it bugs him just a little.

Is that a fair representation?

No.

Fine. *Fine*. So this particular thing bugs him quite a lot.

He doesn't *like* it, see? It pees him off. It rings his bell. It pulls his chain. It sits – it *really* sits, and it presses, *hard* – on his buzzer.

This thing is (has always been/will always be) a source of unbelievable distress to him. It's a thing which he *loathes* / *fears* / *distrusts* more than any other. This thing (if you refer to it, idly) makes him clam-up, then blanch, then shake uncontrollably. He's virtually lethally-fucking-*allergic* to this thing.

Any guesses?

Wheat? Pigeons? Lichen? Jasper Carrott? Dahlias? Lambswool? Beer?

Nope.

Douglas Sinclair MacKenny hates – I said he *hates* – illusionists. And with a passion.

Let me tell you why.

Great Yarmouth. Nineteen fifty-nine. The height of the Summer Season. My dad, still then but a boy, is down on the beach with a large crowd of deliriously rambunctious, candy-floss-speeding, bucket-swinging, spade-waving, snotty-nosed comrades. He's clutching sixpence which his mother has just given him. He is planning to spend this money on – *deep* breath now, Dad, *deeeep* breath – a *Magic* Show!

The magician or 'illusionist' in question is no less (and no more) a man than 'The Great Carrazimo'. Carrazimo is (by all accounts) fairly competent at the magicianing thing. He does some nifty stuff with doves. He can pretend – very effectively – to chop off his thumb. He can throw his voice. He even (and Dad still doesn't know how) stole some little girl's *laugh*. Seriously. He nicked it (she was temporarily hoarse) and then found it again inside her sticky bag of Liquorice Allsorts.

This is all good stuff (I know you're thinking) so why the angst?

Here's why: at the end of his show, Carrazimo pulls a stunt which leaves everyone agog. He gets the kids to dig a hole – a deep hole – in the sand. He climbs into the hole. He then tells the kids to fill it up.

That's right. The Great Carrazimo is intending to get himself Buried 100 Per Cent Alive.

The kids – they aren't a bad bunch – are slightly nervous at the prospect. I mean it's been a good show. The little girl's laugh is back. The thumb's on. The doves are cooing. It's very nearly lunchtime.

But Carrazimo insists. It's the climax of his act.

The kids still aren't entirely convinced. 'And here's the thing,' one especially 'responsible' (read as: 'opportunistic') young 'un pipes up, 'if you don't come back, what's gonna happen to the rabbit and the doves and all the rest of your stuff?'

Carrazimo grins. 'If I don't come back,' he says, 'then you can divide it among you.'

Two seconds later, Carrazimo disappears under a hail of sand.

It takes about ten minutes to bury the illusionist completely. Douglas Sinclair MacKenny has played his part – has even taken the precaution of patting the sand neat and flat on top. He's concerned for the illusionist (yes he is), but he has one (very constant, very careful) eye already firmly affixed on the illusionist's grand collection of magic wands. There's a fat one (the very one he used to fix his thumb back on), and if the worst happens, Douglas Sinclair MacKenny is determined to have it.

When all the work is done, the kids sit down, en masse, and they wait.

And they wait.

Eventually (it's now half an hour past lunch), one of the mums happens along.

'What on earth are you all up to?' she asks.

'We're waiting for Carrazimo,' they respond.

'Well where *is* he?' she asks.

'In the sand,' the kids boom back.

Pause.

'So how long's he been under there?' she enquires.

'Thirty-seven bloody *minutes*,' Douglas Sinclair MacKenny yells furiously.

Another five minutes pass. By now quite a crowd has formed. One of the fathers has asked the kids to indicate *precisely* where the illusionist is buried. The kids are still quite cheerful at this stage (if getting a little hungry), and they happily mark out the spot.

The parents start to dig (the poignancy quotient of this scene is presumably dramatically heightened by the fact that all these men and women have borrowed their

15

kids' tiny shovels). The atmosphere is grave (on the surface, at least), but then – 32 seconds into the rescue operation – an unholy scrap breaks out.

It has finally dawned on the children that Carrazimo might not actually be returning to collect his stuff, and everybody wants first dibs on the things he's left behind. Douglas Sinclair MacKenny is – in his own mind at least – now first in line to get himself that fancy fat magician's wand. But two other boys – at least – have their greedy eyes glued on this exact-same prize.

There is a brief halt to the digging as the tragic magician's possessions are firmly removed from a host of small, grasping hands, and when the digging resumes, the children are duly frogmarched up the beach, on to the prom, and into the warm, distracting embrace of the funfair for 'a couple of rides'.

It isn't a long while after that Carrazimo's body is pulled from the sand. Yes. He'd performed this feat a hundred times before. But it'd rained at breakfast and the sand – for some reason – was just slightly wetter than it usually was in summer.

He'd drowned.

Douglas Sinclair MacKenny was scarred for ever. Not just by the death (although that took its toll – he was, after all, an accessory to the illusion), but by the fact that he was cruelly denied that most tantalising, powerful and *coveted* of items: the magician's fat wand. Carrazimo had *promised*, hadn't he? The perfidious, two-faced, double-crossing *liar*.

Hmmn. Think there might've been any *phallic* significance in all of that?

I know what you're thinking: it was all a very long time ago now (this illusionist stuff). And he's just my old *dad*, after all – I mean if he happens to see me more than twice in your average year – Christmas / birthday – he starts to think the worst.

Suspicious?

Suspicious?!

'Got dumped by your *lady* friend, did you, Adie?'

'Running a little short of money, eh?'

'Thrown in the towel at your job again, then?'

'Still living with that immigrant?'

'Got yourself the effing *clap*?'

'Finally planning to tell your poor mum and me that you take it up the *arse*, for *pleasure*? That you're a dirty (tick one or *all* of the below:) transexual/bisexual/pansexual/disgusting bloody *fag*?!'

(Look, for the *thousandth* time, Dad, I'm *not* a homosexual. It's just the way I wear my hair – I mean if TV's

Vernon Kay can do it *and* marry a beautiful woman *and* sustain a successful career . . .)

Jesus, that illusionist has got a lot to answer for.

And the fact is . . . (to get down to the facts again) . . . *Hmmn*, how to put this into actual *words*?

The *fact* is (to reiterate) that blood is marginally thinner than an iced vodka slammer (and not *half* so digestible) and I've been using . . .

No.

I've been employing . . .

No.

I've been deriving . . .

Score!

. . . *a* certain amount of . . .

Uh . . .

. . . real . . .

Scratch

. . . serious . . .

Scratch

. . . active . . . well, *pleasure*, in getting my own back. On magicians. *Per se*. And on *Blaine*, specifically.

And it isn't (no it *isn't*) just opportunism. It's so much more than that. It's a moral crusade. It's righting the wrong. It's fighting the good fight – *sniff!* – for my trusty old *dad*.

Ahhhh.

(NB. *Please* don't hate me, sensitive Girl Readers. Just try and understand – if you possibly *can* – that vengeance is never a pretty thing. But it still has to be done. I mean where would your girl-philosophy of 'kiss 'n make up' have left Shakespeare? Or *Scorsese*? Or Bridget fucking *Jones. Eh*?)

So I've been (*uh* . . . let's put it *this* way) purposefully (and cheerfully) *avenging* Douglas Sinclair MacKenny (and *myself*, I guess, on *him*, in some strange, messed-up angry-only-son kind of way) in the most uninhibitedly *primal* manner, by cunningly employing the boxed-up Illusionist as my . . .

Now *what's* the word I'm searching for here . . ?

'Pimp.'

Pardon me?

'Pimp.'

A woman – average height, average build, average looks – is suddenly standing before me, grimacing, clutching her forehead, and pushing a plastic bag brimming with Tupperware on to my lap.

Eh?

I refuse to take the bag, rapidly yanking my headphones from my ears. What *is* this?

'Pimp,' she repeats. 'You've been using that poor, starving *bastard* to pimp all the women around here.'

'That's ridiculous,' I say.

'*You're* ridiculous,' she says. Then she drops her Tupperware, groans, slithers down to the tiles, and lies slumped against the wall.

I jump down myself, alarmed. But before I can ask, she waves her hand dismissively, and murmurs,

'Migraine. Mild autumn. The *dust*.'

She's clutching her forehead with her other hand and rocking slightly. I give her the once-over. *Hmmn*. Strangely familiar. I've *definitely* seen her around. I gather up her Tupperware (about twenty small boxes, like the kind you can get at good Thai restaurants to take home your leftovers. Neat. Reusable. Microwave friendly) while I try to remember *where*, exactly . . .

Nope.

'Can I get you a glass of water, maybe?' I ask. 'I actually work in this building.' I point. She has her eyes shut. She is deathly pale.

'Did *you* ever get migraines?' she asks vengefully.

'No.'

'I thought as much.'

'I often get headaches, though,' I squeak, defensively, 'from the glare off my computer.'

She snorts.

I inspect my watch. Lunch is almost over.

'Is there anything I can do?' I ask.

She waves her hand again, 'I'm fine.'

I lean forward, preparing to put her bag down next to her (and then scarper).

'*Open me a box*!' she suddenly yells.

'Pardon?'

'A *box*.'

She lunges for the plastic bag. She grabs a box. She rips off the lid. Then she leans over (quite gracefully) and vomits straight into it. The vomit is thick and glutinous. Instead of detaching itself from her mouth and filling the box neatly, it stretches, in a silvery spider web, from her mouth to the Tupperware.

My God.

She spits and detaches it.

We both stare, blinking, into the container. She sniffs, matter of factly, then reaffixes the lid.

She hands the box back over.

'In the bag,' she orders, feeling around inside her pocket for a tissue. The puke still hangs in fangs down her chin.

A middle-aged man stops, proffering a handkerchief. The be-fanged one takes it.

'Thanks,' she mutters.

'Migraine,' I explain to the Samaritan.

'I know.' The man smiles and squats down in front of her.

'Is it a bad one, Aphra?' he asks.

Aphra?

'Pretty bad,' Aphra murmurs.

'I thought when I saw you leaving,' he says, 'that something was up.'

'The *dust*,' she says, and waves her hand regally towards the magician.

He nods.

I find myself taking a slow step back. I am thinking, 'This is great. They know each other. I'm off the hook. I'm *out* of here.'

The Samaritan turns and peers up at me, 'I work at the hospital,' he says (as if this might prove meaningful), 'Guys. I'm a porter there.'

'Ah.' I nod my head. I'm still holding the bag of Tupperware.

'You'll need to take her home,' he says. He turns to the woman. 'It's not too far, is it?' he asks.

She shakes her head, then winces.

'Shad,' she says, 'just straight down...'

She indicates beyond Blaine, beyond the bridge, to one of the best parts of town.

'Let's get her up,' the porter says.

We slowly manoeuvre her into a standing position (strike what I said before about 'average build'. This girl ain't exactly thistledown).

Once she's up, the porter moves her arm around my neck, and *my* free arm around her waist.

He steps back, appraising his work.

'Good,' he says, smiling. 'Now just take it *nice* and slow, yeah?'

Then he turns and addresses me, exclusively, 'When you get her in, close all the curtains, don't try and give her anything to eat or drink (well, maybe just pour her a glass of water), then gently lay her down and place a moist, *cold* flannel across her forehead . . .'

I scowl. I open my mouth. I close my mouth. I swallow. I adjust the Tupperware . . .

Aw, bollocks, man!

I fucking *nod*.

Pimp?

Pimp?!

Okay. *Okay*. So just *hold* your fire. I'm throwing down my weapon, *see*? And I'm coming out – *very* slowly – with my hands in the air.

I'm *co-operating*.

Now can we please, *please* just try to get this whole thing back into proportion? I mean come *on*. Don't take it all so seriously. This is fun. Just *fun*.

And *another* thing (while we're at it) let's bin *Above the Below* already (cheesy, cheesy, *cheesy*). I've got my own little carry-on a *much* better moniker. I'm calling it 'Above the *Pi*llow', and my current strike rate is five (*five!*) and counting (Yup. It's an Adair Graham MacKenny International Shag-a-thon down here, baby).

Maybe I exaggerate, slightly. Four. Well, three and a half (in one instance I didn't quite get to come. There's been a couple of 'hitches', in other words. But *heck*, who's complaining?). It's early doors (Day *Nine* for Christ-sake), and I'm still – a*hem* – 'feeling my way' – *insert Frankie Howerd-style exclamation of your choice* – around here.

There are several approaches (if you must know. And if you mustn't, then I'm still determined to tell you), but the important thing to bear in mind (morally – *urgh, yawn* – speaking) is that I'm happy – more than happy – to take each and every one of them:

Approach (A) The Girls who Love Blaine

There's nothing more attractive to a sensitive, beautiful, highly-strung girl (who still attends college, believes in Karma and dresses like Nelly Furtado) than an attractive (well, *quite* attractive – if I've cleaned my nails and applied my hair gel), sensitive, highly-strung boy who's ready, willing and *able* to empathise with them over the many complexities of Blaine's tragic predicament.

Girl steps back (temporarily overwhelmed) from the dramatic spectacle of the 'angelic' Blaine. She is shaking her head, bemusedly.

'I mean *why* would people want to throw eggs at him?' she asks poignantly. 'Haven't they got anything better to do? He's not *hurting* anyone, is he?'

Adair Graham MacKenny (doctor on call) shrugs his shoulders, resignedly, 'Nope. Only himself. And that's *absolutely* his prerogative, if you ask me.'

Girl turns to look at A. G. MacKenny, immediately digesting the fact that A. G. MacK. is (like her hero) dressed principally in black.

'Exactly.' She smiles, shyly. 'I mean I think people are threatened by him. By the *statement* he's making.'

A. G. MacK. nods, 'Yeah. And I definitely think people are *confused* by him, and that's half the trouble.'

Girl considers this for a moment, 'You're *right*,' she says, 'I think they are.'

'And sometimes,' A. G. MacK. continues (as if he'd only just thought of it), 'when people are *confused*, they lash out. They do stupid things.'

Girl turns, impressed, the dark pupils in her blue eyes dilating. 'That's sad, but it's so *true*.'

Insert invisible brackets here: I think I might want to make love with you – so long as I'm
(a) not on the rag;
(b) don't have a last-minute history essay to write on the Mau Mau for a bastard tutorial this afternoon and;
(c) my Halls of Residence/your London pad isn't/aren't too far from here.
Oh *yeah*.

Approach (B) The Girls who Hate Blaine

'What a *twat*. What a stupid, self-indulgent, idiotic fucking *twat*.'

A. G. MacK. (on hearing this seductive mating call), rips off his neat, black pullover to reveal his lairy Gunners colours underneath. He commences a conversation with a remarkably pretty – if slightly loopy – girl about the possibility that David Blaine's transparent box might actually be made of glucose (when he thinks nobody's looking, can't you *see* the bastard licking?), and puts forward the additional hypothesis that when the autumn weather *really* kicks in – when it *rains* – the box will gradually dissolve, and that attention-craving American fraud will take the *mother* of all tumbles.

Hah!

Approach (C) The Girls who Have Yet to Make Up their Minds

'I mean what's he *do* up there all day?'

'He pees his nappy, he fantasises about nachos, and he considers the various pros and cons of the British Licensing Laws.'

'*Really*?'

'Yes.'

(Slight pause as A. G. MacK. feels around keenly in his rucksack . . .)

'Fancy an Alco-pop?'

Approach (D) Blaine's Girlfriend

The unbelievably beautiful international model Manon Von Gerkan (hair like wheat. Eyes like forget-me-nots. Lips like a mudskipper – Oh *my*, she's *spectacular*) is reputedly in almost constant attendance (although I – for one – don't often have the privilege of seeing her because she tends to stay in the vicinity of the TV crews' caravans in the private car park, to the rear).

Now *think* about it. Her boyfriend is currently thirty-odd-feet up in the air living on a diet of Evian water.

I am down here.

Va-va-va-voooom!

So far (admittedly) we have only shared one conversation. I was standing directly behind her. She took a small step back (while adjusting her binoculars) and stood on my trainer. She turned round. Our eyes met.

'Sorry,' she said. 'Did I stand on your foot?' 'Yes,' I said, inspecting her indelible bootprint on my *incredibly* precious soft-shoe fabric, 'but don't worry. They're only my very favourite, pristine quality, two-year-old yellow leather plimsoles from YMC. It's *fine*, honestly.'

'Oh,' she said, then smiled and turned back round.

Plenty of room for optimism here, then, eh?

Eh?

Approximately twenty yards on and the tourists are *swarming*. There's a man demonstrating 'the world's smallest kite', there's the hot-dog seller, there's the T-shirts stall and the exotic South American who can effortlessly forge your name out of silver wire. An ice-cream van pulls into a small clearing. A jogger almost runs into him. *Bedlam*.

And swinging high above us – not a care in this world – that crazy Yank magician, smiling down benignly like this chaos has everything and yet *nothing* to do with him.

'*Pimp*.'

She mutters it again (Good *God* she's tenacious). My only compensation (and it's hardly much) is that she's plainly no happier with this arrangement than I am. I yank my headphones back over my ears, and in response, she shoves her sick-smeared hanky into the neat, front pocket of my beautiful, brand new Fendi shirt, and *snorts* (like a *pig*. I presume that's how she laughs).

Right. That's *it*. ODB again, and at full-bloody-*blast* this time. The Tupperware clatters in my 'free' hand as I grimly adjust the volume. A tug on the river sounds its horn, but I don't hear it. Aphra does. She glances, then winces.

I turn the head-set off again (*Aw*, come *on*!).

27

'My name's Adair,' I say, 'Adair Graham MacKenny. Most people call me Adie.'

No palpable response.

'Aphra, *eh*?' I continue, 'Like the seventeenth-century playwright and novelist, Aphra Behn?'

'*Who*?'

She peers up at me, scornfully, 'You honestly think I have the *energy* right now to *listen* to your shit, MacKenny?'

Oh. Right. Good. *Fine*.

Two

You know, I always *really* wanted to make a good film out of that book. *Shane*. You might almost say it's been a dream of mine. They made one in Hollywood, 1953 – starring Alan Ladd, and it was an absolute, fucking disaster. Got six (*six*!) Academy Award Nominations (Including Best Picture, Best Director – George Stevens – Best Screenplay). But how – *How*? – when it was so *bloody* mediocre?

Ladd was a blond for starters (Shane was dark, he was the 'dark stranger', with this huge scar on his cheek. Lean, hungry, like an uncoiled spring. Ladd? Chronically bloated – from what I can recall – and pretty much a *dwarf* off his horse).

Nobody takes it seriously now – I mean the book, as fiction. They *never* took the film seriously … although, having said that, when I looked it up in my flatmate Solomon's trusty *Virgin Film Guide* – 6th edition – the critic had given it a spanking *four* stars (yet then cheerfully starts off his critique with the words, 'Self-important, overly solemn, middlingly paced…' *Huh*?)

He also says – and this is interesting – that Paramount

wanted the film to work in their – then, brand new, state-of-the-art – wide screen cinemas, so they hacked the top and the bottom off Loyal Griggs' – the cinematographer's – visual compositions. The real irony is that Griggs was the only Academy Nomination on the film to actually follow through and *win* (is that messed-up, or what? Although I guess the studio had to do *something* to try to make the short-arse Ladd fill their screens up).

The world has moved on. No point in denying it. Schaefer was writing *Shane* around 1948, 1949, and I suppose there must've been a powerful sense (even then – this was post the first atomic bomb) in which he was already looking back (through Rose Tinteds) to a time when it wasn't entirely inconceivable that one man (one strong man) might've conclusively changed things (this is pre-Kennedy, so I guess there's still a teensy bit of remaining leeway on that particular score).

The world's certainly soured since. It's got bigger (they tell you it's getting smaller, but they're just full of bull. That's how they *control* you, see? Make you feel significant. Lull you into a false sense of security), it's also more complicated, more worn-out, more screwed-up.

And no single man – David Beckham, Justin-*sodding*-Timberlake, US Governor of California, Arnold-blooming-Schwarzenegger – is *ever* going to definitively resolve this one, almighty, dirty mother-*fucker* of an unholy mess we're in.

Uh-uh.

When we finally (*finally*) stop walking, we're still in a pretty-good part of town; the far-end of Shad Thames, beyond the cobbles and the Design Museum. She lives above a line of shops (a fancy supermarket, a dry-cleaners, a swanky film and video store), in a large, smart, modern block called The Square, although (call me a snob) we're not river-fronting it so much as river-*backing* it. Not a damn thing to look at (from her faux-warehouse windows) but the courtyard within – yeah, big *deal* – and the homes of the people *with* something to look at (so *that's* what they mean by aspirational living, *huh?*).

Aphra has practically given up the ghost by this stage. I'm virtually carrying her. She's groaning. She's dragging her feet. She's drooping her head.

'Can't *see* . . .', she keeps mumbling, '. . . the infernal *dot*.'

(She has a dot, a black dot, right in the middle of her field of vision. I believe this phenomenon is fairly common with certain, particularly malicious brands of migraine.)

I actually have to ransack her pockets to find her keys (**note**: *two* different brands of 'ribbed for her pleasure' condom, a parking ticket, a lip salve, a *gonk* on an elasticated string, *five* hair-bands, a plastic fork, a lavender sachet, some cinnamon gum), as she sits on the doorstep, head back, mouth open, legs akimbo. Passers-by – I'm certain – think I've plied her sedate lunchtime glass of Pinot Grigio with the date rape drug (but it's a good quality neighbourhood, so nobody actually bothers to make the time and the effort to stop and find out. *Bless* 'em).

We negotiate the courtyard, some stairs, then the lift (she's on the third floor), then an extremely long corridor, all without too much unnecessary drama. But when we finally make it to the flat itself (explain *this*, if you can) she keeps changing her mind about whether to go in or not (like it's actually the *wrong* flat). We struggle through the door, into the hallway. I turn on the light. She gasps. I turn it off. She blinks a few times. Then she says, 'No', or, 'Uh-*uh*' does a sharp about-turn and staggers outside again.

We briefly reassess ('This *is* your flat, isn't it? Number Twenty-seven? I mean the key opens the lock . . ?') and then we slowly re-enter (no light on this occasion) and then she pauses, blinks, turns, scarpers.

By the third attempt I'm starting to get a little narky. 'This *is* your flat, Aphra?'

She nods an agonised *yes*. 'So can we actually go in and *stay* in this time?' She nods again, but seems profoundly brought down by the idea.

'It's not . . .' She shakes her head, confused. 'It's not *home*, see?'

She gazes up at me, poignantly, as if expecting some kind of profound emotional response on my part.

Uh . . .

Yeah, well, *whatever*.

It's not very big (the flat. My emotional response – I think we can pretty much take this as read – is not huge, either). There's a tiny hall, two bedrooms (one en-suite), a tiny kitchen, a cloakroom, a lounge.

I guide her into the main bedroom and sit her down on the bed. I go and close the curtains. I take off her shoes (fat square-toed, bottle-green slip-ons, with tall, wide heels and Prince-Charming buckles – *eh*?). And above? Lord have *mercy*! *Pop-socks*! To the knee (quite *nice* knees, actually).

'Lie down,' I say.

She lies down, groaning.

I go and find the kitchen. I dig out a salad bowl (for her to vomit in) and find a glass and fill it up for her.

I return to the bedroom. Aphra has (and I don't quite know how) carefully removed the bottom half of her clothing. Skirt, pants, etc. (all folded up neatly and placed on a chair by the bed). But she's left the pop-socks on, for some reason.

Nice touch.

Up top, she's still in her smart but unremarkable French Connection shirt and boxy, denim jacket.

She is asleep, her arms flung out (the two strange shoes I've just so painstakingly removed clutched lovingly – *protectively* – in each of her hands), her knees are pushed primly together, but the lower half of her legs (*wah*?) are at virtual right angles to each other (can that be *comfortable*? Is it even *possible* without detaching a ligament somewhere?).

She looks like an abandoned marionette – tossed down, off-kilter – or a B-movie actress in some tacky *film noir* who's been pushed from the top floor of a very tall tower block.

Splat!

Her skin shines bluely in the half-light. Her pubic bone (I sneak a closer look) is flattish. The hair is thick, tangled and dark. I put down the glass on her bedside table and place the bowl beside her, on the floor. Then I go into the en-suite and search for a flannel, but can't find one, so yank a huge wodge of toilet paper off the roll instead (folding it up, dampening it).

'Hello?'

A voice. A new voice. A *different* voice.

'Aphra?'

A woman's voice.

'Aphra?'

Uh . . .

I freeze, panicked (Now this – *this* – is definitely not good . . .)

I hear someone push open the bedroom door.

'Aphra? Good *Heavens*. Are you all right in there?'

Oh God. Oh *God*. Do I skulk in the bathroom? Try and sit it out? *Hide*? (If I pull the shower curtain over, I can crouch in the bath . . .)

No. *No*.

I casually pop my head round the door.

'Hello,' I say.

The new woman – a smarter, older, more traditionally 'attractive'-seeming version of Aphra, a sister, perhaps – gasps, does a sharp double take and then throws up her hand towards the light-switch.

'*Not* the light,' I exclaim (*sotto voce*). 'She's got a *migraine*.'

'Who the hell are you?' the woman whispers furiously back.

'Adair Graham MacKenny,' I say (and as I'm speaking I see her eyes drawn, ineluctably, to Aphra's naked pubic area).

'She undressed *herself*,' I say, 'while I was in the kitchen, fetching her a glass of water.'

I point to the glass of water by the bed.

The woman remains silent as she angrily appraises the seedy-seeming wodge of damp toilet tissue in my hand.

'She vomited earlier,' I continue, 'so I got her a bowl.'

I point again . . .

'And I couldn't find a flannel,' I stutter, holding up the toilet tissue.

Silence.

'The porter,' I stumble on, 'at the *hospital*, told me exactly what to do for her.'

Nothing.

I clear my throat, I inspect my watch. 'I really, really, really *must* return to work . . .' I announce (with just a tinge of regret), then tiptoe over to Aphra and gently place the wodge of tissue across her brow. She immediately tips her head, with a cattish *yowl*, and tosses it off.

At last the woman finds her voice, 'You're *scaring* me,' she announces (normal volume).

'Well you're scaring *me*,' I shoot back.

I take my mobile out of my pocket.

'This might all seem a little *strange*,' I say (a small laugh in my voice – not entirely successful – *wish to God I hadn't tried that* . . .), 'so I'm going to give you my *phone* number.' I hold up the phone (my technological talisman) as I march on past her and into the living room. I find a stray pen and a random pizza delivery service leaflet and scribble my number on to its corner. I tear it off and hand it to the woman, who, after a moment's delay, has followed me through.

'Adair,' I say, and point to myself (as if English is actually her second language). She doesn't do me the honour of repaying the compliment.

'*Very* nice to meet you,' I add, backing slowly off, 'I'm actually *very* relieved you turned up, because I didn't really want to *leave* her . . .' I pause, still backing. 'I mean . . .' I pause again. 'I mean . . . so terribly *ill* and everything.'

The woman slits her eyes. She utters a single, short,

sharp syllable (but it's certainly a choice one) –
   'Scram!'
   Okay. Yes. Good idea.
   I do my best to oblige her.

God.

There's one thing I'm certain of: Solomon Tuesday
Kwashi (pronounced Solo-mon, and don't you *dare* forget
it), my sarcastic Ghanaian flatmate (I call him my flatmate, but we basically share a house – *his* house – where
he pays the mortgage and I effectively squat) is going to
love this story. There's nothing he enjoys more than a
tragic tale of chronic, psychosexual trauma with 'The
Young Master' (*yup*, that's what he likes to call me; or
'Massa' when he's in an *especially* good humour) as its
pathetic butt.
   We've lived together (like two crabby old queens) in
his house on Cannon Street Road (just off Cable Street)

for eight long years (four-storey – *with* an attic – Georgian, all original features: those brilliant, butcher-shop-style rectangular white tiles in the utility rooms, the well-worn stone floors, the deep enamel kitchen sink with its thick wooden draining boards, the beautifully irregular handmade sash windows . . .).

It's a house deeply imbued with precisely that kind of 'effortlessly pared-down', 'homespun', 'artisan-style' ambience which all those pathetically desperate, head-scarf-wearing, cheesecake-eating, middle-class ponces in Bethnal Green and Whitechapel can only ever aspire to (and slaver over, and throw money at, and *still* come away wanting).

The bricks outside are stained black from a fire (years ago – possibly when the houses opposite were bombed out during the war, and where now there's just a tall wire fence, an expanse of municipal lawn and a block of flats), but the front door is immaculate (the palest pale yellow – with an astonishingly large, antique clenched-fist knocker) and the windows inside (curtainless, of *course*) are pristinely shuttered with a series of wonderfully faded, grey oak panels.

Mwah!

Solomon has an enviable eye (for *everything*, damn him: art, music, fiction, fashion, furniture). And he's rich. And he's handsome. And he's impossibly successful. But it wasn't always so.

(Don't think for a moment that he's one of your proud African princes who wears colourful dresses and a matching tasselled cap. Oh God *no*. Not he. Solomon has yanked himself up by the bootstraps from irredeemably common stock; his mother – I've met her – uses the hem of her skirt to blow her nose on, picks her

37

teeth with a kitchen knife, crosses her arms across her considerable girth, squeezes them – her face set into an expression of exquisite concentration – pushes out a fart, and then *sighs* her relief.

Solomon knows how to box, is a whizz in the kitchen, falls casually into peerless patois, broad cockney (at a push – although he prefers to flirt with perfect modulation), can fix an old Cortina, owns three killer Dobermans, sneers at 'ponces' and 'cunts' and affectation, is principled, has 'standards', lives by his own 'ethical guidelines' – and Christ knows they're strict ones. This man could've roomed with the late Ayatollah Khomeini and have found his morals 'unedifying'.

Clean? You're saying *clean*? Solomon polishes *underneath* his shoes. His toilet habits make the *Japanese* look sloppy).

We went to UCL together. I did Media Studies and English. Solomon did Philosophy. In truth, I couldn't ever have called us 'the best of mates' (we're chalk and cheese – he's *definitely* the chalk. And me? I'm generally served up – slightly above room temperature – on a greasy platter).

His attitude towards me has always been one of genial (nay sanguine) toleration (although he could teach Anna Wintour some lessons in *haughty*. Cutting? *Cutting*?! Like Jack the Ripper's *razor*).

I actually found this house (I *did*. That's my single claim to fame, and – I suspect – the only reason I'm still living here). I brought Solomon on board to remove the locks (he's got himself an O' Level in Breaking and Entering) and we started off as a couple of squatters hanging loose in the basement.

But Solomon 'worked out a deal' (of *course* he did) with an early bunch of contractors. Rented, invested, ducked and dived. Soon got his hands on the ground floor, the first floor, then the second and then the third. Journeyed from 'Social Outcast' to 'Pillar of the Community' (sits on the board of governors at a local school, has four children of various hues on a mentoring programme, fought tooth and *nail* for a new zebra crossing, founded a local 'living history' society to encourage racial integration among the bolshy cockney and Asian populations).

Meantime, I'm still quietly lodged in my original basement room, thinking about girls, playing on my XBOX, listening to Funkadelic; a tragic carbunkle hitched (like a bloated tick) on to the smooth heel of Solomon's relentlessly advancing, righteously ideological, all-conquering life-style.

I mean where's the guy find the *time*, *huh*?

Sometimes (if I'm lucky) he'll bring me out and parade me around when some of his *real* friends are visiting (artists, musicians, accountants, *decent* people) and he'll make me tell them the story of how I shagged a 55-year-old journalism lecturer for six months (to try and improve my grades at college), and then, when it came down to the crunch, she broke my heart and *failed* me (The bitch. And I shouldn't have failed. I was on track for a B. It was my *best* fucking subject. I just wanted the A so bad I could taste it – although, in retrospect, that was probably just the dusty residue of her lily of the valley talcum powder).

Yes that's – 'Ha ha *ha*. That's *very* funny . . . A splash more Johnny W., Martha? . . .'

So what does Solomon *do*, you're wondering. Good question, but not good enough (*Yeah*. Maybe you're

getting a little taste of how it is to be *me* now, *huh*?).
Because the only sensible question to ask in this situation is: 'What *doesn't* Solomon do?'

If you asked him directly he'd probably fob you off with a sarcastic aside about being 'a jobbing inkhorn'. His main gig (or one of them) is at *The Economist*, where he writes complicated stuff about Globalisation, world debt and branding.

Imagine how it *feels* (just for a moment, if you wouldn't mind) to actually be living with someone who read philosophy at university (the degree of choice for crackpots and losers), then graduates, then 'reads a lot', then 'takes an interest in stuff', then 'asserts himself', then 'meets a few people', then 'kicks around some ideas', then 'gets proactive', then 'discovers a niche', then 'earns some respect', then 'makes shitloads of money', then 'blows it', then 'earns some more', then 'has a blast', then . . .

How the hell did he *do* that? I mean I was right *here*. I stood idly by and watched (half an eye on the *Guardian* review of the new Coen Brothers project, fantasising about Rose MacGowan, casually mauling a Pop Tart).

How did he *do* that?

Jealous? *Jealous*?

Fucking *hell*! Wouldn't *you* be?

Solomon is the guy who the 'ideas people' in the advertising industry desperately want on board when they're sourcing a new product. He's the man who knows everything about 'the newest kind of beat', 'the nastiest type of drug', the 'most beezer vitamin', the 'top colour', the 'most innovative fabric'. He's the chap who gets invited to all the best parties but who is too fucking *cool* to ever turn up.

Solomon is the only man I've ever met who can wear

those ridiculously poncey Paul Smith shirts (the ones with the paisley and the frills and the photographic *flower* prints) and still ooze bucket-loads of raw machismo.

Solomon is best pals with Chris Ofili. Bjork thinks he's 'a hoot'. He stole (I repeat he *stole*) Lenny Kravitz's last-but-one girlfriend. He owns two early Jean-Michel Basquiats. He had a cameo in NYC art wunderkind Matthew Barney's *Cremaster 2* (or 3, or 4), where he appeared as a rampant black goat in a golden fleece and stilettos (*coated* in Vaseline).

And you know why? Because Solomon is an archetype. Solomon represents something. Solomon is the *Über*-man.

Solomon grew up – for a year – on the same estate as Goldie, and introduced him to his *dentist*. Solomon got a blow job he didn't really want off a female MP in the locker rooms of the House of Commons ('How could I refuse? It meant so *much* to her . . .'). Solomon told Puff Diddy that he should 'seek redemption through sport' (then Diddy promptly ran the New York marathon, for '*Charidy*').

Want me to go on?

Okay. Solomon met Madonna (yes, that's right) in a NYC bar, and she chatted him up and he turned her down ('Too *muscular*,' he sighs, 'that bitch really needs to soften up'). He told Robbie Williams to be 'more like Sinatra'. He predicted 'a major downturn in MacDonald's economic fortunes' – to the actual *month*, two years before.

Solomon had a *feud* with Palestinian intellectual Edward Said. Alicia Keys claimed he 'broke my damn heart'. He calls Mario Testino 'a sad, little turd'. The people who run *The Late Review* (BBC2, after *Newsnight*) consider him Public Enemy Number One after he casually accused them of 'espousing the worst kind of tokenism' (they asked him to appear, on-screen, to defend his position – of *course* they did – but he told them, 'I'd rather get Meera Syal to lick the cheese off my knob').

Yup.

Solomon's a radical. And he's vicious if he needs to be ('the world never changed yet,' he says, 'through somebody asking nicely'). He has a whole *bunch* of theories about how The Culture is only really interested in rewarding (and exploiting) black mediocrity. 'If they're afraid of UK Garage,' he says, 'then they *kill* UK Garage. Simple as that. Blow the black-on-black violence issues out of all proportion, shit-up the promoters, deny it the radio-play. Stop spinning the discs on Radio One by creating 1-Xtra (Black Music for Black People), aural apartheid, and only available on Digital, remember . . ?'

(Yeah. So *that's* why I catch him listening to it, and with such obvious *enjoyment*, all the livelong day, eh?)

'But then *here's* the master-stroke,' he continues, 'they take with one hand and then they *give* Britain's premier New Music Prize – the Mercury – to Miss Dynamite-*tee-hee*, with the other, as an almighty Garage *sop*, when the person who's innovating that year is The Streets, and he's dynam-*white*-tee-hee. Laugh, Adie? *Laugh*?! I've cum all over my fucking *joggers*.'

'But what about The Rasket?' I ask (and very genially – since Rasket, or Dizzee Rascal – the hottest, most mischievous and cacophonous 'urban-music' pup of this Fresh New Century – has just *won* himself the self-same prize – last *Tuesday*, man. I mean, what to *do* with an ideology of exclusion when the cherry on the cake has just been cordially awarded – *uh* – the cherry on the effing *cake*, so to speak?).

'A blip,' Solomon avers, mildly, then ponders for a moment, then sniffs, and then he's off again.

'This kid's eighteen years *old*,' he rants 'and he has a *history*, yeah? He's an innovator, a genius, and yet his own people *hate* him. They're full of *envy* . . .'

(Dizzee was stabbed, earlier this summer, somewhere in Ayia Napa.)

'And that's what *happens*,' he throws up his hands, 'when a racial group is denied *real* opportunity. Because when success involves cherry-picking, bet-hedging, compromise, pretence, a subtle diminution of creative *integrity*, then a culture – a *confused* culture – turns in on itself. Instead of celebrating its achievements, it hacks them down out of *jealousy*. And can you blame them, Adie? Can you *blame* them?'

'But I thought The Rasket *was* the real deal,' I mutter, confusedly.

'He is,' Solomon confirms. 'And they're making him safe. By sanctioning his brilliance they hope to defuse him. This time is *critical* for Dizzee, see? He needs to stand tall. He needs to be unbowed. He needs to grab the initiative, be irreverent, be young, and black and *fucking strong*.'

Uh. *Okay*, then.

Solomon listens (you're getting tired, *yeah*, me too, so let's try and wind this up now, shall we?) to Lee 'Scratch' Perry and Fela Kuti, Franco, Dancehall and R&B. He deejayed on a Pirate Jungle Station 'back in the day'.

Solomon is obsessed by black sci-fi. 'The black man,' he explains, 'can feel a deep and strangely comforting *resonance* between his own experiences of slavery and the experiences of the UFO abductee . . .'

Yeah. *Enough* already.

So I get to live rent-free in this joint. But just imagine sharing your TV *remote* with this guy.

Three

Oh *shit*.

Oh SHIT!

It's 2 a.m. I'm stewing in the bath having just briefly recounted – to a slightly-stoned Solomon – the perplexing tale of Aphra's pudenda, when it comes back to me in a flash – I suddenly *remember*.

I remember where I *saw* her. I actually *remember Aphra*!

Now hold on a second . . . *hold on* . . .

So it's a ludicrously huge bathroom (to set the scene), made up, in essence, of the entire attic area. There's a sloping roof, a wooden floor, a free-standing bath and a free-standing shower. Solomon is sitting in his favourite, ancient, red leather armchair, tapping his boot to the erratic beats of Wayne Shorter's post-bebop masterpiece, *Juju*, smoking weed, sipping Rooibos tea, encircled by Dobermans (I'm uncertain of the collective noun here – Dobermen? Dobermens? – but suffice to say, that there are three of these viciously angular, prick-eared bastards, which – in my humble opinion – is three too-damn-*many*. Especially when I'm in the buff and they haven't actually eaten since 8 a.m. yesterday).

Solomon is currently (but of course) holding royally forth on his current subject of choice: David Blaine (seems like this canny illusionist is cheerfully perching on the tip of everybody's tongue in this town right now).

'You honestly think Blaine wants to be *Christ*?' he asks, snorting derisively (in caustic response to something utterly uncontentious which I just idly tossed into the discussion-pot), 'but you're barking up the wrong tree *entirely*, Adie. Blaine doesn't want to be Christ, he wants to be *black*.'

'But what about . . ?'

'He wants to be a *brother*.' Solomon marches defiantly on, '*That's* why he invented "street magic", don't you see? He wants to be "down", yeah? He wants to be . . !' (Solomon performs a satirical hand gesture) 'where it's *at*. Most fundamentally,' he continues, 'he wants to be the stranger in the room, the "unknown quantity". He wants to be the mystery, the alien, the *refugee* . . . Because that's what blackness denotes in this country, *and* in America, for that matter . . .'

Even I (full as my mind is of Aphra, *and* Shorter's maddeningly persistent sax, which is rather like having an irate wasp lodged inside your alimentary canal) can't let this pass.

'Well I've rarely seen,' I state provocatively, 'so many people, from such diverse ethnic backgrounds, in such constant attendance at a single, live event, *ever*. (Even En Vogue at the Hammersmith Apollo, 1993.) 'And I think – by and large – that they've mostly come to show their support, not to mock or to denigrate. If *they* sense a fraud or a wannabe, then they're certainly not making any big *fuss* about it . . .'

Solomon waves me away. 'We natives *love* a spectacle,'

he opines grandly. 'We aren't threatened by the theatre of life. Or by the pain of it, either. We *embrace* all that. Only Whitey shies away from the essentials. Whitey needs to live in his box, see? To make his point – to feel secure – he builds his own prison. And he fashions it with such apparent *care*, such *deliberation* – so fucking *painstakingly* – but then he forgets to include the windows, he forgets to include the *doors*. He builds these constructs out of *fear*, Adie, and then tries to make everybody *else* live inside of them. We Melanic* Peoples are different. We build our palaces out of language and music, sex and chaos. These palaces have no ceilings and they have no walls. The White Man may've *caged* our bodies, ruined our economies and appropriated our *cultures*, but our souls remain unencumbered and our spirits, vibrant. More than almost anything, the White Man *loathes* vibrancy . . .'

'Guff,' I say, and fart in the water. A neat row of bubbles rises to the surface.

'Why so needlessly *oppositional*, Massa?' Solomon enquires tenderly. 'I mean why allow yourself to be *restricted* by that intellectually reductive configuration of either/or? It's so pale, so obvious, so horribly *predictable* . . .'

'Fuck *off*!' I glug (over a frantic Elvin Jones drum solo), then sink down even lower in the water and drape my face with a flannel.

Five seconds 'silence'.

*Sorry to interrupt Solomon's *flow* and everything, but when he uses the word 'Melanic' he's referring to the dark skin pigment, melanin, which is found in far greater proportions in those skins of a darker hue – now let's dive straight back in again, *eh*?

Solomon inhales on his spliff, then exhales, with a little cough.

I pull the facecloth off.

'I remembered,' I said, 'while you were talking just now, where it was that I saw Aphra before...'

'Aphra,' Solomon muses, '*Aphrah*. "Declare ye it not at Gath, Weep ye not at all; In the House of Aphrah, roll thyself in the dust."'

I sit up (the water sloshes), '*What*?!'

Solomon remains impassive, 'Micah, 1:10.'

'The *House* of Aphrah?'

He nods, 'In Hebrew, the House of Dust, no less.' (Does this dude have a well-manicured afro-cockney finger in *every* pie?)

He sips his tea. 'So where?' he asks.

I lie back down, musing, spreading the flannel across my chest. 'Remember Day Five or Six,' I say, 'when I met that angry girl with the miniskirt and the terrible hair?'

'No,' Solomon says.

'The girl,' I continue, 'with the corkscrew perm, who slipped on a stray tomato and nearly twisted her ankle?'

'*Ah*,' Solomon exhales.

'Monday night. About twelve o'clock. There's this nasty half-riot under way and we're *right* in the middle of it. The police have just turned up...'

'I remember.' Solomon sounds very bored.

'And I grab this girl and take her up the back exit...'

Solomon snorts.

'Of the *bridge*, you *twat*. The stairs out the back. And we got to that cosy little corner, halfway up...'

'Spare me the gory details,' Solomon groans.

'But that's the *point*,' I expostulate crossly. 'There *were*

48

none. Things were just starting to get nice and steamy, up against that wall – she had her tongue down my throat, I had my hands up her skirt . . . when suddenly the girl freezes on me.'

Solomon doesn't look nearly as astonished by this revelation as I think he perhaps should. 'Halitosis?' he ponders ruminatively.

I scowl.

'Faulty *technique*?'

'Thanks,' I deadpan.

'Someone's *coming*?' he finally offers (rather more helpfully), then ruins the effect by gently adding, 'Prematurely?'

'Yes,' I nod (pointedly ignoring the ejaculatory slur). 'Another woman. And instead of just walking by, like most people would, this other woman pauses and then whispers . . .'

I pause myself, as I recollect (*then* I digress), 'I mean *obviously* I have my back to her, and the girl has *hers* against the wall, so she can see her better. But we're in a clinch . . .'

Solomon slowly rotates his hand to move me on.

'But when she hears a *voice*,' I continue (ignoring him), 'she pulls away slightly, opens her eyes, and she sees this other girl. This woman. And this woman in standing there, smiling, like something from *Fatal Attraction* . . .'

'And she says?' (Solomon obviously finds the film reference a step too far.)

'And she taps me on the shoulder and she says, "*You*. In Bow. The VD Clinic. Six o'clock. Last Tuesday evening."'

Solomon snorts so hard that he spills ash on his trousers.

'*Fuck*,' he curses, and quickly taps it off.

'But that was *her*,' I say, 'that was *Aphra*. I turned round and I saw her, from the back, retreating. But it was definitely her. I remember her hair, and her shoes. These strange green *shoes*. The noise they made . . .'

Even Solomon is perplexed by this story. 'But why'd she want to do that?' he asks. 'Out of sheer mischief, you think?'

I scratch at my neck for a moment, saying nothing.

'I mean you said she had an axe to grind . . ,' Solomon continues musing. 'When she approached you today she called you a *whore* –'

'No,' I interrupt, 'she called me a *pimp*. Then she claimed that I was using Blaine to pimp *for* me . . ,' I pause. 'It was all a little confused, actually.'

'*Argh*, pure *semantics*,' he waves me away.

'Although I suppose,' I start off nervously, 'I mean, I suppose she *might've* said it because . . .'

I clear my throat, 'Because it was true.'

It takes Solomon a moment to catch up, but when he does, he starts, '*What?!* You got yourself cock rot, Massa?'

'Leave *off*! I had an appointment. Amanda – three exes ago – got chlamydia. She said I needed to get a check-up. But I'm *clear*, thank you very much.'

Solomon's still perplexed. 'But how on earth did she *know*?'

As Solomon speaks, one of his three Dobermans stands up, stretches, sniffs the air, trots over to the bath, dips its head down and laps at my water.

'The million dollar question,' I say, trying to push the dog away with my toe. The dog lifts its head and growls at my foot.

Okay.

The foot rapidly retreats.

Solomon clicks his fingers and the dog, Jax (who completes the foul triumvirate with Bud and Ivor), trots mechanically back to his side again.

Man. How'd he *do* that?

'You think she's following you?' he asks, glancing towards the window (Solomon's had three girl stalkers in his time, one of whom subsequently had a successful career in children's TV presenting. *See!* Even his *freak*-followers are interesting).

'What else to think?' I say.

'You believe she actually *had* a migraine?' he asks.

I pause for a second, mouth slightly ajar –

Uh-oh –
Head-fuck time . . .

'She *didn't!*' Solomon jumps in, roaring with glee, slapping his thigh. 'She just Ian McEwaned you, *man*, and you're *still* none the wiser!'*

(He seems indecently delighted by this thought.)

But, fuck . . .

My mind is racing.

And the porter? Even the *porter*? Was *he . . .*?
Nah!

'No,' I say, 'I really think she was sick. I honestly do. She *seemed* sick. She *was* sick. She *smelled* sick.'

---

*I once loaned Solomon a copy of Ian McEwan's *The Comfort of Strangers* where a couple on holiday get drugged, tied up and tortured by an apparently genial pair of bogus holiday-makers. Solomon called the book, 'morally void. A pointlessly sadistic exercise in controlled, middle-class degeneracy.'

'But did you *like* it?' I asked.

I remember the smell. Like rotten milk mixed with cheap lager.

'And so you get her home, and she's *sick*, like you say. And then you leave the room, and she takes off her skirt . .'

Yeah. Solomon's recall seems disturbingly *on point* this evening.

'Then the sister comes home, or the *friend* . .' he chortles.

I sit up, panicked.

'*What?* You think they set me up? You think they're planning to *mess* with me in some legitimately fucked-up, McEwan-like way?'

'Blackmail,' Solomon sniggers, 'or *worse*.'

'I gave her my phone number . .'

Solomon throws up his hands, ecstatically. 'But of *course* you did, Massa. Of *course* you did.'

I stare at him, in silence, while the genius McCoy Tyner hammers away discordantly on his crazy, plinky-plonk piano.

'Karma.' Solomon grins, taking a last, long draw on his spliff and then leaning forward and proffering it to me. 'Pure, undiluted, *genius* karma.'

Wow. Thank God *that* album's over.

No matter what your views happen to be on the subject (love him or loathe him etc), there's still no escaping this one essential thing (no, I'm *not* evading the issue, because this *is* the issue, see?): it's like a bloody 24-hour *party* down here. And everyone's invited – the famous, the infamous, the rich, the poor, the pretty, the ugly, the lovers, the haters. *Everybody's* invited. Seriously. And everybody's equal; they simply wouldn't *dream* of turning you away. Because they want you, no matter what, to be a part of the spectacle.

It's an event. It's a happening. It's fluid – like an organism. It has integrity, it flows, it's vital and screwed up, and ridiculous and ongoing . . .

It's a pure, fucking *blast* (I mean let's just *shelve* the moral whys and the wherefores for one moment, shall we?), because *man*, what a backdrop! Tower Bridge! The Pool of London! I *know* I keep harping on about it, but it really *is* astonishing – like a picture postcard suddenly come to life. Almost as though (and, yes, hyperbole is my middle name, but a person *needs* to get excited about this shit sometimes, don't they?) something which was previously virtually *entombed* in its own history (and significance and tradition; conserved, mothballed, *mummified*) has suddenly been reinvested with this incredible *immediacy*.

The spectacle of Blaine (hanging there, quietly, on his workaday green crane) has made this bridge come alive again (*and* the water, even, damn him – although the water, in my opinion, was doing just fine on its own). Even the sunset. The fucking *sunset*. Even *that*.

This preposterous magician (Jesus Christ! How'd he *do* this trick?) has *reanimated the vista*.

Everybody's feeling it. The lovers are loving it. The angry people are getting angrier (I mean he's a foreigner, a fraud, an affront, a squatter, eh? How *dare* he take on this noble landmark – out of his depth? Out of his *depth*?! – and then casually twist it around him like it's his own private ampitheatre?).

Fact is, it almost seems like the quieter *he* gets, the more vibrant his surroundings grow. His weakness (his 'hunger') kind of *vivifies* the whole area.

Yup.

So where's this strange, new N-R-G coming from, exactly? Us? Him? Is it (God forgive me), could it possibly be: pure, undiluted, honest-to-goodness *charisma*?

Shhiiit!

Hat's *off* to the geezer, I say. Because I didn't think it could be done. No, *seriously* . . . I really didn't (I mean what is this now? Day 10?).

How'd he *do* it (any clues out there?)?

Number 1 (in my opinion): Passivity. The dude just *sits* (this part comes from him). Number 2:

Raw *emotion* (and this is *our* contribution). Love and hatred. Empathy and bile. Fury and benevolence (a great, uncontrollable fucking *wave* of reaction), and all – so far as I can tell – in fairly equal measure. The stuff of *life*, no less. The stuff of art and cinema and fiction. The stuff of all great narrative – comedy, horror, farce, tragedy . . .

It's the whole package (Blaine is merely the prompt, or the *twist* which makes the plot start moving).

And *we're* bringing it along. We're getting all Dickensian again, all Rabelaisian, all 'how's yer father'. We're reconnecting to a long social *history* of public *spite* (and – credit where credit's due – public adoration).

'Tonight, Matthew, I'm going to be . . .'

British. So fuck you, *right*?!

Jeez.

Let's get back to the vista, shall we?

Now *here's* the thing . . . (if you haven't come along yet, or if you're unfamiliar with these surroundings – *Unfamiliar*?! Where've you been *buried* all these years? – or if you're *still* not quite following). You know how it is, sometimes, when you see the most beautiful flower in the world – or girl, for that matter, or scene, or *view*, even – and you're so drawn to it – or her – that you feel this incredible urge to pull closer: you want to touch, lick, smell . . . But – as you'll invariably discover – the most beautiful is rarely the most aromatic, or the most smooth, or the most tasty, or the most *interesting*? Yeah? It's just the most beautiful. And that's simply that.

Uh . . .

Well *not any more.* No siree. *Not* here. This bridge is starting to twitch in its supports, whistle in its masonry and creak in its hinges. Like Frankenstein's Monster, it's starting to thud and gag and shudder and *breathe* again. It is! It *is*! I swear to God.

So let's give that hype-crazy, quick-fingered New Yorker his due: Blaine has altered the dynamic of this spot (don't know if he actually *meant* to; don't know if it'll last for ever – I seriously doubt it, somehow . .), and that's a kind of magic there's no palpable explanation for. You can't just hire the video and watch it all in slo-mo (look for the sleight of hand, the cut in the *flow*). Nope. You simply have to *be* there. It's subtle. It's perplexing. It's pretty fucking *intangible*. It's all (a-*hem*) in the 'atmosphere'.

(*Phew*. Why's my head suddenly filled with this over-powering vision of that smug SOB Solomon rubbing his hands together, rocking back on his heels and basically pissing his damn *pants* at my naive enthusiasm. *Huh*?)

Okay. Enough of the big spiel, the heavy sell . . . Let's get down to brass tacks. Let's hone in on the *mechanics* of the thing. Let's try to get to grips with all those deeply perplexing anthropological and behavioural *niceties*, yeah?
    Yeah?

The Insiders vs. The Outsiders

Right. Because of the way the fencing works, the actual crane (and the box – 7 feet by 7 feet by 3 feet, flying at a steady altitude of 30 feet – and the scaffolding 'tower' adjacent to the box – where they keep the magician's water – so that's the entire *site*, effectively) is cordoned off (it's a rough 50 yards in diameter, I'd say, although my spatial awareness is not all it might be), for security, partly, but also because they're filming the whole event – Blaine's 'great friend', the universally acknowledged nut-job/*enfant terrible* of the US film world, Harmony Korine (he of *Kids* fame, i.e. small group of spoilt, underage brats hang around taking drugs, being twats, having sex and basically setting the refined moral senses of the chattering classes on *both* sides of the Atlantic madly *twittering*), has landed the gig (Nepotism, you say? *Nepotism*?! But the guy's a *genius*, man. Didn't you *see Julien Donkey-Boy*?).

This means (inevitably) that to step inside the cordon is to voluntarily submit to the eye of the camera, which has – but of course – necessarily facilitated the gradual evolution of two main, basic 'types' in the DB watching arena; two very distinct 'divisions', you might almost say: the Insiders and the Outsiders.

(i) The Outsiders

Since they raised the fences (and increased the security – an average of eight men, now, most days, more, even, some especially rowdy Fridays and Saturdays) the distinction between the inner and the outer has become all the more apparent.

The Outsiders are extremely keen to maintain their veneer of indifference (are – by and large – what you might call exquisitely 'British' in their demeanour). They always stay firmly – *decidedly* – on the outer perimeter (wouldn't consider, for a moment, actually going *inside* the fence, proper – *What?!* – that'd be like...*uh*...tantamount to taking a carnation off a Moonie – maybe accepting their cordial invite round to 'afternoon tea'.)

The Outsiders often sit on the river wall, swinging their legs, having a quick fag, reading their papers. They might even – and this, I find, is *ultra*-duplicitious – turn their backs on Blaine and look the *other way*, towards the river – the Pool of London (*Yeah*. Maybe they'll raise the bridge soon...Is that an original nineteenth-century schooner...? Did you actually *see* the harbour master before, on his little blue and white boat down there...?).

They may possibly decide to take a dispassionate (nay, smirking) interest in the nutty-seeming banners bedecking the fences (the fan letters, posters and other detritus) while casually peeking up at Blaine, every few seconds (perhaps muttering angrily, or – you never know – *supportively*, under their breath), like suspicious badgers blinking up into the daylight from the dark and reassuringly musky confines of their underground lair.

Sometimes the Outsiders don't even stop at all. They walk by, but very slowly, as if out for a casual afternoon stroll (like the thought of actually *stopping* would be absolutely inconceivable to them.

Stop? *Me*?! And *here*? But *why*?).

There's a couple of wide, concrete steps up from the embankment, on to what's actually the 'park' proper (Potters Fields – a small, paltry assemblage of dusty grass and tired trees), where the perimeter fence duly kicks in. Climbing up the steps *definitely* denotes something. It's a little concession. And the concession is made out of either aggression (easier to yell – and throw – from this position) or a desire to announce that you're unintimidated by the event (I'm bloody *here* aren't I?!) even if you don't quite consider yourself a real Blaine-groupie.

Some Outsiders like to sit on these steps (mainly tramps and teenagers – once again with their backs to Blaine), like angry silverbacks in the jungle, asserting a strange mixture of (on the one hand) indifference/hostility or (on the other) intimacy/inclusion. If they've brought along a sleeping bag, or a bottle of wine, say (as they often do), then it's almost like they perceive their slightly-raised selves as *part* of the drama. This is *my* show now, see? This is *my* life. This is *me*.

(ia) Eating

Many Outsiders come to eat. It stops them from being bored, it gives them something to toss (or to *think* about tossing), it keeps their hands busy, and it's an *explicit* slight to the High and Hungry One. To come here and *eat* is the number one indicator of real hostility (they say the smell of fried onions from the vans has been driving the Illusionist almost wild with frustration).

It's a curious fact, but I often see packs of women in late middle age standing around and devouring fast food with a far greater sense of malicious *gusto* than almost anybody else from any other sex/age group (apart from the schoolboys – but then these testosterone-fuelled imps are a law unto themselves).

These aren't old slags – uh-*uh* – but polite-seeming women (Matrons. Mothers. *Grand*mothers). The sorts of people who would normally not even *dream* of consuming a hot dog (let alone in public, and from some shonky old *van*), but who come down here and queue and pay and and scoff with a real sense of vindictive *glee*. Stand and *eat* and smirk. ('Oh my *God*, Jemima! You've got an awful slick of chilli sauce on your pashmina. Lucky I've got a handy pack of Wet-Ones in my bag . . .')

'We are London's mothers,' their smug, munching faces seem to announce, 'and while our fundamental instincts are to provide and to nurture, in your particular case we simply don't *care*. You're a stranger. A *nothing*. We despise what you're doing, what you're attempting to do, what you represent. We despise your *Art*, your Magic, your deceit, your *pretension*. We despise what you *are*.'

I read (in some random newspaper article a while back) about how Blaine lost his own mother when he was 21. And I might be going out on a *limb*, here, but I can't help wondering whether this wholesale matronly rejection might not really *sting* that lonely magician a little (*some*where).

Well get *me*, coming over all empathetic, *eh*?!

(ib) The Bridge

The real troublemakers like to stand on the bridge. On the right-hand side (at the southern end of Tower Bridge) is one of the best views available (Blaine is at eye level, here, but about twenty-five yards away). This is the place where the crazy-angry types like to stand and aim their laser pens, or hurl their eggs and their other consumables (no chance of the beefed-up security wrangling you here   too many stairs, too many exits, and then there's always the opportunity to clamber into a waiting car and *scoot* etc.).

Their aim (like their fruit) is generally rotten. There's a spot down below on the embankment (not even in the *park*) where their missiles tend to land, and usually it's outside the cordon, slap-bang in the middle of the 'Outsider' contingent.

Egging their own people. But *still* they keep throwing – *Weird*, huh?

(ii) The Insiders

The Insiders must legally submit to being filmed (like I said before), both by the maverick Korine and by the TV people at Sky (who have a million dollar deal and access to Blaine 24 hours a day).

And you know what? The Insiders fucking *love* that shit. That's partly why they're here. They're dizzy, fuckin' extroverts. They just wanna come on down, pay homage, dance around, show off and be a part of the fiesta.

Yup.

They've brought along their knapsacks and their fold-up chairs, their phones and their cameras. They've brought along their binoculars, their banners and their bunches of flowers (the gerbera is currently the Number One flower of Insider choice. I can only guess that this is (a) because of their cheerfully lurid – almost fluorescent – colours, (b) because of the big flower-head, which means that when you poke them through the wire – to suspend them, *for* David – they stay in place more easily, and (c) because these people are so obvious, so benign, so *craven*, and the gerbera has exactly that classic child-drawing-a-picture-of-a-flower-style-quality – a visual *naïveté* – which these credulous folk – in my lofty opinion – would instinctively go for.

Aw.

Blaine – of course – shows a slight preference for the Insiders. These are the fans. These are 'his' people.

But he doesn't ignore the others. Already he has this dazed quality, this exhausted veneer, this kind of 'wandering focus'. He sees a new face in the crowd, and he smiles, and he weakly lifts his hand. If it's someone he knows, or a person of colour, or a beautiful woman, he might wave, then do a 'thumbs up', then the peace sign. It's got to the point now where he doesn't even think about it. It's totally automatic.

So who's conforming? *That's* what I can't help wondering. And who are the deviants? The Insiders or the Outsiders? Both? Or neither? Is it all just in the *context*? i.e. in the world, in general, the Insiders might be considered to be the erratic ones (the hippies, the Art-freaks, the slavish followers – take a straw poll right now, on any major UK high street and the vast majority will still say they think Blaine's a total madman, a troublemaker, an opportunist, a maniac), but when you're *here* (when you're breathing it), it's the Outsiders who come off seeming just that little bit buttoned-up (repressed, tight-arsed, *scared*). They've come to stand and to watch, but not to support. Not to commit. Not to take part. They're the ghosts at the feast (*Uh* . . . Or at the *starving*, so to speak).

Above and beyond everything, the Outsiders seem to feel this overwhelming terror at the prospect of being 'caught in a lie'. Or of being duped. Or diddled. Or bamboozled. (Blaine cut off his own *ear* in the pre-publicity for this stunt, didn't he – in front of dozens of reporters? And it was all just a trick, a joke. He rode on the top of the London Eye, pretending he was risking his life – just like he is now, apparently – but he was actually wearing a harness, all the while. In terms of inductive knowledge – i.e. basing your views on what's gone before – Blaine's looking like a pretty poor bet to all those cynical Outsiders down here.)

Seems like the need for real 'truth' (whatever *that* is, in the bleak-seeming aftermath of the Iraqi war) has – at some weird level – become almost a kind of modern mania. Perhaps without even realising, this loopy illusionist has tapped into something. Something big. A fury. A disillusionment. A *post*-disillusionment (almost). He personifies this sour mood, this sense of all-pervasive *bafflement*. And he's *American*. And what's even more perplexing is that he's starting – with the dark skin, the beard growth and everything – to look a tad, well, *like an Arab*.

He's the ally *and* the enemy (which, *either* way, symbolically, is pretty bad news for the guy).

So is this thing real?

Is it an illusion?

He *can't* lie, people are thinking, he's *transparent*. And he's *moving*. He's *there*. He's not a puppet, an imposter or a hologram. But how can we be sure? How can we possibly *believe* in a person whose very career (their wealth, their celebrity) is entirely based on casual deception? Even if we wanted to? Even if we *needed* to? How?

How?

The Haters

Now the way I'm seeing it, these certifiable anger-balls are standing *way* outside more than just *one* restrictive cordon. They're outside Blaine's world (that's for sure), and almost (I said *almost*) outside the world of social acceptability (alongside the truant, the graffiti artist, the petty-criminal and the football hooligan). They live *inside* a tabloid feeding frenzy, where everything's in bold and italics and capital letters –

FUUUUUCK! RUN, TONE. MATE! RUUUUN!!

They're that tiny, violent, whistling and juddering release button on society's pressure cooker. They're serving a function. They're expressing what Solomon might resignedly call 'the Dionysian'. And they are *plump* with rage. They are *bloated* with self-righteousness. They stand tall and replete, in a world *stuffed* to its well-fed *gills* with jealousy and distrust and hatred and terror.

(*Man*, we're living in the degenerate West – so where's all this shit even *coming* from?)

The Haters are standing outside a fair few circles, in other words, and inside a lot of others . . . But you know what? You know *what*? Wherever the hell it is they're currently situated, it seems pretty damn *crowded* in there.

So you'd better, *uh* . . .
Duck!

Wow.
Wow!

Damn good shot.

Four

I don't see her again for two whole days. Then I'm wandering out of the office, mid-morning, to buy myself a packet of Lockets (sore throat – too much cheap herb the night before) when I see her, sitting on one of the two benches (I didn't mention the benches yet, did I? Well they're situated at the base of the bridge, side-on to the embankment wall, slightly out of the way; and while the view of Blaine isn't all it *might* be from here – because of the angles, etc – he's still moderately visible from this particular corner).

She has her plastic bag with her, full of Tupperware (but of *course*), and she's wearing what appears to be a bleached-denim shirtwaister (which looks disturbingly like last season's *last* season Marks and Spencer), a neat, tiny, chiffon-style scarf at her throat, some round, pearly-grey Jackie O earrings . . . and her *shoes*? Platforms. Like the kind which almost did for Baby in *Spiceworld*. Grey suede. Square toed. With an obscene burgundy *flower* covering the buckle.

She has nice ankles, actually. But a thick midriff (too thick, if you ask me, for that pinched-in kind of frock). Skin slightly too pale for a brunette, but her arms are pretty. Plump but shapely. Hair looks good – short and shiny (smooth, in general, but enlivened by a good bit of modern chop at her nape).

A plain girl (no getting around it – eyes the shade of a city pigeon, haughty nose – sensitive nostrils – and a full lower lip, but a too-tiny upper one). Past her prime (must be thirty-two, at least – thirty-four?), but with an interesting kind of solidity, a creaminess, a half-absent quality (a washed-out, much-lived-in well-fedness that's strangely hard to resist . . . I mean, for a boy-*whore*, anyway).

So what do I do? Avoid? Approach? Mollify? *Threaten*? Be cute? Make a joke? Get sarcastic?

She's boredly reading an article from a broadsheet paper (just a page – and the article is folded over, as if it's been stored in somebody's pocket). I glance to her right. A man is sitting next to her, also in his thirties; square-set, ruddy-cheeked, chaotic-looking, with slightly-thinning, coarse-seeming, strawberry blond hair, wearing old combat trousers and an extremely ancient, well-ripped 'Punk's Not Dead' T-shirt underneath a *proper* shirt made out of musty-looking black moleskin.

Are they (by any chance) 'together'?

I walk straight over.

'Headache gone?' I ask.

Her eyes don't even flip up.

'*Migraine*,' she hisses.

'Migraine gone?' I ask.

'Uh-*huh*,' she says.

I begin to say something else (something *very* witty, in actual fact) and she raises a curt hand to silence me.

'*Reading*,' she barks.

The hand is held high, and then retained aloft, to stop me (I presume) from moving angrily off.

Punk's Not Dead sneers, superciliously.

'Punk *is* Dead,' I say, 'and that's *exactly* the reason why they designed that T-shirt.'

His superciliousness transmogrifies into pity, as he quietly surveys *my* immaculately well-thought-out look (60 per cent Marc Jacobs, 40 per cent Issey Miyake).

'*Nice*,' he eventually murmurs.

Oooh. *Cutting.*

Aphra finishes reading and glances up. She stares at me, blankly. 'So who the hell are *you*?' she asks.

'Adair MacKenny,' I stutter (falling – but only momentarily – a little off my stride). 'I kindly took you home when you were ill the other day,' I continue, in tones of determined affability, 'was *extremely* late back to work as a result, and subsequently received a rather nasty formal *reprimand* for my crimes.'

(So I exaggerate for effect sometimes.)

'Don't be ridiculous,' she says.

She passes the article back to Punk's Not.

'*Vicious*,' she murmurs.

'What is?' I ask.

'Article in the *Guardian*,' Punk's Not says, 'about Blaine.'

He proffers me the article. I take it and give it the once-over. 'Oh yes,' I say, recalling having read it a few days earlier (Wednesday? Thursday?), 'I remember this . . .'

In the article, a slightly sour pussy called Catherine Bennett holds scathingly forth about what a ridiculous *ass* the magician is, and how unspeakably *proud* she's been rendered by our unstoppable British urge to ridicule and debunk him – our cocky, cockney lawlessness, our innate willingness to lampoon and pillory.

Yip yip!

I mean, that's our Great *fookin'* British Democratic *right*, to rip the damn *piss*, *innit*?

Maybe Blaine (to paraphrase) might've got away with his pretentious pseudo-art rubbish in the US of A, but not *here*. Oh no. Not in good old Blighty, where we stands up proud and tall and we speaks our minds and we calls a spade a spade (then breaks it, in half, across our work-manlike knees).

'*Jew*-hater,' Punk's Not opines, taking the article back off me and folding it up, carefully.

'You think so?' I ask (neatly maintained brows trimming my beautiful fringe in a fetching display of polite middle class alarm).

'But of *course*,' Punk's Not scoffs, 'what else?'

I glance over briefly towards the Illusionist. He's got the little window in his box open (did I mention the window before? A tiny, hinged square, cut into the plastic, which he can easily unlatch if he feels the sudden, overwhelming urge to shout something down to his disciples below). He's currently up on his knees (looking unusually vital), gazing down and out of it at a small huddle of people in brightly coloured, semi-transparent costumes who suddenly strike up (gypsy-style) on five violins and play something cheerfully mundane, which would – by *any* kind of standard – render 'lift music' scintillating.

'Catherine Bennett . . ,' Punk's Not quips, 'if I'm not very much *mistaken*, being the famous heroine of Jane Austen's "Pride and *Prejudice*".'

(Note the dramatic emphasis.)

Man. This kid's *good*.

'But it's not Catherine, it's Elizabeth.'

Aphra – coincidentally – is paying no heed to our

literary jousting. She is standing up and staring – in sheer wonderment – at the musical Didakais. The magician (meanwhile) has collapsed back down (at the start of their second number) and is looking a little wan again (maybe the music's reminding him of all those lousy meals he's had in poor quality Spanish restaurants over the years).

'Same difference,' Punk's Not mutters furiously.

I suddenly realise that Aphra has adjusted her focus and that *I* am now the lone recipient of all her attention.

'I simply don't *remember*,' she says, inspecting my nose and cheek and lips as if I'm some kind of dated – and slightly distasteful – nude hung up in the National Gallery. 'What day was this, exactly?'

'Two days ago,' I say, 'Monday.'

She draws close to the back of my ear and gives a little *sniff*.

(What is this girl? A *collie*?!)

'I did have a migraine then,' she regretfully concedes, drawing back again.

'The *dust*,' I sigh, and wave my hand (the way I distinctly remember she'd waved hers).

'Yes,' she murmurs (not registering my satire), 'it certainly *has* been bad for this time of year.' She pauses, turns, and sits back down. 'So you took me home, you say?'

I nod.

'Did I *ask* you to?'

I shake my head. 'A porter from the hospital asked me,' I explain.

'Good *Lord*,' she expostulates, and then is silent for a while. Punk's Not and I appraise each other, blankly.

'Do you remember the *address*?' she suddenly asks, slitting her dirty pigeon eyes, suspiciously.

'The Square,' I say.

She grimaces.

'Which floor?'

'Third.'

'Which *number*?'

'Twenty-seven,' I say, 'or twenty-eight.'

She digests this information for a moment.

'And *then* what?' she asks.

'I took you inside, but you kept on walking out again. You kept saying, "This isn't *home*...".' I pause. 'It was actually rather irritating...'

'Oh *really*?'

'Yes.'

'And then what?'

I glance anxiously over towards Punk's Not.

'You honestly want me to go *into* all of this right now?'

She snorts, contemptuously, 'And why *wouldn't* I?'

I turn to Punk's Not and hold out my hand. 'I don't believe I got your name before,' I say (by way – *Aw*, *Bless* – of a gentlemanly distraction).

Punk's Not stares at my outstretched palm in open disgust.

Long pause (but still, I persist).

'Larry,' he says, finally.

'Larry?' I repeat.

'Yes,' he says.

'*Good*,' I say.

'*Tell* me,' Aphra butts in impatiently.

I clear my throat. 'Well...' I murmur.

'Cat got your *tongue*?' she enquires smartly.

'*Well*,' I continue (and you can Fuck *Right* Off), 'we got inside and I led you straight through to the bedroom...'

'How'd you even *know* where the bedroom was?' she asks haughtily.

'Instinct,' I respond, still more haughty.

She merely grunts.

'Then I removed your shoes...'

'Oh *really*?' she asks.

'Yes.'

'Which shoes?' she asks.

'Green shoes,' I say, 'with ridiculously huge buckles and ugly, square toes.'

As I finish speaking, she leans forward and quietly inspects *my* shoes (*the* trainer for summer 2003 – according to the Fashion Gestapo at *Arena Magazine* – the Adidas Indoor Super: red, white, blue, with oodles of beige suede trim, *totally* now, yet *totally* then).

She concludes her perusal and glances back up again with a small snort (*Hey*. I *remember* that snort – must be some kind of awful *trademark*).

'Craven,' she intones, darkly.

'Pardon?'

'And *needy*,' she continues smartly, 'you're just *so* incredibly needy, Adair *Graham* MacKenny.'

(Shit. This bitch has absolute recall...*Uh*. Or *does* she?)

Larry sticks both arms behind his head and lounges back on the bench, chuckling.

'Bull,' I say.

'Classic,' she sighs, 'neutral,' she adds, 'retro,' she concludes.

What. A. Cow.

Before I can offer any kind of formal defence for my Indoor Super (and God knows I could've, and it would've been stringent), she turns her lacerating tongue on Punk's Not.

'And *you*,' she says, 'with your *shite* Dr Martens. I mean, it's a new *millennium* now, so let's move *on* a little, shall we?'

I think it would be fair to say that Larry does not particularly relish this unprovoked sartorial dressing down.

'So I take off your *shoes*,' I boldly interject (yeah, wanna play by the Big Boy's rules, do we?), 'and I close the curtains. Then I go into the kitchen and I pour you a glass of water. I find you a bowl to be sick in . . .'

'Well *bully* for you,' she says, crossing her arms, yawning, and glancing back over towards Blaine and his didicoi army.

'And when I come back into the bedroom,' I continue (just a subtle *hint* of smugness in my tone), 'you've removed the bottom half of your clothing . . .' I pause, with relish. 'The pants, the skirt. And you're clutching your ugly, green shoes in each of your two hands, *naked* as the day.'

Larry's spirits (I think it would be fair to say) have suddenly revived. His hands are squeezing his knees and he's leaning forward.

'Naked?' he repeats.

'From the waist down,' say I.

'*Unbelievable*,' Aphra mutters.

'Then I go into the bathroom,' I continue, 'to try and find you a flannel, but there isn't one . . .'

'Flannels,' she harrumphs, '*disgust* me.'

'So I dampen some toilet roll, and then this strange woman comes in . . .'

'Oh my God,' Larry intones.

'A *woman*?' Aphra looks stunned.

'Yes,' I nod. 'I mean in retrospect, it *was* a little awkward . . .'

Aphra stands up.

'Gotta go,' she mutters, and simply walks off.

Bam.

I gaze at Larry. Larry gazes back at me. He shrugs, bemusedly. I glance down. She's left her bloody Tupperware.

'She's left her *bag*,' I tell him, and lean down to grab it.

Larry darts out a restraining hand. 'From the *waist* down?' he asks (hungry for confirmation).

'Yeah,' I say.

'*Hairy*?' he whispers (still holding on, defiantly).

'Let's put it this way,' I say. 'The closest *that* girl's ever got to a Brazilian is the time she did the tango with her salsa instructor.'

Larry releases my arm. I grab the bag. We do a spontaneous high five (*Yup*, that's boys for *ya*), then I dart off, into the crowds, and after her.

Can't find the girl. Not for love nor bloody money. Guess she must've turned a sharp left and headed up the stairs. The crowds are dense, and time is marching, so I head back to work, lugging the bag of Tupperware along with me.

No sooner have I stepped foot back indoors than I'm

caught up in the middle of an excited throng of staff in the foyer.

'Were you *outside*?' someone asks. 'Did you actually *see*?'

Uh?
Wha?!

I quickly make my way over to the window, as dumpy, ginger-haired Bly from Human Resources burns my ear.

'I mean it was all getting a little *frantic* for a while,' she says. 'I don't know if you noticed ...'

Frantic? *What*? The Gypsies? The *Lift* Music?

'There was a big *crowd* of them,' she continues, 'just making this *huge* racket ...'

There was?

'Right inside the *fences* and everything. And then suddenly this man is climbing the thingummy ...'

She points.

'*What*?' my jaw slackens. 'The *Support* Tower?'

'Yup.'

'You're *kidding* me?'

I glance out. I see two Z cars and a frantic cluster of security.

How'd I miss this shit, man?

(How? *How*?! I'll *tell* you how: fucking *Aphra*!)

'Nope.' Bly grimly shakes her head. 'This guy climbs the tower – and nobody's even really *trying* to stop him – and when he reaches the top, he's just standing there, not entirely sure what he's gonna do next. Pretty soon he starts screaming and shouting. Then he starts hurling all the bottles of water everywhere ...'

'I can't believe I missed this ...' I wail.

'Nor can I,' she murmurs, wide-eyed. 'It was pretty,

bloody *scary*.'

'Then what?' I turn back to appraise her. 'Did they get him?'

'Eventually, but it seemed to take hours to sort everything out. It was a really serious breach. A totally *calculated* attack.'

She shakes her head. 'I mean having a bit of fun is *one* thing, but this was just . . .'

She shrugs. 'Humiliating. I mean for *us*.'

Us?

'The British,' she continues (obviously spurred on by my blank expression), 'the *host* nation.'

I turn and gaze out through the window again, but my view of the Illusionist is compromised by a tree.

'And what was Blaine doing all the while?' I ask (thinking it best not to embroil myself in a dialogue about National Responsibility, etc.) 'Was he *shitting* himself or what?'

Her eyes widen. 'The guy started yanking on his *tubes*, you know? The ones for his urine and *uh* . . .' (she pulls exactly the kind of face you'd expect from any well-bred girl under the circumstances).

'Did they come loose?'

'Couldn't see. Maybe.'

'And Blaine?'

'He was standing up and kind of *watching*. But very calm. Unbelievably calm. Someone who was out there said he was just looking at the guy and smiling. The guy was going *potty*. Then Blaine waved at him. A friendly wave. Like he was totally unfazed by the whole situation.'

'Really?'

I hear my own voice, from the outside, and it sounds . . . well, *almost* disappointed.

'Yup. That's what they said. *Totally* unfazed.'

'And he just waved?'

'Yeah. The guy was psycho *before*, but the wave sent him *completely* loopy. He was just thrashing around, screaming, making a real tool out of himself. But Blaine was unflappable. The person who saw it all said he was very, *very* cool. He really handled himself. His behaviour was impeccable.'

She smiles up at me.

Uh. Hang on, now . . . *Is* that a smile?

(So why's this ridiculously amiable girl-pudding suddenly *smirking*? And why am *I* the clueless recipient of her unexpected bitcheroony?)

'Well that's great,' I mutter uneasily. 'I'm *pleased* for him.'

'*Good*,' she says (still the smirk. *Why* the smirk?), then she glances down. 'By the way,' she whispers, 'never really had *you* down as a Christian Radio kinda guy.'

She saunters off.

X-squeeze me?

I frown. I scratch my head. I look around. I pause. I glance down.

I slowly lift up Aphra's Tupperware bag to eye level.

Ah.

Yes. Ha *ha*.

Premier Christian Radio.

Very funny.

I mean is this girl determined to *massacre* my street credibility?

It was full – the Tupperware. It was actually full of *food* (no, not of the regurgitated variety. I checked). And because I'm obliged to slog my way through lunchtime (Yeah. *Big* surprise), I do the neighbourly thing and try to drop it off at her flat in The Square after work.

Major wash-out. Nobody answers the buzzer, and the porter's clocked off, *dammit*, so everything's firmly shutdown and locked up.

I cut my losses and drag the bag (turned neatly inside out – a boy has his pride, doesn't he?) all the way back home with me.

When Solomon comes in (with his current mainsqueeze; a fantastically ferocious, too-skinny, bespectacled, headscarf-wearing poetess called Jalisa – American, originally, but who currently 'brings rhyme' to the schoolkids of Bermondsey – *some*body has to, *eh*?) he finds me seated in a deep meditation at the kitchen table.

I am attempting to commune with the culinary Aphra. So who *she*?

Well, *you* tell *me* . . .

We have the *whitest*, moistest, de-boned, de-skinned, de-everything-ed steamed chicken (flavoured, Solomon later tells me, smacking his lips, joyously, with handfuls of fresh bay). We have an intense green mango and shallot salad, dripping in lemon and dotted in mustard seeds. The most *finely* chopped (this girl must have a *degree* in manual dexterity. . .*Ho-Ho*) coconut, cucumber and coriander concoction.

Then there's this – frankly, unbelievable – savoury dish made out of large, fat, fresh gooseberries, a series of chutneys, relishes and salsas – carrot and ginger, tomato and chilli – some tiny multicoloured worm-like slithers of grilled mixed peppers, *two* types of curry created principally out of mung beans, a side dish made from roasted yams, some fat, sloppy, deliciously *singed* tomatoes baked in spice, a huge *tub* of finely grated raw beetroot and lemon juice, another tub filled with the most *delicately* handmade filo triangles packed with spinach, onion and marinaded tofu. A quarter-portion of nut, seed and heavy-*heavy*-herb soda bread.

Then, the desserts: half an apple pie (which Solomon later informs me is made with quince, cinnamon, and sultanas dipped in rum), and a phenomenal rice pudding – cold, thick, imbued with nutmeg, coconut milk and crunchy cashew nuts fried dark brown in butter . . .

'Wha tha?' Solomon asks, pointing at the assortment of plastic bowls which lie colourfully arrayed on the table before me.

'Aphra,' I say.

He cocks his head, 'Oh yeah?'

He turns off the radio (Zane Lowe's Radio One show, featuring a Strokes interview, which I was actively enjoying) and bangs on a CD by the unbearably tedious tub-thumping mystic Nusrat Fateh Ali Khan instead. Once he's effortlessly dismantled my angry-pimple-ridden-street-kid-style ambience (you think this shit comes *easy* to a boy from north Herefordshire?), he approaches the table.

'*Hmmn*,' he hmmns, picking up one of the containers and sniffing at it, quizzically. 'Dusty girl she make picnic for we?'

I say nothing. He takes off his coat. Jalisa produces a bottle of wine and goes off to locate the corkscrew.

'How long you sit here?' Solomon enquires.

I check my watch.

'Hour,' I say (*Yeah*. Two can play at *that* game).

'So what've we got?' Jalisa asks, returning to the table with the wine and three glasses, setting them down, sitting down herself, pushing her spectacles back up her nose again and leaning greedily forward on her pointy elbows.

'Feast,' Solomon opines, removing a stray pistachio from one of the aromatic salads.

'*Stop* that,' I say, 'We *can't* eat. It's here for safe-keeping.'

'Pity,' Solomon opines.

I glance up, sharply. 'Why?'

'Because how better to get to the *heart* of this girl's messed-up, stalkerish, beaver-baring psychology than through the delicious repast she's prepared, *eh*?'

'Really?'

He nods.

I frown. 'But can't we do all that simply by *looking*?'

Solomon shakes his head. 'No *way*. That'd be like singing a song without knowing the melody.'

'Oh.'

My face drops, disconsolately.

Solomon sighs.

'Okay then,' I retract, 'just a tiny taste. A *tiny* taste.' (*God*, am I this boy's *patsy*, or what?)

Solomon pads off to grab a muddle of cutlery – we each select our weapon of choice – and he's just about to dive in (the yams. He *loves* yams), when I raise a warning hand . . .

'One possibility,' I murmur, 'worth bearing in mind, is that it was *no accident* she left this behind today.'

'*Huh*?'

'Spiked.'

'*Ouch*.'

Solomon withdraws, then he whistles, then he peers down, fondly. 'Bud will know,' he says, reaching out a tender hand to the savage beast's muzzle, 'he's a *ludicrously* fussy eater.'

'Talking of hunger,' Jalisa says, sipping on her wine as Solomon slowly waves tiny portions of Aphra's food in front of Bud's twitching snout, 'I heard someone attacked Blaine today.'

'They did, too,' I confirm, 'climbed right up the Support Tower. Pilfered his water. Tried to yank out his colostomy bag . . .'

'*Hard*core,' Jalisa whistles.

'I was *there*,' I continue excitedly, 'on site, when it happened, but I didn't actually *see* –'

'Ah,' Solomon solemnly interrupts me (Yeah. Try and

say *that* in a fast wind), 'blinded by the stench of pussy, were we?'

I accord this comment all the credit it deserves (none – the mixed-metaphor is a dubious device at the best of times. I mean blinded by a *stench*? I *ask* you) and from here on in I dutifully address all further conversational snippets to Jalisa, exclusively. 'I was having a chat with this fruit-loop – just a few minutes before the attack,' I say, 'who was labouring under the illusion that the whole anti-Blaine thing is actually a mask for widespread anti-*Jewish* feeling . . .'

'Anti-schmanti,' Solomon grumbles.

Jalisa grins. 'Poor Solomon's *worried*,' she goo-goos (almost tickling him under the chin). 'He guards his Social Oppression *jealously*, in case there isn't quite enough to go around . . .' (Solomon shows his irritation by clucking his tongue at Bud, whose nose – he suddenly decides – has drawn slightly too close to a tub).

'Anyhow, *Kafka* was a Jew,' Jalisa casually continues.

'Pardon?'

'Kafka,' she repeats (not a little patronisingly), '*Franz* Kafka. The writer. His short story, "A Hunger Artist", was the inspiration behind this entire thing.'

It *was*?

'You didn't know that?' she purrs, then tops up her wine, smugly.

'Isn't Kafka German?' I ask (struggling to disguise my furious bemusement – I mean I saw Orson Welles' cartoon version of *The Trial* when they played it on Channel 4, late-nite. Shouldn't that be *enough* for this harpy?).

She rolls her eyes, 'German *Jew*, dumbo.'

'He lived mainly in *Prague*, I believe,' Solomon boredly interrupts.

We both ignore him.

'And I don't know if you happened to catch his earlier TV shows,' Jalisa continues, warming to her theme, 'but the whole *Jewish* angle is definitely significant in Blaine's general psychology. He used to have this – frankly kinda *strange* – "radical-rabbi" look (was *well* into it: black clothes, black hat) . . . And when I saw him on the news the other week and they asked him how he was preparing for his ordeal, he said something like, "My biggest inspiration has been reading the work of Primo Levi. Those people went through *real* trials."'

She pauses. '*Those* people,' she explains, as if to a dim 4-year-old child, 'The victims of the *Holocaust* . . .'

She pauses again. 'The *Jews*?'

(Yeah. *Thanks*. Think we *just about* sorted that one out.)

Bud (as she rattles on) has given his seal of approval to at least 70 per cent of the dishes at the table (all credit to the animal and everything, but I've actually seen him devour other dogs' *shit* in the park, so forgive me if I don't consider fastidiousness his *watchword*). He tips his head (somewhat ironically) at the bowl of green mango. Solomon pushes it aside.

'You seem very well informed . . .' I fight back manfully (yes, I'm eaten up with rage – I mean overanalysing Blaine is *my* hobby, isn't it? How *dare* this haughty faux-African queen muscle in on it?). 'A big *magic* fan, are we?'

'*Her*?' Solomon sniggers. 'This is *Jalisa*, man. *She* only became interested in Blaine when he pulled his Art Trousers on.'

Art Trousers?

Art Trousers?

(So who exactly designs *those* unwieldy sounding garments?)

'Here's another irony,' Jalisa continues, pinning Solomon to his chair with a Death-Star smile. 'Harmony Korine is filming the video, yeah?'

I nod, smugly (now this I *do* know . . .). 'Talented director of the legendary *Julien Donkey-Boy* . .' I swank.

'Did you *see* it?' she asks.

Uh . . . (damn, damn, *damn* her).

I slowly shake my head.

'Well it's basically a film about family dysfunction,' she explains. 'The lead is this young kid – Julien – who's a little simple, I guess. But the star of the show is no less a man than Werner *Herzog* . .'

She pauses, as if waiting for the significance of this fact to utterly pole-axe me (I remain politely unpole-axed). 'The legendary German *film* director,' she clucks. '*You* know . . . *Nosferatu*, *Cobra Verde*, *Fitzcarraldo*?'

She quickly and efficiently tucks a stray frond of hair into her headscarf. 'I mean if you actually stop and *think* about it, there's quite a fascinating intellectual art-*link* here . .'

(My face – for your information – is a picture of total bewilderment at this point.)

She turns to Solomon, almost excitedly, 'Remember *Fitzcarraldo*?'

Solomon nods, boredly.

(Solomon remembers it? He *does*?)

She turns back to me again. 'Basically it's this wonderful story about a rich madman – played by the superlative German actor, Klaus Kinski – who has this crazy idea to build an opera house in the middle of the Amazonian rainforest. The film is about his futile attempt to fulfil his dream. The project turns into an absolute disaster when the river they're using to transport all their materials dries up (or *something* – I don't entirely remember the details) and they end up dragging this huge, *huge* boat, full of wood and building equipment, over a massive hill. People are crushed and killed. It's a total catastrophe . . .'

She pauses for a moment, thoughtfully. 'And when you're actually *watching* the film . . .' she eventually continues.

'Does it have subtitles?' I ask (she immediately delivers me the kind of look which could easily maim a small child).

'When you're actually *watching* the film,' she repeats, 'it's almost difficult to believe that the disaster isn't really *happening*, you know? It's kind of like the film itself is *part* of the catastrophe . . .'

She smiles (at her own genius, no doubt). 'And the fact is that it *was*. Herzog got a guy called Les Blank to make *Burden of Dreams* – which is a documentary – about the making of *Fitzcarraldo*, to illustrate this point. I mean Herzog's a kind of madman, too, just like his main character – he's *equally* obsessed. The entire project was wildly over budget, the locations were virtually unreachable, it was incredibly dangerous, and the whole production spiralled into terrible chaos . . .'

Out of the corner of my eye I see Solomon 'taste-testing' one of Aphra's prodigious gooseberries. He swallows and his face actually inverts (like Schwarzenegger's does at the end of *Total Recall*).

'Hang on.' Solomon finally gains control of his juiced-out tongue again. 'So *where's* the actual irony here?'

'I'm still working it out,' Jalisa snaps, 'if you'll just give me a *moment*. And anyway,' she continues, 'I didn't *say* it was ironic, I said that there were signs of some kind of interesting art *legacy*...'

(For your information – and so you don't need to back-track to figure out this girl's inherent *duplicity* – she *did* mention irony before...

What?

Bitter?

Me?)

'So?'

Solomon tears off a piece of herby soda bread, and dips it into a mung-bean curry.

'This is just high-spirited *speculation*,' she says, 'but the powerful parallel between Blaine's "stunts" and the sense of physical extremity in Herzog's cinematic oeuvre seems more than self-evident to *me*...'

As she talks she tucks into a mouthful of chicken.

'Nope.' Solomon is obdurate. 'I'm not linking the dots.'

'Well so far as I'm aware,' Jalisa continues doggedly, 'Herzog totally had Korine down – *Korine*, remember? Blaine's best mucker – as the man who was going to change the face of modern cinema (after *Gummo*, this was). He talked the big talk about him all over the media. He made his admiration for Korine widely known...'

She sucks up a thin slither of mixed pepper.

'So what does Korine *do*? How does he go about *thanking* him? He casts this eccentric German mono-maniac in the part of a monstrous, frustrated father figure in *his* film, thereby both celebrating *and* diminishing him. If you ever get to *see* the film,' she glances my way, witheringly, 'you'll almost be able to *taste* Herzog's fury and frustration, both at the role, and at the direction the film seems to be taking...'

'A dodo?' I ponder.

'Let's just say,' she grins, 'that it asks quite a *lot* of the viewer.' She shrugs. 'But then that's not necessarily any bad thing, huh?'

I commence scratching at my head like a wild dog with eczema.

'And the *Jewish* factor?' Solomon asks.

'I dunno.' She dips her fork a second time into the bowl of grilled mixed peppers. 'But it does seem *strange* that Korine symbolically belittles Herzog in the film, because – intellectually speaking – it's kind of like, "Kill the Father", if you know what I mean...'

(I don't.)

'... or in *this* case, "Kill the *German* Father", which resonates at an even deeper level, actually...'

'It's a *film*,' Solomon says, 'a fiction. The *meta* stuff's all just fanciful conjecture.'

'Don't be so fucking *pedantic*,' she growls, 'the performance art aspect is definitely important. *Fitz-carraldo* – Herzog's masterpiece (and remember, this was *pre*-Dogma) – was both fact *and* fiction. Blaine – via Korine – has used Kafka's story, a *fiction*, to underpin a *real* drama.'

'Do you provide study notes with this lecture?' I ask.

They both ignore me.

'I think you exaggerate Korine's influence,' Solomon growls (through a mouthful of the 'poisoned' mango).

Jalisa shakes her head. 'When Blaine and Korine first met,' she tells him, 'Blaine's desire to impress the film-maker was so intense that he spontaneously climbed into a pizza oven.'

'*What*?'

Now I'm agog.

She nods, scooping up some yams with her fingers. 'The old fashioned kind. The sort that takes hours to cool down. And apparently he remained in that oven for literally *hours*.' She grins. 'It was a total – what would you Brits call it? – *wank* off? I mean if you were *related* to either of these two men, you'd seriously really want to keep an entire continent between them. They're plainly a horrendously bad influence on each other.'

'It was probably just a trick or a scam on Blaine's part,' Solomon debunks her (through more herby bread filled with chicken and topped with chilli salsa). 'Either that, or part of some carefully constructed "imagined" history they've since invented, which cunningly serves to fire the so-called myth of their "partnership", in order that people like you – and simpletons like Adie – can jack-off all over it.'

(Oh. *Thanks*.)

'I certainly don't have Blaine down as an intellectual,' Jalisa says, 'or even as a radical. He's an entertainer, a performer. He's very commercial. Korine, on the other hand, is *totally* art-house. He's self-destructive. But he's extremely clever. This is basically an Art/Celebrity union of the highest order. It's a powerful partnership, but it's a destructive one. Korine's agenda – to his mind – is plainly better acted out on an international *tabloid* stage, rather than on merely an Art one. Art wasn't enough for him. And the mystery of *magic*, i.e. *bullshit*, was obviously wearing a little thin for Blaine. This recent stuff is a *real* challenge. A *real* mystery. But Korine's definitely the intellectual. He's definitely the spur . . .'

Solomon performs a – frankly offensive – wanking gesture with a triangle of filo in his hand.

'Korine had a long-term film project,' she calmly continues (while devouring yet *another* portion of the mung-bean curry), 'in which he walked around the streets of New York, provoking people of different racial and cultural backgrounds to get into physical fights with him. And he filmed each encounter.'

'Hang on,' I say. 'Now just *hang on* . . .'

'The guy has no sense of self-preservation,' she shrugs. 'He's chaotic. He does everything to excess. But even *he* had to rein in a little. I mean he's only small. He's quite puny. There's only so many Czechoslovakian bricklayers you can provoke into punching you in the larynx before things start to turn kinda *nasty*. So what does he do? He turns to Blaine. The Big Man.'

'How *convenient*,' Solomon intervenes, 'that the stooge was so accessible.'

'And so rich,' I say.

'All the "doing stunts" stuff definitely comes from Korine,' Jalisa fights on. '*Think* about it. The stunt is arbitrary. It's uncontrolled. Magic, as such, is about setting things up, about meticulous pre-planning in order to create the mere *appearance* of arbitrariness . . .'

'It's a fucking *love* affair,' Solomon trills.

'You could just be right there,' Jalisa smiles, 'and I certainly get the strong impression that when Blaine does these "stunts" of his – you know, standing on that ninety-foot pole, packing himself in ice, all the rest of it – he's completely neglecting to research into the likely consequences of the things he's doing. They represent a kind of leap into the darkness. A leap of *faith*.

But also an act of total *nihilism*. And that's Korine's influence. Blaine wants to impress Korine. He wants to *embrace Art*. I'm certain.'

She pauses. 'Is that dessert?' she asks, reaching for the apple and quince pie, and taking a big spoonful of it. 'I do think we're dealing with a generation of young Jewish men,' she muses, 'who are, at some very fundamental level, acting out the pain and the guilt they feel at perhaps not loving life *quite* as much as they think they should do after all the sacrifices made by those who went before them . . .' She gradually peters out. 'Or perhaps they're clinging on to the . . . the *drama* . .' (she's re-energised by another mouthful of pie), 'or to the sense of *belonging* . .' she swallows, 'or perhaps this is a fundamental *uncertainty* which they're now experiencing as a direct consequence of Israel's current belligerence which makes them feel this overwhelming *urge* to rediscover their victimhood. I mean, *'Don't let those damn Muslims take it away from us . .'*

She sighs. 'The end of the Millennium kind of drew a line under that jumble of feelings . . . and yet, somehow, paradoxically, it also brought them back, ever more acutely.'

Solomon merely snorts as he experiments with his second and third gooseberry. Jalisa starts counting things off on her fingers – *'First* there's all the Herzog stuff,' she says, 'which I think is terribly symbolic, and *then* the double irony of Blaine, in that tiny box – totally re-kindling all those images of Jews being shipped in those cramped railway carriages to the concentration camps, without food, you know? The sense of something unspeakable taking place, but in *public* – and finally, there's the fact of the "*Jew*", Blaine, being guarded as he starves in that box by his beautiful *German* girl-friend . . .'

Solomon chokes on his grated beetroot. '*Now* you go too far,' he almost bellows.

(*What*? The king of controversy, finally on the run? Arse-whipped by a *woman*?)

Jalisa doesn't turn a hair.

'Why?' she asks insouciantly. 'This is just *Art*, after all . . .'

I step in. 'Do you approve of what Blaine's doing?' I ask.

She rolls her eyes, boredly. 'It's not a *question* of liking or disliking,' she says. 'Good or bad. This kind of Art is like a Stop sign. You can either put on your brakes or decide to run through it. You don't get *angry* with the sign itself, or *love* the sign. That'd be kinda inappropriate.'

'So are Blaine and Korine *feeling* guilty or *representing* guilt?' Solomon asks.

'Both, of course,' Jalisa says pertly, helping herself to another chunk of pie.

'Well I suppose *you* should know,' Solomon smiles, icily.

'Pardon?'

Jalisa glances up.

'The *headscarf*.'

Solomon enunciates his words so cleanly I can almost hear them squeaking. A short, tight silence follows. Then Jalisa merely shrugs. 'You're *right*,' she says, 'perhaps that's just the culture we find ourselves in,' she takes a defiant swig of her wine, 'where looking back is, in a sense, our only real way of looking forward.'

She gently puts her glass down again. 'Everybody

90

nowadays feels this overwhelming urge to source the root of their own perceived oppression,' she says, 'victimhood is the new black, or green or whatever...'

Then she pauses, 'But fuck you, anyway.'

Solomon says nothing, but he's plainly utterly delighted by the impact he's had (am I just out of my depth here, or does this man have *no* idea how to secure himself a shag?).

Man . . .

You'd struggle to chip this atmosphere with an ice pick. I shift in my seat and look down at the table. It's then that I observe how almost *all* of Aphra's food has been casually ingested during the course of this 'discussion'. And none of it by *me*.

Jalisa suddenly gets up and stalks off to the bathroom. Solomon marches defiantly upstairs in the apparent pursuit of weed. I go to the fridge and grab myself a Coke (Nusrat Fateh howling away rhythmically in the background about the eternal love of bloody Allah – and only my heathen ears to hear him), when *bugger me* if I don't turn around at the critical moment to see those three evil curs forming a vile, black tripod across the table and decimating the paltry remainder of Aphra's fine repast. Bud even goes so far as to snatch a Tupperware container – holding the fragrant chicken – in his gnashing white teeth and carry it off.

You fancy getting that thing back off him? *Huh*?

Nope.

Me neither.

Five

'There's an apple pie in *Shane*, actually. The book. It features quite prominently in chapter 3. The narrator's mother – Marian – bakes this huge, succulent, deep-dish pie, in the pathetic hope (at *some* level) of impressing "the dark stranger", Shane, with it, but then she gets distracted and the pie burns and she goes absolutely loopy – in that fantastically "repressed housewife of the developing American West" sort of way.

It's a *classic* interlude . . .'

Aphra – who is currently holding my (recently re-discovered) copy of *Shane* in her hoity hand, having just that second dug it out of her (recently returned) Premier Christian Radio bag – gazes up at me, blankly.
Oh *dear*.

So it's the morning after the feast before and I'm just blathering on meaninglessly to a – frankly, strangely laid-back-seeming – Aphra as I struggle to explain *why* exactly I (or *not* I) demolished her succulent food-store.

'While I'm *incredibly* impressed by your literary critique,' she says (casually leaving the entire food-theft issue behind her – which I'm extremely grateful for), 'Westerns don't really ring my bell.'

She tries to pass the book back over to me.

'Don't judge a book by its cover,' I say, taking a step back and refusing – out of principle – to take it from her.

'I'm not a great *reader*,' she says, scowling.

'I'll bet you a fiver,' I say, 'that you won't be able to put it down after the first two chapters.'

She rolls her tired eyes (been working the hospital night shift, maybe? I mean this girl has 'nurse' written all over her. *Uh*. Except for the *feet* part, where today she's wearing the most alarmingly flirtatious pair of scarlet, patent-leather, pointy-toed, kitten-heeled creations I've ever beheld). 'You honestly think I'm gonna be fatally *seduced* by the story of a burnt *pie*?' she asks.

'The pie is *symbolic*,' I sniff.

She merely shrugs, shoves the book roughly back into her bag again (it's an *early edition*, for Heaven's Sake), and glances down along the embankment wall where – about ten feet away from us – two rookie coppers are lounging disconsolately.

'Looks like *somebody* took yesterday's attack seriously,' she observes.

'*Hmmn*. They certainly seem over the moon to be here,' I murmur.

It's a dull old autumn morning. Grey sky. Nippy wind.

'Been here long yourself?' I ask, shivering involuntarily, then sneezing, then yanking my short, beige, heavy canvas Boxfresh jacket even closer around me.

'Bless you,' she says (sidestepping my question with typical finesse), then casually adjusting the Tupperware bag in her hand, before pausing for a second to inspect the contents more closely.

'How hungry *were* you?' she asks, lifting out a badly mangled dish.

'The *dogs*,' I cringe. 'Sorry. We all got a little distracted after my flatmate and his girlfriend had this unholy *row* about Blaine . . .'

'Really?'

(Is that a *glimmer* of interest?)

'Yup.'

As I speak her bleary eyes settle quietly just above my left shoulder (it almost feels as if I have an extremely entertaining parrot crouching there). The magician (for it is he who crouches, not a bird) is still asleep (yeah, *not* crouching then, so scrap that), bundled up inside his bag – corpsing it – just a dark, slightly poignant, elongated blob.

'Remember what your friend Larry said yesterday?' I ask. 'About there being this whole, unspoken, anti-*semitic* agenda against Blaine?'

'Larry *who*?'

'Punk's Not Dead,' I say.

'Yes it *is*,' she snaps, then yawns again.

'Well anyway,' I continue (why's it always such a *battle* with this girl? Is it simply dispositional? Is it her? Is it *me*?), 'my flatmate's girlfriend, Jalisa . . .'

'Ja-*who*?'

'Lisa.'

'Oh.'

'. . . was saying how Blaine is actually very *into* all the Jewish stuff. She said this entire stunt had been devised as a consequence of Blaine's friend Harmony Korine – the film-maker . . .'

(Absolutely no sign of recognition at this name.)

'. . . having shown him a short story by the German-Jewish writer, Franz Kafka.'

'What's the story about?' she asks (moderately interested).

'Haven't read it yet . . .' I say.

'Ah.'

(The light inside her quietly switches off.)

'But from what I can tell . . .'

'He just moved his hand,' Aphra murmurs.

I blink.

'Pardon?'

'He moved his *hand*,' she says.

I turn around.

Yup. There's his hand. Out of the sleeping bag. Scratching weakly at his trademark mop of dark hair.

The hand disappears again. I turn back around.

'Gone,' she says, mournfully.

Her eyes return to my face for a moment. Sad eyes. Grey eyes.

Okay . . . (So I've temporarily run out of steam. I open my mouth to say something but nothing emerges. So I inhale, deeply, and close it again.)

'Were you clear?' she suddenly enquires.

'Pardon?'

'The *clinic*,' she says, 'were you clear?'

I frown, somewhat taken off my guard (Now this is a *whole* other can of worms . . .)

'Yes,' I finally mutter, 'I was, actually.'

'Good,' she says, her eyes sliding back over towards the Illusionist again.

'How did you know?' I ask (maybe a *touch* of aggression in my voice – which I try my best to temper on the grounds of our recent – and still potentially delicate – food-theft situation).

She just shrugs. 'An old friend of mine was temping there. I met her from work for a drink that night. I was with you in the waiting room . . .'

She smiles. '...And because I'd already had the benefit of observing your antics around *here*...'

She stops smiling.

'Two and two, et cetera,' she concludes.

I scratch my head. She looks down at her watch.

'Don't you have a *job* to go to?' she asks tartly. (Well that's a Summary Dismissal if ever I heard one.)

I half-turn but don't move. Instead I pretend to busy myself with methodically fastening my jacket (it has one of those magnificently chunky, 'work-wear', lumber-jack-style zips), then immediately *un*fasten it, then *re*fasten it, like a boy standing outside his school science lab, debating whether to head inside for a practical, or bolt off across the playing field and down into the ditch beyond where all the bad kids like to hang, during lessons, and sniff solvents, and make out, and share a smoke (or was that just *my* school? *My* science class? Was that just *me*?

Yeah?

So *fuck* the universal).

She straightens up and jumps down from the wall (plainly preparing to head off herself), and as she does, one of the security guards waves at her, jovially, from inside the fenced enclosure. She waves back.

'See you *later*,' she yells.

He nods, does the thumbs up.

(Great. *Another* rival.)

'Hey...' she suddenly murmurs (much softer, now, and in my direction).

I glance up, briefly, from my zippering hell (*man*, all that friction's starting to burn off my *thumb*nail).

'So next time you want a free feed, MacKenny...' She rattles her bag at me, smiling, rather tenderly...

(*Sweet Mary Mother of Jesus* – is she actually gonna ask me round for *dinner*?)

The smile suddenly drops. 'Why not bring your *own* fucking Tupperware, *eh*?'

Gets me *every* time, damn her.

But come *on*, the shoes were *hot*.

Back to last night:

'She can cook,' Jalisa informs me as she returns from the bathroom. 'God *knows* she can cook.'

(Solomon – too – is rendered virtually *rhapsodic* by some of the more 'esoteric' culinary productions.)

'I mean everything in tiny pieces and portions,' Jalisa murmurs, 'as if prepared for a sickly child or a fussy dowager . . .'

'Bizarrely *aromatic*,' Solomon announces, 'did you happen to notice that?'

Uh . . . I cock my head (I mean I didn't get to *eat* much yet, but smell . . ? Yeah. Maybe.)

'Low-fat,' Jalisa interjects, informatively.

'And succulent,' Solomon continues, 'if unbelievably *fussy* . . .'

'Yeast-free,' Jalisa raises her voice slightly (*Wow*. Think that crack about her headscarf might still be stinging her?).

'Yeast-fucking-*free*?' Solomon scoffs.

Jalisa stares at him, heavy-lidded (*Ay*. The hypnotic glare of the angry polecat).

'*And* gluten free,' she growls.

'What about the *bread*?' Solomon raises one sceptical brow.

'*Spelt* flour,' she hisses.

'And the filo *pastry*?'

Silence.

'So you basically think that this food is intended to appeal to someone sickly?' I jump in (before the actual *blows* commence – *Hmmn*. Is Aphra sick? She doesn't *look* sick . . .)

'Perhaps an allergy sufferer,' Jalisa ponders, 'or a *very* healthy hedonist . . .'

'Given that we're dealing with what could essentially be described as your basic south-east Indian cuisine here,' Solomon shrugs his ridiculously manly, steel-grey-lambswool, John Smedley-encased shoulders, 'by *your* estimation . . .' he delivers Jalisa a pitying look, 'the entire Indian sub-continent should be peopled by allergy sufferers.'

Jalisa stares at him for a while, her expression, quizzical. 'I'm not sure who built the *road*, Solomon,' she eventually murmurs, 'but you seem to be experiencing some kind of temporary *charm* bypass.'

(No comment is forthcoming from the guy wielding the tarmac.)

The overall impact of this scathing attack is marginally undermined by the fact that as soon as Jalisa finishes speaking she picks up a stray spoon and finishes off the rice pudding with it.

'*I* wanted some of that,' Solomon finally hisses.

Jalisa smacks her lips, defiantly.

(So he's *definitely* not getting any tonight, eh?)

I slowly tiptoe away from the table and towards the door, hands raised (perhaps) in the slightly defensive attitude of a frightened hamster.

'Well this *has* been fun,' I mutter, rapidly exiting.

'Yes, *hasn't* it,' Jalisa tosses back.

The guard's name is Seth and he's extremely garrulous. Within five minutes he's told me where he's originally from (Greenwich), which part of London he currently lives in (Battersea), what his last assignment was (some shonky American Wrestling deal at the London Arena), what his next will be (the new Bridget Jones film), how much he's earning (£100 per day), the duration for which his mother *breast*fed him (Okay, so now I'm just showing off – the dude was *bottle* fed, as it happens).

As I'm sure you can imagine, it doesn't take a man of *my* subtle conversational abilities long to lure him around to the fascinating subject of Aphra.

'*Lovely* girl,' he says cheerfully, 'but a total fucking *nutter*.'

'Really?'

'Didn't you notice yet, guv?' he chortles.

'Well, she's certainly a little . . .'

I raise my brows, suggestively (Could that *possibly* be constructed as ungallant?).

'Believe it or not,' he runs effortlessly on, 'the first time she ever came here she didn't have the first *clue* about who David Blaine was or what the fuck he was doing up there . . .' He smiles, fondly, at the memory. 'She's like, "But *why's* he in the box . . .?" "Won't he get *sick* if he doesn't *eat* for all that time?", "And how will he go to the *toilet*?", "*What*? With everybody just *watching*?"'

He cracks up laughing, 'I mean she was *totally* concerned for the guy. Just standing there, in her funny little shoes, open-mouthed, staring up at the box in sheer wonder. Like a kid at Christmas, pretty much.'

'She'd never even *heard* of Blaine before?'

I'm shocked.

'Nope. Says she doesn't have a *TV*. Never reads a paper. Didn't have a *clue*, I swear. Like she'd just landed here from *Mars*, it was.'

'But now she's here most days . . .' I casually muse (Sherlock, eat yer heart out).

'Most *nights*,' he corrects me.

'Of *course*,' I murmur.

'Only comes when he's sleeping,' he sighs, glancing up towards the magician who has – just that minute – lifted his head on to his hand and is now lying on his side, still warmly ensconced in his sleeping bag.

'Arrives at around ten or eleven, most evenings,' Seth continues, 'then usually stays right through. Some of the other lads worry a bit about her – I mean it gets quite *wild* down here sometimes. But she's *fine*. She told me once how she has a nice little flat just down the cobbles a way . . .' he points.

'She does,' I confirm.

He gives me a straight look. 'Been there, *huh*?' (And I don't think he means the *flat*, either.)

'Why,' I ask (quick as a flash), 'have *you*?'

He slowly shakes his head (and not a little regretfully).

At this point one of his colleagues calls him over. He turns, waves his ready compliance, then glances, briefly, back at me. 'Amazing *nose*, though, eh?' he murmurs, in a strangely inscrutable parting shot.

Amazing *nose*?

'Yeah. *Yeah*, absolutely *amazing* . . .' I bluster pointlessly after him.

And the tits aren't half bad, either.

Did *I* just say that?

I charge into the office, crash down in front of my computer, and dive straight on to the internet.
Wham!
Amazon...
Bam!
Bookfinder...
   After sniffing around for a while I pull out my Master-card and order:

(1) *The Complete Short Stories of Franz Kafka* (Vintage Classics, £9.99).
(2) Primo Levi, *If This Is a Man/The Truce* (Abacus, £8.99).
(3) David Blaine, *Mysterious Stranger* – 'The Sunday

Times Bestseller: His secrets will become yours'
Pan, £12.99).

I do a mite more surfing, but find out surprisingly little
of personal interest about Blaine. The full-on autobiographical detail is sketchy, at best . . .

- Born in Brooklyn, New York, 1973 (no actual date
  available).
- First got 'into' magic aged four, when he saw a man
  performing conjuring tricks on the Subway.
- His mother remarried when he was ten (no information about his real father or stepfather –
  although someone did mention something about his
  dad having died when he was very young) and the
  family moved to New Jersey.
- As a teenager Blaine became an actor, attending a
  Manhattan acting school and then appearing in a
  few commercials and playing some cameo roles in a
  couple of soaps.
- His mother died in 1994, when he was twenty-one.
- He started doing 'magic for the Movie Stars in
  Hollywood', so consequently has many 'celebrity
  fans', including Leonardo Di Caprio, Al Pacino and
  Robert De Niro.
- He sent an amateur video of himself to ABC and they
  responded by offering him a million dollar contract to
  perform what they called 'street magic' on TV (So he
  didn't invent that phrase himself? Well this makes
  Solomon's theories look a little dodgy, *eh*?).
- Apparently – now I *like* this – Blaine absolutely
  loves Tower Bridge. Always has. That's why he's
  doing the stunt here.

(*Hmmn*. Think this 'loves Tower Bridge' thing has that distinctively *feculent* aroma of a big ol' pile of wheedling PR).

On one of the fan-sites there's passing reference to Blaine's (now almost legendary) 'public demeanor of vacant detachment', which strikes me as fairly interesting . . . I mean is all that very flat yet very deliberate slow-moving, slow-talking stuff just a *public* persona? (Does he jerk and buzz like Woody the fuckin' Woodpecker in private?). More to the point: doesn't *everybody* talk that way in Brooklyn?

Of course *then* there's the reams of people trying to cash in on the whole *magic* side of his work (i.e. 'Make all your friends gasp in astonishment . . . buy this video/ DVD/book . . . put your hand through a glass window . . . levitate . . . do a card trick . . . bring a fly back to life . . .' *blah blah*).

I also happen across Wakedavid.com, 'the site dedicated to keeping David awake for 44 days and nights'.

God, I really *dig* that about the internet: you're banging through an apparently endless, incredibly turgid pile of fan-shite one minute, then the next – and completely without warning – you're suddenly entering a world peopled entirely by *haters*. And yet here they are, rubbing up benignly against each other, almost as if – underneath all that careful packaging – they're actually just one and the same thing . . .

Which they *are*, effectively (i.e, two sides/same coin etc.).

'Cos that's Modern Life, *huh*?

Wakedavid.com . . .

ENTER

104

Wow. It's a flashy old site, though, for something so apparently *ad hoc*.

And the first thing I notice – apart from the unnervingly detached, yet effortlessly *jocular* tone – is how incredibly keen these people are to make it clear, up front, that their campaign against David Blaine has *nothing whatsoever* to do with any kind of *racial* motivation –

Good *God*, no!
Never!
Uh-*uh*!

I call Bly over at lunchtime to take a quick peek.

'You okay?' she asks, in passing.

'Huh?'

'You look a little *pale*,' she says.

'Did you see this before?' I ask, pointing at the screen.

She puts her hand on to the back of my chair, leans in closer, and commences reading.

'I had a boyfriend once,' she informs me, a short while later, as we share a sandwich, walking along the river, 'who was *really* into his four wheel drive Landcruiser . . .'

Okay . . .

'. . . And you might well think that this has nothing

whatsoever to do with the Blaine thing...'

Yes, I might.

'And you may well be right...'

'But?'

(*Jeez.* This girl's certainly no Jalisa on the information front. It's like pulling fucking *teeth* with her.)

'But when I read that Wakedavid stuff just now it *totally* reminded me of the kind of tripe *he* used to download. The general *tone*,' she says, 'and this particular kind of...uh...*mind*set...'

'Was the boy a Nazi?' I ask sweetly.

She slits her eyes at me. 'At least credit me with more discrimination than *that*.'

We grind to a halt in front of a dazed if cheery-looking Blaine. I peer down at my half of the sandwich. It suddenly looks quite unappetising. And while there's a chill in the air, I feel a little...*phew*...hot.

'Oh *fantastic*,' Bly suddenly gasps (between urgent mouthfuls of her tomato and mozzarella ciabatta), 'it's Hilary, Adie, *look*...'

I turn to where she's pointing (somewhat irritably – I mean when does she finally *elucidate* on the improbable 4x4/Wakedavid connection?) and see that the individual who's generating such excitement on her part is sitting on Aphra's bench, two spaces along from a currently blissfully dozing Punk's Not (doesn't this guy have a *home* to go to?).

He's this slightly overweight, conventionally dressed, smug-looking, bespectacled, 30-something guy who happens to be wearing a preposterous headscarf – red and white, the kind favoured by Middle Eastern politicos (Yasser Arafat probably has the copyright).

To say the scarf looks a mite *incongruous* would be

to dabble in a grotesque world of profound understatement (If he's not wearing that thing for a *bet*, then I certainly wanna know why).

The scarf is literally just *tossed* over his head (like someone threw it at him and he didn't quite duck in time). Next to him (and I mean *directly* next to him – in the gap between himself and Punk's Not) is a small, rather scruffy, home-made sign which goes some way – I guess – to partially explaining this fabulous head-apparel: 'Fortunes Read', it says.

'You actually *know* this creature?' I murmur.

(*Jesus*. The Illusionist is certainly drawing all the freaks out of the woodwork.)

'It's *Hilary*,' she says. 'Remember? Worked as Mike Wilkinson's PA last year?'

Nothing clicks.

'Fourth floor?'

Nope (This chick isn't in Human Resources for nothing, *huh*?).

'Think he has the gift?' I ask.

Bly nods. 'He told my fortune last December,' she says, 'and he was *really* good.'

'Oh yeah?'

She nods. 'He said my father would lose his arm. And he did, three months later . . .'

I jolt to attention. 'Your father lost his *arm*?'

She nods. 'In an accident at work.'

'And he said *that*? He said, "Your father will lose an arm?"'

She chuckles. 'No, not *exactly* . . .'
Ahhh.

'So what *did* he say?'

'He said, "A close, male relative will lose a limb."'

107

'Good God.'

'I *know*. Weird, huh?'

She pauses. 'And the strangest thing was that my mother's brother, Marty – my favourite uncle – lost his toe to gangrene literally a *month* before my dad had *his* accident, and I briefly thought he was the person Hilary was talking about...But at the time I just kept thinking, "A toe is *not* a limb..."'

She gazes up at me, full of emotion, 'I mean it just *isn't*, is it?'

'Wouldn't it've been *awful*,' I interject, 'if, on top of everything else, Hilary's *linguistic grasp* had been found wanting?'

She continues to look up at me, but now more cautiously.

'You're *harsh*,' she eventually mutters. 'I'm going over to say hi. Coming?'

Oh yes. Of course. I remember now. He's put on some weight and he's changed his glasses, but underneath that baroque headdress he's fundamentally the same strait-laced, cynical, world-weary, *unbelievably* punctilious *tool* from the fourth floor that he always used to be.

We had an argument, once, about photocopying paper. His department had over-ordered, our department had run short, so I 'borrowed' a couple of packs without bothering to fill out the relevant acquisition slip and he got all snooty and snitchy and up on his hind legs about it.

Man.

Who *needs* that shit?

So get this: I am approximately five feet away from this would-be Paragon of the Paranormal when he glances up from the book he's reading – a particularly lovely (deliciously battered-looking) American paperback edition of the collected works of Richard Brautigan, with a fantastic black-and-white front cover (featuring a charming, old-fashioned photographic image of the author and his hippie-chick girlfriend), and then a beautiful, bright red *back* cover with only the word 'mayonnaise' written on it, in white, dead centre (*Wow*. So isn't this itinerant paper hoarder *quite* the man of the moment now with his independent life-style, mystical leanings and iconoclastic *reading* matter?) – when he looks up, frowns and yells, '*Stop!*'

(About ten tourists freeze and turn around, in shock. Punk's Not wakes up from his light doze, with a gasp.)

Bly and I both grind to a sharp halt.

'Go home,' the Paragon tells me in shrill, ecclesiastical tones (while pointing, rudely, like Moses on the damn Mount). 'You have a contagious virus.'

'Fuck off,' I say.

'You do,' he says, 'Australian *flu*.'

'*Urgh*'

Bly takes a step back.

'But how can you possibly *tell*,' I ask, 'when I didn't even cross your sweaty, petty, embarrassingly *opportunistic* palm with silver yet?'

He waves my insults aside: 'It's an especially *virulent* strain,' he cants (causing shocked inhalations from the small audience which his bogus proclamations have already amassed).

'Well lucky for me you're sporting that industrial-sized *hanky* then,' I say, pointing (somewhat gratuitously).

'Done any inter-departmental *thieving* lately?' he snarls (*Yup*. Old wounds).

109

'Still have the name of a *girl*?' I sneer.

'I believe you'll discover,' Punk's Not cordially informs me, 'that Hilary is actually derived from the Latin, *hilaris*, which means "cheerful". And up until the late nineteenth century it was used entirely by the male. There was both a pope *and* a fourth-century saint –'

'And *then* it became a *girl's* name,' I interrupt, 'and that's all that matters *now* . . .'

'Fuck off, germ-farm,' Hilary scoffs.

'. . . And not even a *nice* girl's name,' I continue, 'but the name of a pear-shaped girl with no tits and fallen arches, who wears moccasins and *tweed*, and collects novelty *liqueur* bottles, and smells of radishes . . .'

(Novelty *liqueur* bottles? *Woah*, there.)

'You ignorant, pointless, fluffy little *fop*,' he splutters (plainly mortally offended for the girl he might've been).

I take a step closer, and pant, provocatively.

He cowers away from me, drawing some of his excess scarf fabric across his mouth, like a heavily bespectacled Lawrence of Arabia.

'I'm going to *lick* you,' I announce.

A booted foot kicks out at me.

The crowd steps back.

Then I jump, like a wildcat, and set my tongue to work on him.

What?

Has this man never troubled *acquainting* himself with soap and water?

Hmmn. Is it just me, or does Punk's Not have an unexpectedly *magisterial* aspect from down here?

Six

So I got the flu. Bully for *him*. And it *is* virulent (just like he said): I have shooting pains in my head, my chest, my legs, my nuts. Fever, nausea, the runs.

Night sweats (really bad ones). Exhaustion. Chapping. Am skiing through a veritable *avalanche* of phlegm . . .

And the Illusionist thinks *he*'s doing it tough? (Experiencing 'A funny taste in the mouth?' *Eh*? While I lie shivering, in the foetal position, looking like Marilyn fucking Manson after three hours in make-up?)

Hey. But Bly *did* end up telling me about the 4x4/Wakedavid connection (yeah – I *know* you've been literally on the edge of your *seat* over that one) although I'm far too ill now to know if it's relevant or not (and if it *is*, what – if anything – it's relevant *for* . .).

I guess you could just say that I'm gradually building up some kind of basic, three-dimensional *jigsaw* inside my head; piece by tiny piece (as if David Blaine, the *rage* he's generated, the logistics of his actual 'stunt', are some kind of magnificently fractured, profoundly perplexing, antique ceramic *pot* . . .

So will it hold together when I'm finally done? Will it be waterproof? Are all the fragments in place? Are my fingers clean? Is the glue strong enough?).

Okay. *Okay.* Try and be *kind*, will ya? I'm sickening. I'm gummed up.

Remember earlier, *much* earlier, before the plague?

'All this damn *rancour*,' Bly grizzles, once she's hauled me off the pavement, apologised profusely (on my behalf), retrieved Hilary's (not so 'hilarious' *now*, eh?) headscarf from my frenzied clutch, returned it, and cluckingly dusted down the arms and elbows on my heavy-wear jacket, 'what's the *point* of it?'

'Rancour?'

I do the wide-eyed act.

(My philosophy: if in *any* doubt, deny, and deny passionately.)

'You *attacked* him.'

She gives me a reproachful look.

'He kicked me first,' I squeak, 'and anyway, I only licked him. In most "advanced" cultures a lick is a sign of overwhelming benevolence.'

'To a dog, perhaps.'

'All that bloody *piety*,' I growl (conforming to type), and setting my (now, slightly wonky) sights back on work again. 'I mean who suddenly gave all these skanky New Agers such ready access to the fine, moral high ground? They have no *right* to it. They don't pay any damn *rent*. They're just Ethical *Squatters* . . .'

(Bly neglects to congratulate me on what I feel is my peerless use of morality-based real estate imagery.)

'You're honestly trying to tell me,' she scoffs, 'that Hilary offends your "Christian sensibilities" in some way?'

'Yes,' I gabble defensively, '*and* fucking Blaine, for that matter...'

'How?'

Uh...(Now I'm flummoxed. Just give me a second ... I'm harbouring the *pox*, remember?). 'Well ... the *adverts*, for starters. The TV adverts. And before this whole thing even *started*, there he was, like the proverbial bad penny, hanging around town and behaving – at every opportunity – like a real celebrity *dick*. Cutting off his *ear* at a press conference. Getting tough-nuts on the streets to punch him in the guts. Prancing around on the London Eye. I mean big fucking *deal*. Is he meant to be an *Artist*, or some kind of low-rent *carnival* entertainer?'

I pause and cough.

(*Shit*, man, I'm pent *up*.)

'Is it really any wonder,' I continue, 'that people've got so confused and pissed-off?'

'The TV ads...' she nudges me.

'*Yeah*. The TV ads. They were *unbelievably* provocative...'

'Not so's I remember...' she debunks.

'You don't have a problem, then,' I gabble, 'with some trumped-up, two-bit American magician – best mucker of those social *stalwarts*: Uri Geller and Michael Jackson – drawing casual but *explicit* parallels between his million-dollar, Sky sponsored, money-making antics, and the trials and tribulations of the Son of *God*?'

Bly merely cocks her head.

'The dark *corridor*,' I twitter, 'the raised *arms*, the grandiose *music*, the portentous *voice*-over...'

'So *what*?' She throws up her hands. 'Who cares?'

'Who cares? Who *cares*? *Lots* of people care. Because

it's sacri-bloody-legious. It's arrogant. It's outrageous. It's *wrong*.'

'Oh. *Fine*,' Bly snipes, caustically. 'It's suddenly against the law now, *huh*, to employ basic Christian iconography in other walks of life?'

(Iconography?! *Man*. What's *happening* to these females lately?)

'Yes. *Yes*. It *is*. Against the laws of good *taste*,' I gurgle: 'Just look what the Muslims did to *Rushdie*: a fatwa, for writing some crummy piece of undigestible *fiction*. But when Blaine compares himself – his so-called "struggle", his theatrics – to the trials of Jesus Christ, we're all just meant to go, "*Uh*, oh, good, *yeah* . . ."'

Bly puts up a hand to stop me: '*How* did he compare himself?' she asks.

'In *every* way. The imagery. The whole *presentation* of the thing. All the "forty-four days in the wilderness" malarkey . . .'

'Forty days,' she chips in.

'Pardon me?'

'Forty days,' she yells. 'You're standing here as Christianity's chief defender and you don't even know the number of *days* involved.'

'So Blaine cocks a snook at Christ by going *four days longer*!' I exclaim. 'Wow. You *surprise* me.'

We enter the foyer. 'Okay . . .' Bly pauses thoughtfully by the front desk. 'I'm perfectly willing to concede to your idea that the Christ thing is implicit in what he's doing . . ,' she frowns, 'but you already told me how it was the *Kafka* story that inspired the whole stunt. You were burning my damn *ear* about the subtle ramifications of the so-called "Korine connection" all bloody morning . . .'

'So what?' I shrug. 'Blaine's just cherry-picking. He's trite. An opportunist. A cultural slut.'

'Uh-*uh*,' she uh-*uhs*. 'It's not simply a question of cherry-picking, it's about experimentation, about pushing buttons, crossing boundaries. He's *transgressing*.' She pokes me in the chest with her beefy finger. 'He's making you *think*.' Another poke. 'He's making you *question*. He's being intellectually flirtatious ... and – at some fundamental level – I think he's probably just taking the *piss* a little...'

'Maybe he is,' I squawk (I hate this idea, somehow – to be the punchline of Blaine's *joke*? How infuriating is that?). 'Maybe he *is* taking the piss, but how can we possibly be expected to *tell*, when he's so unreservedly smug and pious and American and *humourless* about it? *Funny?*!' I point, dramatically, in the general direction of the Illusionist's box. 'You call *this* funny? Slumped in a plastic *tomb*, twenty-four/seven? Waving occasionally? I thought he was meant to be a fucking *show*man.'

'That's his style.' Bly rolls her eyes. 'That's his trip. And maybe – bottom line – you just don't get the joke. Or perhaps what he's doing is more complicated than you think. Maybe it's the very multi-layeredness of the whole thing which is putting your back up. He's confusing you. He's challenging your preconceptions. You don't *like* that.'

I sneeze. She ducks.

'We're all such rugged bloody *individualists* lately,' she murmurs, searching in her bag for something: 'The ex I was just telling you about – *he* was a perfect case in point. And the people on that site you showed me, the stay-awake bullies, *they* all think they're standing out from the crowd, that they're *defending* something, that they're really cutting a dash . . .'

She hands me a tissue: 'But they're not individuals at *all*. They're just deluded conformists.'

'How so?'

I cover my nose and blow.

'Well this guy – my ex; his name was Steve – was completely obsessed by his Landcruiser. He lived in Stratford, for Chrissakes, and the parking was a nightmare. But he loved that car . . .'

I blow again.

'. . . Because it was big, for starters, and utilitarian-looking, and tough, and it made him feel like an outsider, like someone who *would* drive over the pavement if he needed to – bend the rules a little, you know? He felt armour-plated in that thing, like an urban *warrior*.'

I look around for a bin to throw my soggy tissue in. There's one by the lift. She follows me over.

'I mean this guy was so anti-corporate – in his own mind – *hated* what he liked to call "The McDonald's Mentality", saw the rest of the "developed" world as burger-munching imbeciles. And there *he* was, standing out from the slavish crowd in his magical 4x4, guzzling his petrol, "up-grading" his tyres, threatening local schoolkids with his repulsive crash bars . . .'

'You're right. That *is* wack,' I say, and press for my floor.

'But the *hypocrisy* of these people! The ignorance! They think that just by *owning* something, by buying *into* something – a car, an idea, a certain type of boot, a Boxfresh *jacket* . . .' She slaps at the open flap of my coat with her free hand . . .

Oi! Watch it!

117

'. . . that they're defining themselves against "the system". But the system is all *about* people defining themselves through certain objects, or fads, and summarily rejecting others. That's capitalism at its zenith. That's the *disease* which consumes us . . .'

She pauses, dramatically. 'And which we, in turn, consume.'

(Think this girl might have a future in politics?)

I gently remove the flaps of my jacket from her slapping orbit by zipping them up.

'*Jesus*,' I murmur, 'I mean didn't these fools even watch *The Matrix*?'

The lift arrives. We climb in.

'Those Wakedavid people share that exact-same mentality,' she sighs. 'They honestly think they're defining their mental toughness, their sacred individualism, their righteous *Englishness*, against something which – if they just stopped and thought, and took a proper *look* – is actually much more honest and individual and vulnerable and subversive than they could *ever* be . . .'

'Too bloody *true*,' I say.

'Their hatred is just *jealousy*,' she splutters.

'Hear *hear*,' I incant.

The lift stops. The doors open. I step out. She stays in.

'See ya.' I wave.

She nods, reaching out her hand distractedly for the fifth floor button. 'He was right about the arm, though,' she mutters ominously, '"Ethical Squatter" or *not* . . .'

(*Ah*. So she *was* listening . . .)

Then she suddenly frowns, peers into her bag, begins patting at her pockets, glances up.

'Did I actually *finish* my ciabatta before?'

I nod.

The doors start closing.

'Did I eat the whole thing without even *noticing*?'

I shrug, then nod again.

The doors close. Her voice is very muffled . . .

'Are you *sure*?'

I mean where's the *trust* between a man and a woman?

So you probably think this is just a *cold*, and that I'm simply making a big, male *fuss*.

Wrong, wrong, *wrong*.

I'm sick as a whippet.

Even the *dogs* have stopped growling at me on my occasional, poignant trips to the refrigerator (of course I'm not eating . . . That's just where the citrus is). They know, see? *They* can tell.

The first three days are simply a blur (I can't – I *won't* – remember). On day four, however, Bookfinder comes up trumps with the Kafka short stories, and I feel well enough to leave the sordid confines of my fetid hutch, stagger upstairs, wrapped in a blanket, and slump down, wheezing, on to Solomon's chic but unbelievably impractical cream suede sofa.

I read for twenty solid minutes, accompanied by my four-part *Pet Sounds Sessions* Beach Boys CD. I'm on disc 2, listening to Brian Wilson barking out jovial instructions about the perfect setting for the organ, bass and drums on 'Good Vibrations' (Yeah. Hearing that so-familiar stereo backing track slowly coming into its own from virtually nothing kinda sets my skin a-tingle. It's like seeing this giant, disembodied hand pushing up into a bright summer sky and casually turning all the clouds around . . .

Okay. So no more paracetamol for me, *eh?*)

I'll tell you this for nothing, though (Wilson's despotic meanderings aside): that story is *damn* strong meat:

A *Hunger* Artist.

It's vicious. It's merciless. It's bleak and uncompromising.

I check out the useful chronology at the back of the book and discover that the story was published just a handful of months after Kafka's death in 1924. He was only 40 years old. He died of consumption.

Twenty years later (when I move down the chronology a little further) I see how the Nazis murdered all three of his sisters. Then Grete Bloch, the mother of the son he never knew he had. Then the Czech writer, Milena Jesenska'-Pollak, to whom he entrusted his precious diaries . . .

Man.

The list just goes *on.*

I suppose Jalisa might've had a point re the Jewish

angle. Because from what my puffy eyes can divine, Kafka *really* got into being a Jew in his mid to late twenties (prior to that, he'd read German literature, studied law at the German University, etc.). But in 1910 everything changed. He bought tickets to go and see this Yiddish theatre company, and was apparently so inspired by their work, that he began to bury himself in Jewish folklore, started studying Judaism seriously in 1912, then actually *lectured* on Yiddish a short while after.

He rediscovered his Jewishness just on the cusp of the First World War – not the greatest timing, I guess, on one level (but *superlative* timing, really, on another).

When you actually stop and *think* about it, things must've been pretty tough for all Europeans back then (ancient boundaries irrevocably altering, traditions in total flux, an entire *generation* of young men about to be haplessly slaughtered . . .); and starvation? *Hunger*? Basic facts of *life*, not just mildly diverting literary metaphors.

Hmmn. That's the best I can do for context. Let's get to grips with the actual *story*, eh?

So the basic *gist* of 'A Hunger Artist' is as follows: there's this professional Hunger Artist (the main character – *duh*) who works alongside a clever impresario. He starves himself all over Europe. This is back in a time when fasting was still considered to be 'in fashion' – those are the actual words Kafka uses. Most adults find the whole thing slightly ridiculous – 'just a joke' – but the children are totally bowled over by it (I've *seen* the kids at Blaine, *and* the adults, for that matter, who also *totally* conform to type: even the most diehard supporters can't help smirking slightly. But the kids? They all just fall madly in love with the spectacle. The

kids are hypnotised. They're agog. They're intoxicated
...A crazy combination of doubtful and exhilarated. And
instead of allowing one impulse to counter the other, to
win it over – like any grown-up would – they simply
experience it *all*, as a *whole*. And it's joyful. It's almost
– kind of...*uh*.., *ancient*, somehow. You know? *Primal*.

But *woah* there a moment...

Time *Out*!

Because what are these parents even *thinking*, bringing
their kids along? What kind of fucked-up message is this
depraved tableau sending out to them? 'Hector, get little
Fifi's coat on. We're going to a public starving – And
tomorrow? A man is devoured by a python. Friday? Public
fucking execution.'

That's wrong, man. That's *really* wrong).

Anyhow, the parallels (at this juncture) are fairly overwhelming. I'd quote you the entire relevant section from
the story if I could, but remember that bored SOB in the
copyright department of that Big-Ass publishers in
Swindon? Remember him? *Yeah*.

So let me just, *uh*, paraphrase, if I may. And compare.

Kafka describes the Hunger Artist on page one (I've high-
lighted the important words and phrases in bold, to
further ease the comparison):

(1) He's dressed in **black** (*tick* for Blaine).
(2) He is '**self-contained**,' and '**courteous**' ... (*tick, tick*;
    Blaine's nothing if not both).
(3) He answers questions with a '**constrained smile**'
    (big *tick*).
(4) Every so often he withdraws, into a kind of

122

thoughtful trance, where nothing can distract him (*Tickus Majorus*).

(5) Next to him is a large **clock** (*tick* – although Blaine's is digital).

(6) Every so often he takes a small, restrained sip of **water** from a cup (*tick*, Blaine swigs his straight from the bottle).

Okay, so before you go and get all *narky* on me, I know full-well that the art of hunger-striking isn't going to be something which a person necessarily 'makes their own'. I mean there's only so much an individual can do to innovate in this field (apart from, say, riding on a tricycle, while fasting, which would – quite frankly – be utterly ridiculous). Even so, I think the comparisons are telling (okay, Jalisa was right. *Bully* for Jalisa. *Hip hip* etc.).

In the story, the Hunger Artist (note 'artist') has 'watchers' to keep an eye on him. Butchers, mainly (nobody really knows why, exactly). He pays them for their services by feeding them a huge breakfast each morning (which is consumed – with palpable relish, directly in front of him) . . .

(7) The 'watchers' **eat** in front of him (*tick*, cf. the burger van).

Sometimes the watchers huddle up in a corner and play cards together. They don't take the watching seriously. This drives the Hunger Artist crazy, because he *wants* people to guard him, he *wants* to dispel all doubts about the fact that he's really starving. He *needs* people to know that he's not cheating.

Kafka says that all initiates into hunger-striking know that it would be literally impossible to cheat if you were even remotely serious about it. This is because the fast is primarily against *oneself* (not the watchers or the audience). It's almost entirely an 'interior' act.

He's definitely got a point there. Fasting is about endurance. Maybe some people confuse the concept of a fast with the idea of – say – a diet. When you diet you are hoping to achieve some kind of result (weight loss). If you cheat, then maybe you don't lose quite as much weight that week as you might've hoped, but the diet continues. The diet is predicated on the *end results*, not on the actual *process* of dieting.

A fast is entirely different. When you cheat on a fast, it's no longer a fast. The act of fasting is predicated entirely – nay exclusively – on *not eating*. To eat on a fast would be like spending six months reading *War and Peace* (entirely for your own pleasure) but not actually digesting the words, just sitting, every evening, and holding the book, turning the pages, moving your eyes etc. but taking nothing in.

What an unholy waste of energy. How utterly self-defeating.

Kafka readily admits in his story that suspicion is 'a necessary accompaniment' to professional fasting. This is because (at the time of writing) nobody could possibly hope to watch the Hunger Artist for 24 hours a day, solid.

Okay. So in Blaine's case 'progress' has made this possible. He's being filmed. He's live on Sky. The hungry American has Moroccan chamber maids and Antipodean businessmen watching him at every available opportunity, waiting – just *waiting* – to catch him out. Blaine has the entire world observing. Millions of eyes, all focusing on him.

But still we doubt (*Wow*. Feels kinda strange for me

to be lying here and pencilling in Kafka as a pessimistic light-weight. If Kafka could only see the *lengths* Blaine and his people have had to go to prove his legitimacy (the water testing, the dispassionate 24-hour scrutiny etc.) only to still – *still* – be doubted . . . *Man*, I honestly think the sallow Czech might crack a dry smile. I do).

Now here's the crux of the story: Kafka says that in the Art of Fasting, *only* the Fasters themselves can know, 100 per cent, that they aren't cheating. And this makes him – I'm gonna steal a sentence, but I'll do it in a whisper, *'The sole completely satisfied spectator of his own fast.'*

Cool, *huh*? Basically, Kafka's saying that fasting is *intrinsically unsatisfactory* as a spectator sport.

(And to think that Blaine *read* this, then calmly continued on with the project. Or maybe – *damn* you, Bly – that's *why* . . . The perverse fucker.)

In case you were wondering, I still haven't reached the narrative crux yet. The crux is this: the Hunger Artist – even when he *is* legit and he *knows* he is – is *also* dissatisfied with his own fasting. This (Kafka claims, but merely in the case of his own fictional character, obviously) is because he alone knows how *easy* (Kafka's word) it is to fast. There's no trick to it. He's not doing anything to *make* it so – there's no 'knack'. He just happens to find the whole process fairly effortless.

Baldly speaking, Kafka's hero *loves* to fast (Some people really thrill to that whole 'endurance' groove. How else to explain all those idiots risking life and limb to trudge to the North Pole? Or 16,000 twats gamely running the London Marathon?). The critical point here is: the Hunger Artist loves to fast, and when the fast ends, he always secretly yearns to fast *on*.

But he's contractually obliged to fast for only 40 days.

His impresario has noticed that the public's interest cannot be maintained for any period longer than 40 days (even with heavy advertising – *yup*, believe it or not, this story is brimming with a really modern kind of cynicism about 'the media', and is totally keyed into the whole idea of the potential manipulativeness of publicity, etc).

The 40-day thing is non-negotiable (I can't really comment on *why* Kafka has chosen this particular timescale – or his impresario, either. He just does. Maybe it's unconsciously biblical. Who knows).

So on the 40th day, the Hunger Artist's flower-bedecked cage is duly opened –

(8) The Hunger Artist sits in a '**flower**-bedecked cage' (*tick*: Blaine has his gerbera, remember?)

– and two doctors enter, with megaphones, to check exactly how much weight the Artist has lost, and to announce their findings to the waiting hordes. There's a military band playing. Then two beautiful women turn up to assist the fragile Artist out of his cage . . .

My fascinating musings are (I'm afraid) cruelly interrupted at this point by the untimely arrival of Solomon Tuesday Kwashi, who charges into the living room clutching a host of newspapers and bellowing something incoherent about how the Beach Boys only play 'music for Jocks'.

'Repressed *meat*-heads,' he thoughtfully elucidates, before turning it off with an extravagant flourish.

Then, 'What the *fuck* you doing out of bed?' he asks.

'Reading,' I say.

'Are you leaving sweat marks on my sofa?'

He lifts one of my legs and inspects underneath. I unleash a spitfire of coughs. He retreats.

'What's with all the papers?' I ask.

'Rasket,' he says (That's teen-dream, urban-music-meister Dizzee Rascal to you and me).

'What about him?'

'So get this...' Solomon rages (one to ten on the fury-o-meter in just a *fraction* under two seconds – this guy's 'fight or flight' mechanisms are second to none), – 'they give him the fucking *Mercury*...' (Mercury Music Prize – remember?)

'...and it's such a *radical* choice, it's such a *brave* choice...'

'And you're absolutely livid about it, as I recollect...' I interject (perhaps unwisely).

He stares at me, blankly: 'Rasket deserve him prize,' he says.

'Nobody's denying *that*,' I backtrack.

'Him problem is *whitey's* agenda...' Solomon hisses, 'Whitey want to castrate him Rasket. He want to make *safe* him music.'

Fine, *fine*...

'But him need to uncover this Rasket *weakness*, to have him his *power*...'

Okay...

'So what did they do?' I ask.

Solomon throws his clutch of papers on to the floor.

'*The music teacher!*' he bellows.

Wah?

'Take a look!' Solomon shrieks, 'they find their weasly, white access to Rasket through his school *music* teacher.'

'Rasket had a music teacher?'

(Why am I so surprised by this?)

'Yeah. Mr Smith or Mr Jones or *somebody*..' Solomon growls: 'Now them feel *safe* with him Rasket: they take him bomb, yeah? And them slowly *defuse* it.'

I stretch out a wobbling hand towards the papers.

Solomon squats down and snatches up the top tabloid himself – the *Mail* or *Express* . . .

He rips it open and flashes a page at me.

There, smiling out of a photo, is a benign, respectable-looking, middle-aged white man sitting next to some kind of convoluted, computerised keyboard-style thingummy. Next to him (in cut-out form) is an ominous image (he don't do no other kind) of the be-capped, be-hooded, be-baggy-panted kid-gangsta, Rasket.

'This the story,' Solomon whispers. 'Rasket he fifteen. He go nowhere, yeah? Rasket truant him school, mugging him the occasional old dear. Rasket troubled. Rasket *angry*. Then one day ..' Solomon's basic intonation suddenly undergoes a profound alteration, 'he gets in with this wonderful *music* teacher who's a source of *unbelievable* inspiration to him ..'

'Where *is* this school, exactly?' I ask. 'East London?'

'This wonderful, enthusiastic, charming, talented, *white* music teacher ..'

'Or did he grow up in South London?'

'*Poplar*,' Solomon snaps: 'And the school has a *ton* of modern equipment, see?'

He points to a particular paragraph in the article then snatches it away again: 'Passed down from all these local Docklands-style do-gooder businessmen who've up-graded their computer systems and wanna do their *bit* for the impoverished community around them. And the teacher – Mr Smith, Mr Jones ...

(Mr *Smith*, in fact.)

'. . . he takes the desperate, degenerate Rasket under his wing, rolls back that heavy stone from the mouth of the cave, and kindly gives him *access* to his inner-artist. He generously *unlocks* Mercury Prize Winner Dizzee Rascal's creativity.'

(*Wow.* This is starting to sound just like British Hip-hop's answer to *The Cross and the Switchblade*! Is it any *wonder* they're filling so many column inches with it?)

'So Rasket now owes everything to . . ?' I murmur nervously.

'*Exactly*!' Solomon hollers.

I'm quiet for a moment.

'How'd they get on to this story?' I eventually ask.

Solomon grunts: 'List of thank yous on the album cover.'

'Ah.'

Solomon glowers at me.

'Well, what's *Dizzee's* take on this monstrous PR jamboree?' I gingerly enquire.

Solomon doesn't appear to hear me.

'I mean, it's not just the *fact* of it,' he murmurs, 'but the sickening *inevitability* . . .'

One of the Dobermen (Dobermens, Dobermans) enters the room, observes Solomon's funk, goes to sit down next to his master, loosens his own stiff spine in an attitude of companionable defeat, and sighs.

'I mean it's not that you don't *want* people to like Dizzee . . .' I nervously mutter.

Solomon's brows shoot up. 'Of *course* I want them to like him,' he insists, 'but they need to like him in the *right* way. They need to be challenged. Dizzee *exists* to challenge, and to confound, and to intimidate, with his youth, with his blackness, with his outsider *cachet*. That's what gives him his power. That's who he *is*.'

'They don't need to like him because of some geri-atric *music* teacher ...'

'*White* music teacher,' Solomon interjects. 'It's like Rasket has to be given *permission* to be creative, don't you see? And that very transaction suddenly makes it possible for these patronising Tory *bastards* to neatly include him inside their fucked-up, self-congratulatory, jaundiced white world-view, when they couldn't – or just *wouldn't* – have considered doing so before.'

Hmmn.

'Maybe it's just one of those chicken/egg situations ...' I volunteer (trying to strike a note of positivism).

Solomon says nothing.

'I mean maybe it doesn't really matter *how* people gain access to Dizzee, so long as they do, and then *he* gets the opportunity to educate them through his music.'

'Absolutely *not*!' Solomon bellows. 'He's an *artist*, you fool, an *innovator*, a *radical*, not some affable, slack-jawed *Mary Poppins*-style figure.'

He suddenly bounces into the air and proceeds to dance around the living room performing a preposterous, ragga-style version of 'A Spoonful of Sugar'.

(If Jay-Z gets his ears on this shit, we're *definitely* in the money.)

'But if the teacher *did* actually help him ...' I quietly interject (secretly hoping he won't hear me).

'That's his *job*!' Solomon roars. 'He had all this free equipment, didn't he? What d'you expect him to do? Lock up the music room and go out and shoot *crack* every afternoon?'

'But if Dizzee doesn't mind,' I murmur (taking a certain amount for granted). 'I mean so long as he sells

130

enough copies of this album, and then he gets to make another. . . .'

'That's basic *capitalism*, you *twat*,' Solomon hisses, 'and since when did an *economic system* have any significant bearing on the dissemination of *genius*?'

He stares at me, intently, holding out the (now rolled-up) paper like it's some kind of disciplinary baton.

'I've got *flu*,' I squeak: 'I can't *think*. I give *in* . . .'

The dog stands up, yawns, turns its back on me (in a *most* peremptory manner), and then *farts* its disdain my way.

Pretty lucky that I'm all blocked up, really.

Good *God*. Where'd that unsightly stain come from?

Seven

Woman trouble. I can smell it a mile off. I mean Solomon's irascible, volatile, highly strung . . . But this Rasket thing just doesn't quite sit right. It smacks a tiny-*wee* bit of what his previous ex but one might've called 'displacement activity' (Her name was Brook. She was sharp, black, French-Canadian, spoke seven languages, worked as a model, was in constant therapy and knew all the lingo – which was partly why he dumped her, actually; Solomon loathes jargon with a passion – calls it 'a short cut to fuck-all' – and was *especially* infuriated when she pilfered one of his dreams – she'd run short – and then found out from her analyst – much to her shock – that the dream was a strong manifestation of sexual indifference. When she confronted him with this information he accused her of 'whoring my unconscious, you castrating bitch'. And that was it).

Displacement?

Yeah. So Solomon is letting off steam about the Rascal (in other words) because he feels conflicted (at *some* level – I mean this man's a multi-storey car park of the emotions) about Jalisa.

If any further confirmation of this fact were needed,

Solomon's music choices that evening totally provide it. At eight we are treated (I'm shuddering in the basement, with a *thumping* headache; but who gives a damn about me?) to the raucous cacophony that is the Wu-Tang Clan-gers (36 *Chambers: Enter the Wu*, for the train-spotters among you). By nine, things have mellowed out slightly and Kraftwerk's pared-down vehicular master-work *Autobahn* can be heard chugging and clicking. By ten, things've obviously degenerated to an all-time low when I hear Cannon Street Road's answer to C L R. James yodelling along to none other than Ms Norah Jones.

Yup. Your eyes aren't deceiving you. Solomon is *voluntarily* submitting his aural senses to Ravi Shankar's dark-haired and dimpled MOR songsmith daughter – that pretty, malty-voiced chanteuse of 'Come Away With Me' fame.

Things must be at a *really* low ebb here (Norah only comes out when the percodan stops working).

Hmmn.

Perhaps I should venture upstairs and offer a supportive shoulder . . ?

But I'm terribly *busy*, see? (I've just spent the last two hours texting all my friends to inform them of how I'm much too *ill* to text them – and I *desperately* need a shot of vapour; my sinuses have transformed into two, throbbing pebbles banging around tortuously in a snotty sea – and then – *then* – there's still the rest of the Kafka to try and get to grips with . . . I mean who could possibly have anticipated that being ill might prove so *agitating*?).

Five seconds sweet hush and then Track Two kicks in. Oh *God*. The dogs start howling.

I rise from my tomb fully intent upon offering him solace (and on fetching myself a glass of water – although this consideration is *entirely* secondary).

Solomon's in the kitchen, sitting on the bench at one side of the table. The three Dobermans (Dobermens?) are sitting, in a neat row, on the opposite bench, facing him. Solomon is drinking (brace yourselves) Amarula (the African version of Bailey's cream liqueur; one of the main ingredients of which is the amarula berry, famous for being the fruit which eight out of ten elephants prefer to get pissed on. *Seriously*). He's actually been mixing this syrupy concoction with Sprite (Why not just skip the alcohol and down a packet of caster sugar?).

He is drunk (a feat in itself – this tipple's the equivalent of Dirty Harry armed with a *pop*gun), and he's slowly working his way through a large salad bowl full of Japanese rice crackers (at his elbow, I observe an empty can of chocolate-flavour Nutriment, a scrunched-up American-style pretzel packet, and a very messy, half-eaten beef tomato.

Urgh).

Each time he consumes a rice cracker himself, he lobs another three (with sure-fire precision) at each of the dogs. '*Bud*! *Jax*! *Ivor*!'

Snap, snap, *snap*.

I take my life in my hands and turn Norah off.

'What're you *doing*?' Solomon roars (The dogs – keen as they are, I'm sure, to defend their master – don't budge an inch. Every panting, salivating *fibre* is focused on Solomon's fingers and the bowl of crackers).

'Norah *Jones*,' I quietly explain, 'in case you didn't already *know*, writes music for love-lorn 36-year-old clerical assistants from Kettering called Samantha.'

Solomon angrily slits his eyes at me.

'Even Jalisa,' I explain gently, 'would hate to see you brought so low.'

'*Bud*! *Jax*! *Ivor*!'

Three more rice cakes are duly thrown.

'*Adie*!'

A fourth rice cake hits me square between the eyes.

'Thanks,' I murmur (my motor skills are a little slow this evening).

'Jalisa,' he suddenly informs me, 'could yap the hind leg off a fucking *donkey* . . .' He pauses, dissatisfied. 'If they could somehow harness the energy in that girl's *jaw* they could provide enough electricity for a town the size of Basildon.' He pauses for a second time. 'Or Stirling. Or *Edinburgh*. It's just *wah, wah, wah, wah, wah*.'

'She dumped you?'

'*Unceremoniously*,' he exclaims. 'It took half a fucking *hour*. That cow used up the *entire* Thesaurus for "you're ditched, you insensitive twat".'

'Discarded?' I ask (rapidly catching on).

He nods.

'Jettisoned?'

He shrugs.

'Scrapped?'

He merely grimaces.

'Junked?'

He scowls.

'Renounced?'

The scowl deepens.

'Pensioned off . . .?'

'*Enough*!' he bellows.

Right. *Okay*. I turn to head downstairs again (I mean I think he's successfully vented now, hasn't he?).

'And I wouldn't even *mind*' Solomon grouchily continues, 'but the main crime she accused me of was not actually *listening*...'

He unscrews the Amarula again.

'Not *listening*!' he repeats incredulously. 'I mean what the fuck *else* have I been doing for the past forty-seven and a half days?'

Oh dear. He's counting the days. Not a good Healing Indicator.

'That's seven *very* noisy weeks,' I tabulate soberly.

'Yes.' Solomon nods.

He inhales. 'And now...'

He looks up at the ceiling, poignantly, 'The *quiet*.'

I look up at the ceiling too. The dogs look up at the ceiling (except for Jax, who keeps staring at the crackers).

'I never, *ever* want to hear that *ridiculous* name mentioned in this house again,' Solomon announces.

Good.

I half-turn for a second time –

'*Never*,' he says.

I freeze.

'Not *ever*,' he says.

'It's a *deal*,' I whisper encouragingly, and mime zipping my lips up.

'*Ja*-lisa... Ja-*lisa*...'

He revolves the unsayable around on his tongue.

'I mean is it *Janet*? Is it *Melissa*? What *is* it?'

'Both,' I say, then blow my nose.

'Opinionated?' Solomon ponders out loud... '*Bud*! *Jax*! *Ivor*!'

Three more crackers are hurled out of the bowl. Ivor's is slightly skew-whiff this time, he lunges, then falls off the bench with a clatter.

Ouch.

Solomon doesn't appear to notice.

'*Opinionated*?!' he repeats (even more incredulously), 'I mean did you ever meet anyone with so many *opinions* before?'

Uh . . .

Does he actually expect me to respond to this question honestly?

(Answer: on reflection: almost definitely not.)

'Yes,' I say (without reflecting), 'I have.'

'Really?' he glances over, momentarily engaged. 'Who?'

'You, of course,' I cackle (through several dried sheets of snot), 'you deluded *cunt*.'

Silence.

(Did I go too far?)

Ivor finally retrieves his cracker (it was stuck in the crack between the fridge and the washing machine), eats it, then jumps back – with a delicious clatter of nails – on to the bench again.

More silence.

I blow my nose, pour myself a glass of water, gently press *play*, and leave Solomon to Norah.

So where the fuck's Chris Ofili when you need him, eh?

Yeah. Some *pal* he turned out to be.

In 'A Hunger Artist' (Yup. I'm nicely snuggled up between the sheets again, patiently nursing one of those strangely disorientating sick-bed erections) Kafka says how the two beautiful women who are sent into the Artist's cage to retrieve him from his fast are 'apparently so friendly and in reality so cruel'.

(I know, I *know*. I'm growing far too bold with my summary quotations, but I'm planning to plead this one under 'diminished responsibility'. Because I'm virtually *insensible* with fever here.)

And that's all Kafka *needs* to say, really: 'so friendly . . . so cruel'. He has no reason to elaborate any further. His point is made. Because we all know who these girls *are* . . . . They're the kinds of females who – in modern times – might enjoy a 'written correspondence' with a serial killer. Or the type who – in far distant history – might've discovered a 'deep affinity' with a particular saint, then've become a nun (with a heavy sideline in self-flagellation), then've had a series of hysterical fits, then've experienced a 'revelation', then've participated in a series of degenerate sex-acts with a 15-year-old monk in the neighbouring monastery as 'an expression of God's True Will' etc. (Is this nun-related scenario *especially* imaginative, or am I just tiredly reiterating the plot of a second-rate porn film which I saw last year? *Oh.* You saw that film *too*, eh?).

They're like Valkyries (these women); carefully picking themselves a nice, neat path through blood-sodden fields crammed with the still-steaming corpses of the recently slaughtered.

Hmmn. I can't honestly pretend that I feel sufficiently familiar with the Blaine situation to draw too many parallels at this stage . . . (*Blaine.* Remember him? Still sitting patiently by the river, a lively crowd milling around restively to the fore, a waxing moon hanging whitely behind . . . *Remember*?).

Although there was this *one* woman . . .

I happened to catch a glimpse of her whilst idly flipping channels (on the late-nite rerun of the Channel 4 reality TV hairdressing series, *The Salon*). She came in to the salon to tell the nation how she was planning – *tah-dah*! – not to *wash her hair* for the duration of the Illusionist's spate in his box.

I say again: this simpering dim-wit fully intended to let no shampoo or water *touch* her (already rather rank-looking) blonde locks (and she *was* a blonde. I see no point in evading that fact) for the 44-day period of Blaine's dramatic fast.

Wha?!

Is this sympathetic madness? Hard-boiled (but utterly deluded) exhibitionism? A deep-set follicle-related sense of self-loathing? Or does this girl-moron have a sub-terranean grudge against all the friendly folks at Pantene Pro-v, perhaps?

Imagine actually appearing on TV – in a *salon*, of all places – to announce how *dirty* you're planning to get? Not only that, but to 'seek advice' on the 'hair ordeal' you're about to face?

This girl actually brought in a photo of herself – down at the riverside, with all the other punters – hanging out with Blaine's lady-love (the aforementioned Manon of the Big Feet).

Poor Manon – being obliged to have her picture taken with this lank-haired girl maniac on account of some-thing psychotic her boyfriend's done. I mean is this what an international model *expects* when she starts dating a multimillionaire? Is this glamorous? Is this 'spiritual'? Is this meaningful? Is this *fun*?

Uh . . . *Sorry*. Quick five minute break, there, to ponder a little more on the manifold virtues of Ms Von Gerkan.

Yeah.

That's better.

Now where *were* we?

So they take the Hunger Artist out of his cage – he fights it for a while (doesn't *want* to leave – is there a name for that? I don't know why, but I'm thinking it might actually be called 'Hostage Syndrome'. Isn't it what happened to Patty Hearst? Where you kinda *become* your oppressor?), but he's so weak now that they can easily drag him out, even under duress.

Then the band strikes up (to prevent him from speaking – he'd probably ask to go back *in* again, or make a depressing speech and ruin the celebratory atmosphere) and he is set down in front of a table laid with food (a veritable banquet) and obliged to eat some of it.

But he cannot.

So the Impresario crams a few bits and pieces into his hapless mouth as the band plays on. Then the Impresario pretends that the Artist has asked him to propose a toast to the public (although he proposed no such thing) and the toast is made, then everybody disperses, perfectly satisfied.

Time passes (in the story), and a gradual change takes

place in the public's taste re fasting. Kafka says that there may've been 'profound' reasons for this change, but, 'who was going to bother about that?', i.e. he doesn't give a damn what the reasons are. Or *he* does, perhaps, but society doesn't. So what the heck, eh?

This apparent 'indifference' eventually turns into an active hostility (which is where we are now, fasting-wise, I guess – except for in India, maybe, and some other Eastern countries where doing without still has strong associations with devotion and piety).

The Artist and his impresario go their separate ways. The Impresario is just an opportunist – your typical shonky manager – and within the story he basically represents Capitalism (note, capital C). The Artist subsequently sells himself to a circus who simply want to trade off his famous name (and have no interest in his craft, *per se*).

And *then* (to cut a short story shorter), he's just left in his cage to starve and nobody actually gives a damn about him. Because the Impresario isn't there, he just carries on (he never *stops*). He breaks all these fasting limits and records, but nobody even notices (in essence, Kafka's implying that while the Impresario was merciless he was also an essential *cog* in the fasting machine – because in his own, rough-hewn way, he was committed to the Artist. You know? The way McDonald's, say, are committed to the *cow*).

Anyhow, the Artist fasts and fasts, but nobody even sees him any more. He's just this bag of bones in an old cage under a pile of dirty straw.

One day the circus 'overseer' observes that the cage is empty and asks why. They shift the straw and expose the Hunger Artist. He is still alive, but only just. He's in a terrible state – not at all blissful or victorious (as you might've imagined) but full of hatred and self-disgust. He whispers (in his last breaths – and to an indifferent audience) that his fasting is in no way 'admirable', and then he explains why . . .

Man – you're just gonna have to go out and buy the book. Because I can't quote this entire section, even though I'd love to. Suffice to say, the Artist whispers to the overseer that the only reason he ever fasted was because he couldn't ever find 'the food I liked'.

Then he dies and they replace him with a panther.

Fin.

After I throw down the book, I can't help dwelling on it. This idea (this – a*hem* – 'grande dénouement') that the Artist is only what he is (*who* he is) because he actually *hates all food* is rather an ingenious one. And it's not just *literal*, i.e. it's not so much food he rejects as life itself (love, ambition, Art, sex, who cares? *Everything*).

Did Blaine sympathise with this tragic creature (I wonder) when *he* read the story? Or did he hold him in contempt? Is this how *he* feels? Is this *his* psychology? I mean are his stunts about holding life precious (which I suppose would have to be the official PR – or they'd *section* him, basically), or are they about holding it cheap (or even holding it *at bay*)? Because surely if you hold life cheap, the risks you take *don't actually signify anything*? They're just empty gestures. And the stunt itself is stripped of all meaningfulness.

What makes *us* so angry (we puffed-up, sensitive, Western *ticks*) is seeing all the aspirations of capitalism degraded by the man who has pretty much everything (this young,

143

handsome, charming, intelligent, multi-*multi*million-aire). He has it all – everything we yearn for – and yet he casts it casually, haughtily – *publicly* – aside . . .

Well, for the princely sum of five million dollars . . .

The ultimate Capitalist gesture of *Anti*-Capitalism.

No *wonder* we're so pissed off.

He's magnificently lit. *Blaine*. I ponder this fact as I turn *my* light off.

At night you can see his bright little glass pod from miles around. In 'A Hunger Artist' Kafka says how the Artist loves to have the full glare of artificial light upon him. The Impresario actually provides especially enthusiastic 'watchers' with pocket torches so that at night they can shine them full in his face as he tries to rest.

And the Artist welcomes this. *Screw* sleep! He *loves* the light. He wants everything to be seen. He wants the light – he *needs* the light – to dispel all doubt.

Blaine is also lit – day and night – for TV. I'm not certain how he feels about it. But I suppose this masochistic urge to be focused upon is all very much part and parcel of the modern idea of celebrity. Why else would they call it 'the limelight'?

The light brings truth and it brings validation ('If everybody wants to *look* so badly,' the tragically hounded yet horribly insecure star reasons, 'I *must* be worth looking at . . .').

The light also brings moths. And mosquitoes. And all manner of other pests.

But that's just the arse-end of showbusiness, I guess.

Can't sleep.

I lie in bed, shivering, my mind *infested* by the Kafka. To temporarily distract myself, I try and remember Blaine's TV shows. I half-recollect seeing them – ages ago now – the one with the pole-standing stunt and the one when he was packed up in ice. The stunts (so far as I can recollect) were interspersed with Blaine wandering around the place, just doing his tricks.

He had this one scam with a discarded beer can: approached a couple in a park (lying on their picnic blanket), picked up this spent beer can next to where they were sitting (was it their can? Or his can?), tipped it up (it was empty) then ran his hand over the ring-pull so it looked – for all the world – like he'd *resealed* it (how he do dat?). Then he opened the can again and started pouring. Beer spills out in apparent abundance. He even offers the can to the blanket man so that he can drink some, and he does.

Right.

So it doesn't take a genius to figure out how that particular trick worked . . . Some kind of tiny, sliding door inside the can which – when you tip it a particular way – latches back and allows a portion of beer – previously trapped in the can's bottom, to pour forth.

Then there was a trick with a pigeon, a dead pigeon. Blaine (apparently arbitrarily) attracts the attention of a passing eccentric (this oldish guy, walking about the place, 'exercising' his pet budgerigar on his shoulder) and shows him this pigeon lying dead in a patch of sun . . .

I open my eyes in the dark

Yeah like your average New Yorker is gonna be so incredibly *distressed* by the premature demise of a 'Rat o' the Air'.

Anyhow, Blaine holds his hand over the bird (like a Healer, if I remember correctly) and after a short while it stirs, then it stands up, then it flies. Apparently (if my investigations on the internet are anything to go by) he does the same trick with a fly (maybe the fly was just a dry-run for something bigger).

This prank is *all* about timing, the way I'm seeing it, and refrigeration. The only thing that'll simulate death in any sentient creature is the cold. So Blaine sticks some godforsaken pigeon into a refrigerator until it passes out, calculates the time it'll take for it to come back to again, then engineers the entire 'meeting' to take place at the exact midway point in this process – keeps the guy talking for as long as he thinks he needs to etc.

I presume his 'team' will've picked on this guy for a reason. He probably exercises his bird at the same time in that park every day. He obviously *likes* birds, maybe he feeds the pigeons or something – I mean this trick is hardly gonna work out so well if Blaine randomly picks on some passing neurotic female who happens to think pigeons are a pest – has 3,000 of the fuckers ruining the masonry on her building, shitting everywhere etc. or is *phobic* about them (just imagine, he calls her over, shows her the dead bird – a cause, in her mind, for righteous celebration – and then brings this vile creature straight back to life again. Good *God*. I see a major lawsuit pending).

I clearly remember him doing a load of tricks on kids, and one particularly bad one where he takes this young boy's penknife and sticks it – with much *oohing* and *aaahing* – through his tongue.

The kid isn't entertained. He's absolutely fucking *horrified*.

And Blaine? Totally delighted. Eyes shining. Feeding on his disquiet. Smiling crazily. *Eating* it up.

Now I don't want to come over all Mary Whitehouse (and if I do, and it creeps you out, then just bear in mind

147

the traumatic legacy of Douglas Sinclair MacKenny, Post Officer *extraordinaire*), but wasn't that tongue-stabbing thing just a little bit too much? Kids are suggestible, and that makes them vulnerable. So maybe (and I have to give the guy a fair *go*, I suppose) Blaine showed the boy how he'd done the trick, afterwards, to make sure he wasn't utterly fucked-up by it.

Maybe.

(*How'd* he do it, anyway? Has he got a pierced tongue? Was it an optical illusion?)

His public manner (magic-wise) – now I come to think about it – is not at all what you might expect. In interviews he can be difficult (unhelpful, sarcastic, slow, monosyllabic – that's all part of his mystique) but on the TV shows he's almost sycophantic. He *really* wants to please. He actively *seeks* approval. And he's *clumsy*. Most of the tricks depend on him distracting the attention of the trickee for a second, so he drops an object or stumbles. Then he repeatedly apologises (another distraction, you fucking moron, so stop saying 'that's okay', and start looking at what he's *doing* . . .).

He's not a scary magician. He's a friendly one. He smiles a lot. He maintains plenty of eye contact (can't be shifty, can't look down, can't seem uncertain . . .)

Shit.

(My own eyes fly open again.)

I suddenly remember how he did this whole section on one of the shows from Haiti (or somewhere), a place where magic isn't just a beguiling branch of the entertainment industry, but a fundamental part of the culture – a *religion* – and he's doing all these tricks for these people who plainly think he's the Devil (or at the very least, the Devil's proxy – his American catspaw). And they're scared.

Really scared. And – at points – *he* seems a little scared (by the fear he's generating). *Man*. That was so . . . *Uh* . . .

A second later – I remember how, in another episode, he went into the South American rainforest and met this tribe of primitive people and did a bunch of tricks for them. In the commentary he's going, 'They could quite easily kill us if they get at all frightened or suspicious . . .', then the next thing we see is Blaine on his knees in front of a pack of rainforest *children*, cutting circles with a knife into the flesh of his hand, then telling one of the kids to open up *his* hand, where he sees – to his palpable horror – that he has the exact-same blood-mark etched into his own tiny palm.

What? You're telling me that the tribal elders wouldn't've lopped his damn *balls* off if they'd actually witnessed this baroque spectacle for themselves (and were as 'dangerous' as he said they were)? And are *we* – the viewers – seriously meant to believe that these 'dangerous' pygmies would just stand casually by and applaud as he fucks around with their young 'uns delicate minds and go, 'that's weird, how'd he *do* it?' *Eh*?

Uh-*uh*.

Hang on . . .

I suddenly sit bolt upright.

Korine!

I must ring Jalisa and see if Korine was involved. Because this idea really *smacks* of Korine. That bizarre and unsettling conflation of cynicism and simplicity . . . Isn't that *just* his style?

The more I think about it the less I *like* this whole rainforest/Haiti element. Because what's Blaine saying, really? What's he trying to make us think? In some senses he's undermining the culture of these peoples (because we know he's just performing tricks, but to them, magic and mystery are a part of the dark side. They're real. They're life-threatening).

Effectively he's telling all us complacent Western viewers that these 'primitive' people are fools (I mean they're so honest, so *credulous*!) but at the same time their fear is informing us, subconsciously, that magic is real, that *his* magic is real, that it *can* be serious. And Blaine is the route between these two worlds. Blaine is the short cut. He proposes himself as the bridge by which we cross back and forth (from cynicism, to disbelief, to naivety, to believing).

Hmmn.

Interesting journey.

I suddenly need to get up.

I go for a piss. I stand by the window. When I look at the clock it's 2 a.m. and I'm fucking *wired.*

Hot.

Next thing I know, I've pulled on some jeans, a T-shirt, grabbed my trainers, my portable CD-player, my jacket, and I'm heading out of the house and towards the river.

Eight

And there she is. Aphra. Sitting quietly on the wall. Alone. Chin jinked up. Ankles crossed demurely. Hands resting on her lap. Tupperware bag on the floor by her feet. Like a riddlesome Sphinx. Totally rapt.

I'm up on the bridge – in a light sweat, a feverish *fug* – staring down at her.

She has eyes for no one but the magician. She doesn't see me there. So I lean over (gradually catching my breath), and watch her, watching him. And then I watch the magician (to try and tap into her fascination – but he's fast asleep, tucked up inside his sleeping bag, not moving). And then I watch her again.

It's quiet, except for the occasional van horn (some cheesed-off Monday-morning joker on his way to the early shift), the buzz of the lights on the bridge, and the wet sounds of the river.

Eerie.

Only me, and her, and some tramp huddled up in a blanket on the floor, and three security guards (but they're miles off, in a far corner of the compound, chatting over a flask and a fag), and (but of *course*) there's David Blaine, the International Superstar.

Eventually I make my way down on to the embankment and hitch myself up casually on to the wall a short way along from her. She doesn't seem to notice me at first and I dare not speak. She's in some kind of trance. But peaceful. Just sitting on that wall, staring up at the box. Lips slightly parted. Breathing shallow.

When ten long minutes have ticked by she glances over and says, 'You don't smell right. You're ill.'

'Had the flu,' I confirm croakily.

'Still got it,' she says, then takes my hand and sniffs at the palm. She pulls a face. 'Wank,' she says, then tips her head, speculatively, 'at about eleven o'clock last night, I reckon ..' She sniffs again. 'A blackcurrant Lemsip at twelve..' She pauses, frowning, then inhales for a final time. 'And you stroked a *dog*. A male dog. A *big* dog. Just before you came out.'

How'd she *do* that?

I leave my hand resting in her hand.

'How'd you *do* that?'

'It's my job,' she says, matter of factly.

'It's your job to know I had a *wank* at eleven?'

'I'm reading your book,' she says.

'*Shane*?' I stutter, slow to catch up. 'You are?'

'Yeah.'

'Are you enjoying it?'

'I've reached Chapter six,' she says, 'the summer's almost over and Fletcher's back. He's got a big contract. He wants the Homesteaders off his land ..'

'Ah.' I nod, sagely.

'I feel a little sorry for him,' she says.

'How's that?'

'Because he used to own it all, the entire *valley*, then he had some bad luck after the drought and hard winter

152

of '86.' She sighs: 'And everybody started moving in on him, stealing his grazing...'

Typical *girl*, eh? To get everything the wrong way round.

'It's the American *West*', I explain. 'That's how the nation was *built* – individuals, staking their rightful claim...'

'Rightful?' she looks quizzical. 'Fletcher was there first.'

'The Native Americans were there *first*,' I hiss. 'If you want to get all pernickety about it.'

Her eyes widen. 'Then maybe Fletcher should give the land back to *them*,' she says, 'not just a random bunch of greedy white settlers.'

'The point of the book,' I growl, 'is to celebrate the struggle of the underdog.'

'Well maybe they're celebrating the *wrong* underdog,' she persists.

'There's no right or wrong in fiction,' I mutter, 'the story's just the story.'

She's quiet for a moment.

'And the mother's a bloody *tramp*,' she suddenly says (cheerfully ignoring my meta-textual input).

'What?'

'A tramp,' she reiterates.

'Marian? A *tramp*?' I gasp, snatching my hand back. (The *sainted* Marian? She of the deep-dish pie?)

Aphra nods, then she grins. 'You have a problem with that?'

I shake my head. 'Of course not. You're just...' I struggle to find the words (I've got *flu*, remember?). 'You're just *merciless*, that's all.'

She's wide-eyed.

'*Moi?*'

Ha *ha*.

'The whole *point* of the book is this wonderful sense of the subtle interplay between the three adult characters,' I crisply lecture. 'Marian is attracted to Shane, but she loves her husband. It's a dilemma. It's interesting. It's subtle.'

'Life must be pretty bloody dull . . .' Aphra concedes, kicking out her feet (purple-suede eighties-style pixie-boots with lethal-looking three-inch stiletto heels) 'on that dusty old Homestead . . .'

'Precisely.'

'Just stuck in a shack all day with an infuriating kid . . .'

'What?'

My back straightens (now this *is* fighting talk). 'You think *Bob's* infuriating?'

She shrugs. 'He just never stops talking.'

My eyes bulge. 'But he *narrates* in the first person. The boy *tells* the story.'

She bursts out laughing.

'I *know* that,' she says, nudging me. 'I'm just *kidding*.'

Oh.

She gazes up at the magician for a while, then cocks her head, inquisitively. 'Was it a good wank?'

(Is nothing sacred?)

'So *was* it?' she prompts.

'A little feverish, perhaps,' I sullenly mutter.

'*Everybody* gets horny when they're ill . . .' she says. 'Remember that angry old bastard on Oxford Street who used to march up and down with his neat little placard saying "Less Protein, Less Lust"?'

I nod.

'He was *right*,' she says. 'Too much meat. Too much sitting down. That's at the heart of it.'

'And you've been sitting here *how* long?' I flirt.

She clucks on her tongue, then glances up, then falls deep into her trance again.

'D'you think *he* gets horny?' I ask, a few minutes later, 'just lying there all day.'

'Of course he does . . .'

She frowns. 'But then after a while *everything* gets imbued with it. The original urge just filters down into each movement. Each spasm. Each blink . . .'

'How very Zen,' I say, tartly.

'The way the box rocks,' she sighs 'His breathing. The *hunger*.'

She falls quiet again, smiling.

'You love watching him,' I murmur thickly.

'When he's sleeping,' she says, slowly nodding. 'Yes I do. When it's quiet . . .'

(Is that a subtle hint, perhaps?)

'Are you a fan of his magic?' I ask (already knowing the answer).

'No.' She shakes her head. 'Not especially. And it might sound ridiculous, but I never really *intend* to come . . . I mean, sometimes I'm on my way somewhere else, and then . . .'

She shrugs.

'You get distracted?'

'You probably think it's pathetic,' she mutters, glancing over at me for a moment, then straight back up at Blaine (as if she's driving the *car* of Blaine – has to keep her eyes on the road at *all* times), 'but being here while he sleeps, before he wakes, *as* he wakes . . .'

She grimaces, 'It just makes everything feel better. Feel

155

whole again. And often – if I concentrate really hard – I can hang on to this feeling for the rest of the day – this quiet, this hopefulness. I can cook and wash and go into work...'

She smiles. 'Remember Christmas time, when you're a kid, and the presents are all laid out under the tree? Nothing opened yet? Just *pure* anticipation?'

'Yes.'

'It's like that.'

Okay. I nod.

'And it's the *tiniest* things...' she continues (warming to her subject now), 'the way he *holds* himself as he sleeps. I find such amazing *comfort* in that. And in all the insignificant stuff. All the details.'

I gaze up at the magician myself, hunting for the minutiae. I see a dark blob in a bag. The lights. The glass.

'Either he's flat on his back ...' she says, observing my interest, and (much to my delight) responding, 'and I imagine him just gazing up at the sky, at the stars, at the vapour trails at dawn, or having these astonishing *dreams*. Oh my *God*. The hallucinations ... Can you imagine how wild they must be by now?'

She doesn't wait for an answer. 'Or else he curls up, on his side, like a boy. Like a little kid. And there's something so fragile about him. So lonely...'

Her voice is softer, almost tender.

'Then as he actually *wakes*,' she continues, her eyes sparkling now, with a real sense of drama, 'he moves his hand. Just this *tiny* bit. And then he adjusts his head on his pillow. And then he rubs his fingers through his hair – you'll have noticed his hair is getting longer, and curlier...'

(Oh will I?)

'And then he has a little scratch. Of his beard. A real root around...I mean it's nothing significant, just trivial details. Things you wouldn't notice if he was right there in bed with you. You wouldn't *see* them then. Or you might even find them irritating...'

She ruminates on this point for a while. 'Or maybe if you *knew* him, they'd just be a part of a picture which was already *drawn* – if you know what I mean...'

She glances over at me. A nod appears necessary, so I nod, accordingly.

'But there's so much in so *little* here...,' she says, her eyes sliding back again. 'When he wakes, for example, he wakes very quickly. He has a lovely no-nonsense approach to rising. He's like, *yup*, I'm awake. Let's sit up...And then he sits up...'

Her voice is full of wonder: 'And his eyes are so *innocent*. Like he's washed *clean*. And then almost straight away he sees us watching him and he feels a moment's anxiety – you can sense it, this tiny *tremor* – then he responds. He lifts his hand. Very weakly. Automatically. The hands are beautiful. I *love* to see his hands – I know it's kind of corny – but his hands say everything about him. They're the way he *speaks*. They're his *tongue*...'

She inspects her own hands for a moment. 'After two seconds, maybe three, he switches off. He picks up his pen and his notebook, looks down, frowns. And it's a lovely moment, somehow, that brief closing off. And really *necessary*. Because often when I see him in the day – when I'm wandering past on my way out shopping, or to the hospital – he's so empty. Just open. Resigned. Everything's simply flooding in. But at that moment, when he awakens, he's entirely *himself*, and

157

you get to see all this confusion and sweetness, this incredible *unease* . . .'

She smiles.

'That's why I come.'

I sneeze (I've been holding it back for a while, now, not wanting to ruin her moment or anything – I mean God forbid I should impair her charming description of his delicate *hands* with my barbaric, phlegm-racked expostulation).

'Bless you,' she says.

'So you never saw him do a trick?' I ask.

'Nope.'

'That's weird.'

She shrugs.

'He cut off his *ear* . . .' I say, wiping my nose, 'at the press conference.'

'Did he?'

She's barely even listening.

'It was like he was going out of his *way* to kill his credibility,' I bumble on. 'And when he's finally *finished* – all this grunting and groaning, all this false blood and gore – some guy in the press corps goes, "What about the *other* one?"

'I mean to pull a stunt like *that*. And right *then*. These are hardened professionals. These are probably the same people who laughed at David Copperfield for flying around on wires, pretending like he was Peter fucking Pan.'

She frowns. 'David *who*?'

Oh dear.

'In one of Blaine's films,' I say, suddenly *determined* (more than anything) to make her interested, 'there's this little kid, just walking along a New York street with his mother, and Blaine goes up to the kid and says, "Hold on a minute . . ." and reaches out and pulls a strand of cotton from the collar of his sweater.'

I inspect the collar of *her* sweater and pull off a stray hair.

'Why'd he do that?' she asks (glancing down, worriedly, at her own shoulder).

I don't answer.

'So Blaine shows the kid this strand of cotton,' I continue, 'and then puts it into his mouth . . .'

'Into the *boy's* mouth?'

'His *own* mouth. He chews on it for a while – really concentrating – then he swallows, then he opens his mouth and sticks out his tongue to show the kid that the piece of cotton's not in his mouth any more . . .'

I stick out my own tongue, to demonstrate. She winces. I guess it might be a little furry.

(But so far so good.)

'Then he waits for a while. Looks a little confused – like he's not entirely in control of what's happening – then he winces, lifts up his *shirt* and starts inspecting his chest.'

I lift up my own shirt.

'Why?' she asks, staring at my belly.

'That's the *trick*,' I say (pulling it in slightly).

'Oh.'

'He inspects his chest with his *fingers* for a while, and then he suddenly locates something. Like an imperfection of some kind, on the skin. Right in the middle. And he starts to pick at it, and to pull. And he pulls, and he pulls . . . And suddenly you can see that he's pulling a strand of cotton, through his skin. Actually *through* his skin. There's a close-up and everything. The skin is actually *tenting* under the pressure of his fingers and the cotton . . .'

'That's disgusting,' she says. '*Tenting* . . .'

(She's disgusted by my *vocabulary*, note, yet not even remotely alarmed by Blaine's visceral exhibitionism.)

'I know.'

'My God,' she marvels, 'and it's the *same* piece of cotton . . .'

'You think so?'

She frowns.

'Because for the trick to *work*,' I explain, 'I imagine he implanted a piece of twine into his chest earlier – maybe under his actual flesh, or under a flap of *false* skin. Then he approaches the kid and pretends to pull a strand of cotton off his collar – but he probably already has the cotton in his hand . . . maybe it's normal cotton, or even cotton that dissolves in saliva – and he eats it, then lifts up his shirt. The two events are entirely unrelated . . .'

It takes her a while to digest this information.

'So it's your *job*,' I say, 'to smell things?'

She nods (still frowning over all the other stuff).

'At the hospital?'

She blinks. 'The hospital?'

'Isn't that where you work?'

She shakes her head, almost chuckling at the notion. 'John Lewis,' she says, 'the department store. Years ago, I was a sniffer there.'

'A sniffer?'

'But now I mostly do consultation work. I'm actually a qualified perfumier.'

I stare at her nose. She stares at *my* nose.

'He was an actor,' I say, 'to start off with.'

'Who?'

'Blaine.'

She stops staring at my nose.

'Really? An *actor*?'

(I can tell she doesn't particularly like this idea.)

'A child actor. Adverts. Soaps . . .'

'An actor,' she murmurs, glancing up at the box. 'So you think he's acting in there?'

I shrug.

'An actor,' she says again, then frowns.

'A *sniffer*,' I say.

She flaps her hand, irritably.

'But that's interesting.'

'No. It's boring,' she says.

'Why?'

'Because I'm hypersensitive to stuff. Strong scents. Tastes. Dust. Pollen. I get headaches.'

'Migraines.'

Silence.

'I'd like to smell *him* though,' she says, tipping her head towards the magician.

'You would?'

'Yeah. I could tell his people things. I could help. I can sense minor physical imbalances. Gauge certain underlying stresses . . .'

'Like a horse. Horses smell fear.'

She smiles. '*Exactly* like that.'

She turns and appraises me closely for a second. 'You wear Odeur 53,' she says, 'Comme des Garçons. It's very sweet. Very feminine. I noticed it the first time you walked past. They marketed it as a scent with a *gap* in the middle of the aroma . . .' She grins. 'Like an *anti*-scent. It was very clever. I mean *complete* bullshit . . .'

She pauses. 'But *you* fell for it, *eh*?'

Before I can respond she lifts up her left leg. 'D'you like my shoes?'

She rotates her foot.

I'm still lagging behind a little.
'Uh, *no . . .*' I slowly shake my head. 'I really *don't*.'
'Good. Come home with me,' she says, and stands up.

But I've got the *flu*.
Her shoes are *awful*.
And I *wanked* at eleven . . .

That's only a couple of *hours* ago.

Well, okay. *Four*.

Nine

I am awoken – at ten – by Solomon, who takes the unusual step of journeying downstairs to pay me a brief visit; not out of any concern for my health – it soon transpires – but because Bud (the dog) has devoured the post again.

He holds out a tragic-looking copy of Primo Levi's *If This Is a Man/ The Truce*, and a slightly *less* well-masticated copy of *David Blaine, Mysterious Stranger*.

'I have an earlier edition of this upstairs,' he says, pointing at the Levi, 'if you'd only bothered to look.'

Then he grimaces and adds, 'You have tufts of tissue *everywhere*.'

I paw at my face, blearily.

'*Everywhere*.'

I paw again.

'Have you read it, then?' I ask (as I paw).

'Well that's *generally* what books are for . . .' he murmurs.

'Is it good?'

Solomon ponders this question for a moment. 'Is it good? One of the intellectual titans of the last century writes a legendary first-person account of his experiences of the Holocaust . . . Is it *good . . .*?'

He smiles brightly: 'Yeah. It's a *romp*.'

He tosses the two books on to my bed and then glances down at the abandoned Kafka. He kicks it, gently, with a leather-booted foot.

'Let me get this straight . . .' he murmurs, 'I break up with Jalisa . . .'

'*Shhh*!' I whisper, then peer suspiciously over my shoulder, then perform my (frankly, utterly hilarious) zipping mime. He stares at me, blankly.

'I break up with *Jalisa*,' he repeats, 'and to help me get *over* the whole thing you immediately resolve to transform yourself into her slavering, half-witted, intellectual *disciple*.'

'The Kafka was great,' I shrug, 'for your information she was *right* about the Kafka.'

'Well, *bully* for her.'

His mouth tightens, jealously.

'It's given me a whole new perspective on this stuff,' I say airily. 'In fact I've been making some enquiries of my own and was wondering if you might give me her phone number . . .'

'No way on God's Earth,' he snaps.

'Oh come *on*.'

'You actually *went out* last night?' he asks, pointing at my sweater (which I didn't bother pulling off before I fell into bed).

'For a couple of hours.'

(I'm sounding a little defensive, a little wheedly.)

'Where?'

I don't answer.

'*Where*?'

(Who's he think he is? My *dad*?)

'A *walk*. I was feverish.'

He stares at me, unblinking, and then ... 'Oh my *God*,' he says, 'that *fucking magician*! You went to see *Blaine*, didn't you?'

I shake my head.

'Three in the *morning*,' he gurgles. 'You're half-dead with *flu*. Are you out of your *mind*?'

'I went to see *Aphra*,' I squeak.

'What?' Solomon reins himself in, quite commendably.

'One of the guards told me she was down there most nights. And I couldn't sleep. So I decided to go and take a quick look.'

'And she was there?'

I nod.

'Alone?'

I nod again. 'Aphra, a couple of guards and a tramp. Three fifteen a.m.'

He takes a small step back, stretches out a well-muscled arm and leans against the chimney breast. 'Then what?'

'We talked.'

He slits his eyes. 'You do *fuck*?'

I ignore this.

'We went back to her apartment . . .'

'*Apartment*,' he scoffs.

'We went back to her *flat* and looked at her shoe collection,' I say haughtily. 'She collects second-hand *shoes*.'

'Does she actually wear them?'

'Yes.'

He wrinkles up his nose. 'That's disgusting.'

'She's a sniffer,' I continue (suddenly rather *revelling* in the perplexing wonder that is Aphra). 'She used to work at John Lewis, in the Returns Department. She told me how they hire people with sensitive noses to 'sniff the returns and check if they've been used or not.'

'I've heard about that before,' he says.

'Bull*shit* you have.'

He shrugs.

'So did you do *fuck*?' he asks again (I mean who could *guess* that this horn-ball had just broken up?).

'Well once we got *home*,' I sidetrack, 'she told me I had to be very quiet, because there was someone sleeping in the spare room . . .'

'Who was it?'

I shrug. 'No idea.'

'The *sister*,' he chuckles, 'the one who took your number. She comes out of the bedroom while you're looking at the shoes, buck-naked, and rotates like a small tornado on your lap . . .'

'It might've been a man,' I say, 'I think I heard a man's voice at one point. Heard someone call out, like they were having a bad dream or something . . .'

'Hang on there. . . Let's just wind back a bit. . .' Solomon quickly inspects his watch. 'I need some coffee. I have an appointment at eleven. Come upstairs with me and finish off.'

I don't move. He scowls.

'I'll make it worth your while,' he promises.

'Jalisa's number,' I sigh, collapsing back smugly on to my pillows, 'or no details.'

He gives this some thought. 'Only if it's *really* mortifying,' he says.

'Trust me. It is.'

'I mean *really* humiliating. Really awful. Utterly degraded. Vile. *Sickening*.'

'I can tick all your boxes,' I brag, 'but give me Jalisa's number, up front, or the deal's off.'

Solomon heads for the stairs.

'Gonna pretend I didn't hear that,' he mutters.

God. I should've *known* he'd get his own back.

Twenty minutes later (meeting? *What* meeting?) Solomon is delivering me a lengthy lecture on the myth of the Protocols of the Elders of Zion.

'It was essentially the cornerstone of the anti-semitic idea,' he says. 'This fantastical notion of a shadowy group of Jewish Elders who are holding secret meetings, raising funds, forwarding the Jewish agenda on an international platform and setting serious social and political changes in motion...'

'But they didn't even exist?'

'Nope. Just anti-Jewish scaremongering.'

I blow my nose, bleakly.

'All I'm really *saying*,' he continues, 'is that Jalisa is perfectly good – in fact extremely *talented* – at repackaging the chat and the gossip and the hearsay. She's an intellectual firecracker. A *magpie*. She loves nothing better than to line her nest with all that *sparkles* in the culture. But the dull stuff? The *flat* stuff? The dates? The facts? The context? Uh-*uh*. Nothing. Zilch. Nought. *Zero*.'

I blow my nose for a second time.

'I mean *I* should know. I dated the girl for two damn *months*. If you're looking for *depth* there then you're diving in at the wrong end, my friend.'

'Fine.'

(Let's just *ignore* the diving metaphor, shall we?)

'And if the water's too shallow, you're gonna end up breaking your *neck*.'

(Should've known he wouldn't let us get away with that.)

'Because what's the point of reading the Kafka if you can't set it into some kind of historical perspective, *huh*?'

Silence.

'I mean she didn't even know he was Czechoslovakian. She thought he was *German*.'

'She did,' I eventually murmur. 'That's true.'

'I'll bet you fifty *quid*,' Solomon continues, 'that Jalisa knows diddly-*squat* about the Russian pogroms under the czar...'

I smile, weakly.

'Or the Dreyfus Case.'

I merely shrug.

'*Eh*?'

I shake my head.

(*Ouch.* Headache back.)

'She probably thinks the Beerhall Putsch was a dispute about *lager*.'

I laugh, weakly (Do Jews even *drink* beer?).

'To prove my point,' he says, 'I'm gonna *give* you her number.'

He pauses for a second: 'In fact you can ring her on my phone. I haven't deleted her digits yet.'

He takes his phone out of his pocket, selects her number, sets it ringing and slides it across the table at me.

'There you go,' he says.

I refuse to touch the phone.

'I don't want to speak to her *now*,' I say.

'Hello?'

Jalisa answers her phone.

'*Solomon*!' I growl.

'Hello?'

Solomon just grins.

'Hello?'

I pick up the phone.

'Jalisa,' I say. 'It's Adair. I'm speaking to you on Solomon's phone.'

'Why?' she asks.

'Ask her about the Dreyfus Case,' Solomon whispers.

I close my eyes for a second. I open them.

'Jalisa,' I say, 'Solomon wants you to tell me about the Dreyfus Case.'

A short silence follows.

'Oh. *Okay*,' Jalisa intonates each syllable with a terrifying, clipped efficiency. 'Tell him that Dreyfus was a Jewish officer in the late-nineteenth century French army who was scapegoated in a spying case because of his religious orientation.'

I look over at Solomon. 'She knows about Dreyfus,' I say. 'Jewish officer. French army. Scapegoated in spying case *et cetera*.'

He slits his eyes.

'Beerhall Putsch,' he says.

'Tell that arrogant, fat-headed little *dick*,' she snaps (before I've even said anything), 'that The Beerhall Putsch took place in Munich in 1923 and was Hitler's first, unsuccessful attempt at taking power.'

'She knows about the Putsch,' I say.

He leans across the table and snatches the phone off me.

'I was *right* about the food,' he hisses. 'It transpires that Aphra has a highly developed sense of *smell*.'
Pause.

'I said it was "aromatic",' he squawks. 'I said it was "unusually aromatic".'

Another pause.

'So what were the Protocols of the Elders of Zion?' he asks.

He listens for three seconds and then hangs up.

'What did she say?'

'She didn't have a *clue.*'

'*Really*?'

'Of course not.'

He puts the phone down and picks up the coffee jug. He clears his throat.

'So you're telling me that Aphra actually sits on that wall *every* night?' (*Uh* – excuse me, but am I currently the *only* person in my social circle with any kind of serious commitment to conversational *flow*?)

'That's what the security guard said.' I shrug. 'Sean or *Saul* or something . . .'

'And after you found that out, you *still* wanted to shag the girl?'

'I don't believe I ever actually confessed to such an urge,' I sniff.

'Didn't have to,' he grimaces. 'It's written all over you.'

I glance down at my torso, as if hunting for the lettering.

'Tell me about the shoes,' he says, pulling out a chair.

'I thought you were disgusted by the shoes.'

'I am.'

Right.

Fine.

'Well, she actually had the shoes all lined up on her dining-room table,' I say, 'although she has no dining-room as such, just a corner of the lounge close to the french windows which is a designated "dining area". But the lounge is big and there's plenty of room . . .'

'Could you sketch me out a floor plan?' Solomon asks (the *bitch*).

'Anyway,' I stagger manfully on, 'attached to each pair of shoes – and there must've been about fifty or so – was a small, handwritten tag, and printed on to each tag was a list of information particular to that pair – where they were bought –'

'But *why* were the shoes on the table?' he butts in.

'I don't know. I didn't ask.'

'You didn't *ask*?'

I roll my eyes. 'Do you actually *want* me to get to the part when we have terrible sex or not?'

'Shoes on the fucking *table*,' Solomon mutters. (Yeah. He wants the sex part *real* bad.)

'All the shoes were antique. And even *I* could tell that it was a pretty amazing collection . . .'

'What do you mean, "even *I* could tell . . .",' Solomon scoffs. 'You're shoe *obsessed*.'

'I am not.'

'You *are*.'

'I am *not*.'

'Well, you're the only person *I've* ever met,' he snipes, 'who conducts formal *burial* services for their worn-out trainers.'

'So I have an affection for Chuck Taylor,' I snap. 'What *of* it?'

Silence.

'She actually had a couple of pairs,' I continue (rather sullenly), 'from the seventeenth century. French. Absolutely exquisite. Said she only ever wore them inside.'

'People had smaller feet back then,' Solomon opines.

'Yeah. The shoes were minute. All hand stitched. But Aphra has tiny feet. Size four. So they fit.'

171

'How tall is she?'

'Uh . . . five two? Three?'

'I have this image in my mind now,' he mutters, 'of a girl like a *tent* peg.'

'The feet aren't too small,' I leap to her defence. 'Not at *all*. They're fine. In fact they're . . . they're *nice*.'

Solomon merely grunts.

'They *are*. I saw them. Soft skin. Neat little toes. Finely arched. She actually tried on several pairs for me while I was just sitting there . . .'

'Which shoes did you fuck her in?'

(Does this man have no *concept* of foreplay?)

'On each *tag*,' I persist, 'is a brief description of where she bought the shoes, how much she paid, and a detailed analysis of the previous person who owned them.'

'*Wah*?'

Solomon does a couple of gay blinks.

'*Yeah*. See? *Now* you're interested, eh?'

'Is her nose *that* good?'

I nod.

He leans back in his chair. 'I've actually *heard* about people like that before,' he says.

'Bull*shit* you have.'

He shrugs.

'She had this pair of pale-pink pigskin boots from the nineteen-*fifties* – pearl buttons all up the sides – which stretched halfway to her thighs.'

'You know what?' Solomon shakes his head. 'Not only is that historically improbable, but it's physically *un-appealing*. Is she blonde?'

'Brunette.'

'Even so. The insipid pink of the boot, coupled with all those dimpling *acres* of pale, white thigh flesh.'

'Fantastic,' I gasp.

'Repugnant,' he shudders.

We face a brief impasse.

'You owe me fifty quid,' I mutter (piqued for Aphra's thighs), 'Jalisa knew about the Putsch.'

'True,' Solomon concedes, and pulls his wallet from his pocket. As he opens it up and removes the notes (his gambling credentials are *always* impeccable – he'd rather eviscerate a small poodle than welsh on a bet) I spin his phone around and access his address book.
Good.

'So who owned them, then?' he asks, pushing the notes over.

I glance up, guiltily. 'A Frenchman. Very small. Had corns. Probably a dancer. Addicted to painkillers.'

'And did she try them on while you were there?'

'No.'

(This is a lie.)

'Did you listen to any music?'

I squirm in my seat slightly.

'*Well*?'

'She *has* no music. She doesn't listen to music. I only saw an old portable radio / cassette player and two tapes. *The Best of Joan Armatrading* and *The Best of Abba*.'

'Only the best of *everything* for this filly, eh?' Solomon chortles. 'So a big Fuck-Off TV, maybe?'

'Nothing fancy,' I mutter, 'and the TV was bust. Anyway, she claimed she "didn't have time" for TV.'

'Books?'

I clear my throat, anxiously. 'Loads of cook-books. A *Life on Earth* hardback from the TV series . . .'

'Which she presumably didn't actually *see*,' Solomon murmurs.

'And a dictionary. *Collins*.'

'*Man*, she'd better fuck like a hell-hound,' Solomon observes soberly, 'because *By Christ* this girl's an immortal philistine.'

I merely shrug.

'I mean what did you *talk* about all night?'

I shrug again. 'Stuff.'

'*What* stuff?'

'Her shoes. The weather. I don't remember.'

Solomon frowns at me.

'You're not actually going to spill, are you?'

I blow my nose, poignantly.

'I can see it in your face. You're feeling *guilty*. You're already developing some kind of pointless *crush* on this aspirant, star-fucking shoe-fiend. In fact you're planning a fantasy mixed-music cassette tape for her, probably *themed*, even as I speak . . .'

My eyes widen, in shock (and *hurt*), as he snatches up his phone and marches off to his meeting.

Then I grab a stray pencil and chew ferociously on its tip.

Okay. *Right*. Track Three . . .

Something *really* mellow.

Roy Ayers, 'Everybody Loves The Sunshine'.

Bingo.

Then something jazzy – to show my emotional depth and range – but nothing too scary . . .

Ray Charles, 'Don't Let the Sun Catch You Crying'.

Followed by something *really* poppy (*What*? Adair Graham MacKenny taking himself *too* seriously? Not on your bloody *nelly*). 'Who Loves The Sun'. Velvet Underground.

And I'll call it *Aphra's Autumnal Groové* cassette.
('Twenty-four songs about the sun.')

No. On second thoughts, skip the bit in parentheses.

Can't be *too* obvious.

Ten

She prepares me a cup of White Tea in her tiny kitchen. I stand in the open doorway with a thumping headache and my sinuses prickling.

'Made from the newest leaves on the plant,' she whispers, 'which the Chinese reserve for their most *sacred* tea ceremonies . . .'

She inhales the aroma, ecstatically, her eyes tight shut, then opens them and registers my jaded expression. 'Pearls before swine,' she mutters, passing it over (This girl is the last *word* in hospitality, *eh*?) before hunting around in a wall unit and producing a bottle of 10-year-old single malt (from one of the more brutish of the Scottish islands), unscrewing the lid and drinking a nip from the cap.

(By the way that she winces I deduce that it has a kick to it like a bad gear-change on a Kawasaki 500.)

Perhaps it's my blocked-up nose, but the tea is *incredibly* bland (*Sacred*? My arse). And (can this be *just* a coincidence?) she hasn't poured herself a cup.

We tip-toe through to the living room. She shows me her shoes laid out on the dining-room table. There are dozens of others, too, packed neatly into a large, cardboard box. I pull out the pink, pigskin boots and inspect them.

'Never worn the things,' she whispers so quietly that I have to move closer to hear her. 'Never worn them,' she repeats and I feel the warmth of her whisky-breath on my ear.

She steps back, yanking off her left pixie atrocity and pulling the boot on to her foot (simply leaving the pigskin to flap). 'They were handmade in the nineteen fifties,' she explains, 'owned by a Frenchman, a showman. Maybe an actor. He was addicted to painkillers. Smell that . . .'

She offers me the second boot to sniff.

I point to my nose. 'Blocked.'

'Ah.'

She lounges against the arm of the sofa, holding her pigskinned foot out mournfully in front of her. 'There must be over two hundred tiny pearl buttons.'

'Gotta see them done up,' I say, crouching down and taking a hold of her foot. She promptly collapses – with a gurgle – backwards over the arm (almost kicking me in the face) so all that's now visible from my low angle is her shin and her knee and the boot.

'*Loads* of people bringing along their American flags this weekend,' she murmurs up towards the ceiling, yawning, 'but on Friday he'd scrawled this message on to the back of the box.'

I glance up from the boot. 'How'd he do that?'

(Second button, third.)

'I'm not sure. Maybe just in the condensation. I heard someone saying he must've used his lip salve, but I'm not sure he did . . .'

'And what did it say?'

(Fourth – a little *tight*.)

'I can't remember exactly, but something about how he didn't consider himself to be a member of any particular nation or creed, and that what he was doing was meant to be a demonstration of the strength of the human spirit and how he hoped it would give courage to others.'

(Fifth button – my eyes are watering – I sneeze, *hugely* – sixth, seventh.)

'*Bless* you.'

Another yawn.

'But he was really proud of it. Kept retouching it all day, standing on his knees. It gave him something positive to focus on.'

'Really?'

'Yup.'

She burps.

'Sorry. And there was a really noisy woman wrapped up in this *huge* American flag at one point. She was marching around the compound, waving her arms about, offering support. But he just kept turning and pointing at the message he'd written. I think he was touched by her enthusiasm, but irritated by her patriotism.'

(Twelfth button. Thirteenth is missing.)

'Your thirteenth button is missing.'

'I know. There's this *beautiful* blonde woman who comes to see him most nights before he goes to sleep ...'

'That'll be Manon. His girlfriend. She's German. She's apparently staying in one of the caravans in the car park.'

'She's stunning.'

'A model.'

'Yeah. Well whatever she is, she must be incredibly patient.'

'You're not wrong there.'

'I mean how could you *do* that to yourself? If you loved someone?'

'Live in a car park?'

'Starve yourself. Hurt yourself, and expect them to watch on.'

'His mother died when he was twenty-one,' I mutter, 'after a terrible illness, and his father – so far as I'm aware – died when he was young. Perhaps it's vengeance. Or perhaps that's precisely how he understands love. Perhaps – for him – the *journey* of love is in suffering.'

(Twenty-fifth.)

She pokes out her head, to peer at me round the arm, 'That's *deep*.'

She grins.

'The question is,' I muse, 'how long *any* woman could retain her sense of self-worth in the face of these self-destructive acts. You won't've seen the film they made when he packed himself in ice . . .'

'Nope.'

'Incredibly disturbing.'

She pokes her head out again. 'Really?'

'Yeah. The stunt's underway. He's trapped inside this massive ice-block. There are hundreds of people standing there watching. He's unbelievably cold. He's maybe fifty-odd hours in, and he starts to hallucinate. He's basically going into shock.'

I feel her leg stiffen.

'Doesn't anyone try and *help* him?'

'They can't. He has some kind of release sign – or release word – and he hasn't used it yet.'

'*Shit.*'

'Yeah. Anyway, things are all getting a little strange

180

when suddenly his girlfriend arrives. She's come to see him.'

'A different girlfriend?'

'That's exactly my point...'

(Thirty-fourth – I suck on my thumb for a minute.)

'...*Man*, these things are *pesky*. They're tight *and* sharp.'

'So what happens?'

When I finish sucking my thumb I readjust the boots on her legs, then can't stop myself from stretching out my hand and slipping it along the soft skin inside her knee. In automatic response, her knee jerks straight and she kicks me, squarely, on the chin.

So that taught *me*, then.

'*Ow.*'

'Sorry.'

'Anyhow...' The buttoning recommences. 'The girl-friend is this famous actress. Can't remember her name. Tall, brunette, very beautiful – but she looks absolutely fucking *desperate*. I mean maybe I read too much into it at the time, but my feeling was definitely that she didn't like the idea of this stunt, that she was pissed off, that she utterly *resented* being made to parade in front of the public like that, having her fear, her grief, made a part of the drama...'

'Tough call.'

'*Exactly*. Anyway, she walks up to the front of the ice-block and glances in at him. Her expression is not compassionate, but more – kind of – blank. Then she walks off.'

'And what's *he* doing?'

(She's trying to sit up, but I have her leg held too tight.)

'That's the tragic part. When he sees her walking away he goes absolutely bloody ape-shit. *Frantic*. Becomes unbelievably distressed. Is crying, hitting the ice . . . It's *incredibly* claustrophobic to watch.'

'My *God*.'

'I know. And his team fly into a panic. They can see that he's losing it. So they suddenly start trying to cut him out.'

'How long does it take?'

'Too long. A good while. They have to hack into this huge ice-block with an axe or a chain-saw (I can't remember which) and Blaine, meanwhile, has almost come back to himself, and he's shouting at them – gesticulating wildly – but it's impossible to tell if it's because he does or he doesn't want to leave the block . . .'

'Which was it?'

'I don't know . . .'

(Fifty-eighth.)

I clamber up on to my knees and adjust her leg so that now it's lying across my shoulder. I can see her below me, stretched out on the sofa.

'Hope my knickers are clean,' she muses.

'You're not wearing any.'

'Ah.'

She yawns, 'I'm a little claustrophobic.'

Hmmn. *Okay*.

I'm buttoning, now, above the knee. The skin is very soft here, and I have to pull the boot tight to contain its fleshiness.

'*Ouch*,' she mutters.

'Anyway, so he's finally cut free and he's in terrible shock. Shivering uncontrollably, then every so often screaming out, in agony, like someone's just stabbed him.'

'That's the *cold*,' she says, with a shudder.

'Frostbite. They take him to hospital in an ambulance, and the cameras go along with him. His girlfriend is there. I think she's crying. He's in and out of consciousness. It's *really* grim.'

'But he's okay,' she says, 'isn't he?'

'So far as I can remember, I think his foot's pretty fucked. He's in bed for a month or so afterwards … Although that might've just been PR. But that's not actually the important part. The important part is what happened when he was *in* the block. When he saw his girlfriend approach him and then walk away again.'

'That feels very tight,' she says, shunting herself up on to her elbows, inspecting her leg, which is stiff now, as if it's been set into a pink pigskin cast.

'It's fine,' I say, stroking the leather. 'It's beautiful. It's *meant* to cling like that.'

She frowns and tips her head, quizzically.

'The point *is*,' I continue, 'Blaine says afterwards that when his girlfriend approached the block, he saw her, and he called out to her, but it was as if she hadn't seen him. And he suddenly thought he was dead. He suddenly *believed* that he was dead. That he was a ghost. That she *couldn't* see him. And *that's* why he panicked.'

On 'panicked', Aphra suddenly says, 'You *have* to take it off.'

'Pardon?'

She slides the leg down from my shoulder, over the side of the chair and on to the floor.

'Oh *God*,' she says, scrabbling at the pigskin. 'You must get it *off*. It's frightening me.'

I stand up, confused. 'Don't be silly. It's just a boot.'

'I don't *care*. I don't *like* it. It's scaring me. I can't breathe.'

She puts her hands to her neck, gasping.

I fall on to my knees and start unbuttoning.

She's actually crying now, hiccuping. 'I just don't...*hick* ...like it...*hick*...I can't stand the...*hick*...feeling..'

As I struggle to unbutton, she's pulling at the pigskin, frantically, which isn't helping.

'I *must* bend my knee,' she says, and starts desperately trying to stand up.

'Sit *down*,' I say (loudly).

'*Shhh*!'

She puts her hands over my mouth, looking over towards the door, anxiously, then clasps her own throat, wheezing, horribly. She seems to be having some kind of panic attack.

'Just calm down,' I say, 'and we'll get it off.'

But she simply stares at me, wheezing, her cheeks draining, her eyes glazing.

So I slap her. She gasps, her eyes fly wide, she yells, 'You *fucker*!' then she slaps me back.

(Ah. *Just* what I needed to sort out my sinuses.)

It's at *this* point I hear some kind of call from a bedroom. A quiet voice. A man's voice. Aphra gives no sign of having heard anything. She collapses back on the sofa, covering her face with her hands, sobbing.

I grit my teeth, and continue unbuttoning. She stops crying fairly rapidly and then just sits there, breathing heavily, holding her cheek, watching me, ruefully.

It takes five minutes to get the bastard off. I finally pull it free and throw it back into the box. My thumb and index fingers are almost raw. I inspect them, scowling.

'Sorry,' she says, peering up at me through her fringe,

'I just *really* hate to feel constrained.' We're both silent for a minute, then, 'Sometimes *I* feel like a ghost,' she says, and holds out her two arms (like a pretty ghoul) and inspects them.

'Ghost arms,' I murmur softly.

(They're certainly pale enough.)

She nods. She half-smiles. Then she grabs a hold of my hand (Good *God* that's some grip) and pulls me down on top of her.

Two minutes pass in a chaos of zips and elbows, then suddenly she freezes. 'Are you *crying*?'

(*Crying*? Me?)

'Nope.'

(Gasping a little, maybe.)

She pushes me aside, sits bolt upright, puts her hand to her neck and says, 'But you *are* . . .' Then before I can respond she jumps up. '*Fuck* . . . it's *snot*!' she exclaims. 'On my lovely *neck*.'

('Lovely neck?' Get *her*!)

Oh dear. Oh *dear*. My nose has been dripping.

'I've got *flu*,' I stutter. 'What did you expect?'

'Perhaps you should go,' she says, clutching at her temples.

'The thing about snot,' I try and reassure her, 'is that it's basically just saliva with extra *flavour*. Like a kiss with added *salt*.'

'Fuck off,' she says, then disappears.

I hear her clattering around in the bathroom, then opening a couple of drawers in the bedroom. I hear some furtive muttering. Then nothing.

Ten minutes pass.

I inspect her tape cassettes. I look at her shoes, her books. I finish my tea (cold). I try to get the TV to work.

185

Twenty minutes pass.

Thirty.

Is she ill? Asleep? Pondering the snot/kiss dichotomy?
Waiting? Distressed?

Does she *want* me to go?

Really?

Really?

I give her an hour to change her mind.

Okay. Ninety minutes, tops.

And my flu – thanks for asking – has grown considerably worse in the meantime.

Track six? Are you *kidding*?! Primal Scream. 'Higher than the Sun.'
   Every time.

God *please* forgive me, but I speed-read the Primo Levi as I compile the cassette (I can't commit. I *won't* commit. This is too Big. I just can't *own* it). But every so often (just the same) the strong rope of its narrative lassoes me up, pulls me in and drags me along (spreadeagled, scrabbling for a handhold, bleating out my weak defence of terminal frivolity. I'm totally superficial, *see*? I'm inherently trivial. D'you have any fucking idea how *hard* that can sometimes be?).

They're full of ghosts, these two books, both living and dead. In the Author's Preface (and even *this* isn't a safe place) Levi says how for most people (and most peoples) 'every stranger is an enemy', but that this belief, this feeling, does not exist (in general) as the basis of any formal doctrine, but rather 'it betrays itself only in random, disconnected acts'.

In Paul Bailey's Introduction he snipes at 'the artists who use the terrible fact of the camps for emotional and aesthetic effect'.

So is Blaine doing that? Can we accuse *him* of this crime? Even if it was just a question of *mentioning* the Levi book in passing (like it was vaguely connected, in some way, to the ordeal he was undertaking)?

I ponder this for a while.

But the reference *was* an oblique one.

Is Bailey right, then? Is the holocaust bigger than art?

Is it *beyond* art?

And is Blaine – through this strange, solitary gesture of his – simply pointing a small torch into the huge, black sky of history, and hoping that people might peer up and see – and pause, and *remember* – how very *dark* it is up there?

Seven. Gotta be the Beatles. 'Here Comes the Sun.'

Doo-dun-doo-doo!

At the exact midway point of the Levi (and remember I've got the two separate books published *together* here), I come across this little kid. This 3-year-old kid called Hurbinek. In fact that isn't actually even his real name. Nobody knows what he's called. He doesn't *have* a name. He's just this partially functioning scrag of flesh perched determinedly in a grubby cot.

Levi and his fellow survivors (the Germans are on the run by this stage and Levi is slowly recovering from scarlet fever in the camp's infirmary) think he was born in captivity, but they aren't entirely sure. He has no family. He's simply been left. He's utterly alone.

Hurbinek's disabled – his legs are just two pegs – and thin. Levi describes his face as 'triangular'. Merely an amalgam of bones and skin. But what little skin there *is* on this tot's tiny forearm is tattoed with those indelible digits of Auschwitz.

But the eyes! Hurbinek's eyes! Flashing and seething and alive. Furious. *Blazing*. Because he cannot speak. He's never been taught. So he just sits in his cot, an 'obsessive presence', his eyes burning with this thwarted desire to communicate. And at first no one will speak to him. Nobody can face that indomitable 3-year-old gaze and bear what it might tell them. Except for one person. A boy called Henek. Fifteen years old. Hungarian.

Henek begins to nurture the tiny, isosceles-faced Hurbinek. He speaks to him, hour after hour, slowly and calmly. He's unbelievably patient and tender. Then, after a week or so, he approaches the other men on the ward and proudly tells them that Hurbinek – this incandescent scrap, this 'child of death' – has spoken. He has articulated a *word*. The word (and it varies, slightly, with each faltering pronunciation) sounds something like 'mass-klo'! *Mass-klo*?

There are men from every corner of Europe lying in that ward, educated men, men who – between them – speak every European language, *every* tongue. But nobody knows what Hurbinek's word means. People have their theories (certainly) but no one is entirely sure.

And nobody finds out, definitively, because Hurbinek dies (as he surely must), without his word ever being clearly interpreted, without ever experiencing that reassuring thrill of being truly comprehended. And Levi – who has seen so much, and this is merely more – shakes his head, wisely, and in that sublimely understated way of his, murmurs, 'No, it was certainly not a message, it was not a revelation . . .'

It was just a word – two defiant syllables – which nobody understood.

Mass-klo.
   Some things are beyond the reach of art.
   Some words are meaningful beyond understanding.

It was Blaine. It was *him*. He made me read that book.

Eleven

It's not a criticism of the girl or anything (well, not *exactly*), but don't you just hate those people who automatically sympathise with the baddie in a book (or film, or play) simply because they think it makes them seem 'multifaceted'?

Of course they'll provide you with some perfectly *coherent* reason for their deranged stance: 'Oh *no*, I always *loved* the Child-Catcher in *Chitty Chitty Bang Bang*. I mean he's so *true*, so *rounded*. And he was probably bullied by the other children at school when *he* was a kid because of his misshapen nose and his chalky pallor . . .

'I bet he's *great* to his mother. In fact I'm pretty certain that he's a passionate supporter of Help The Aged's "Sponsor a Granny" scheme, but he just doesn't go public about it (He's far too subtle, too self-deprecating for that). My sources tell me that he sends a *very* regular allowance to an isolated Nicaraguan octogenarian called Rosa Francesca Velasquez. A worn-out mother of twelve. She was destitute before he stepped in . . .'

My *God*. But of *course*. *Now* I realise. You're just so complex, so contrary, so intuitive, so *fascinating* . . .

George *Lucas* certainly isn't helping matters in this respect, now that Darth Vader's suddenly been unmasked as Luke Skywalker's *father*.

'Yeah, so apparently Darth had a stutter as a boy, and it made him feel really socially inept...And then, when he had a kid of his own, he just couldn't bring himself to express real *love*...'

Why can't a baddie just be *bad*? And why can't a good guy just be *better*?

The way I'm seeing it, the rot started at ground level: the British school system in the seventies, when they introduced mixed ability classes and abandoned streaming –

'I'm very sorry Jimmy/Johnny/Jane, but you're just going to have to sit quietly and read your books while I struggle for an *entire lesson* to get *Smeg*-boy here to hold his *crayon* properly.'

Trust *Aphra* to find something appealing in the money-grabbing Fletcher. Maybe she's doing it simply to provoke. I mean to refuse – point blank – to admire a *hero* who fills every page with effortless light and grace and colour, in favour of some wealthy absentee landowner who – for crass, financial gain – uses his hired hands to rough-up the law-abiding local folk? Can that be logical (or emotionally sustaining)? Has she no Social *Antennae*?

Bly interrupts my musings by phoning just before she knocks off work, at five. 'I was just on the internet,' she says, her voice full of horror, 'reading about how Vincent Gallo – the actor ...'

'I *know* who Vincent Gallo is ...'

(Best hair in the business, let's make no bones about it. And biggest *mouth*, come to that.) '... Of *course* you do. Well, Gallo said that he wouldn't have sex with Chloe Sevigny during the filming of *Brown Bunny*, because he didn't want to catch Harmony Korine's *herpes* ...'

As she's speaking I'm lounging on my bed, gingerly trying to unfurl the well-masticated back cover of the David Blaine biography.

Now hang *on* a minute ...

The back cover – which is virtually unsalvageable – has been gnawed away just far enough to reveal a small black-and-white photograph of Blaine himself (underneath a two-page, small-type insert entitled 'Blaine's Challenge', where it would appear that the enthusiastic reader – by following a series of clues dotted throughout the text – might be able to treasure hunt themselves a fantastic $100,000).

But the picture ...

'Isn't herpes transmitted through the saliva?' I interject distractedly.

Bly muses on this point for a second. 'I can't profess

to be an expert on the subject . . .'

I hold the book slightly closer to my face.

'Well, I'm pretty certain that the virus is related to the cold sore,' I say. 'Kind of like an older cousin or something. And if it is, he's definitely going to regret that fifteen minute on-screen *blow*-job Sevigny gave him.'

Bly groans. 'That's *revolting*.'

(And this from a girl who thinks Harmony Korine's genital *health* is an appropriate topic for conversation?)

'Gallo's revolting,' I mutter, 'and a legendary bull-shitter . . . Sevigny's a *babe*. There's no flies on her.'

Short silence.

Then three seconds later, 'I've just *thought* of one,' she yelps. 'That lovely, catchy, pop/dance thing from the early nineties. . .*uh*. . .Zoe: "Sunshine On A Rainy Day".'

'Violent Femmes,' I shout straight back (don't ask me why – probably spurred on to new heights by her crushing mediocrity), "Blister In The Sun"!'

'"Waiting for the Sun", The *Doors*!' she bellows.

Hmmn.

I quietly weigh up the pros and the cons. 'Great *idea*,' I cordially allow her,'but a shit track. Sorry.'

I mean whose themed mix tape *is* this, anyway?

Two minutes later I'm on the phone to Jalisa.

'Who gave you my number?' she asks tightly.

'So you fell a little short on that pesky Elders of Zion question, *huh*?'

(Not that I want to dab vinegar on the wound or anything.)

'*Protocols* of the Elders of Zion,' she corrects me. 'Do you have any idea what protocol *is*, Adair?'

'Of *course*,' I kinda, sorta, half-lie.

'Well, if that's actually the case,' she informs me primly, 'then you'll fully appreciate how many you've just *breached* by ringing me today.'

Pause.

'I'm just worried about Solomon,' I lie.

'No you're not,' she corrects me.

Okay . . .

'So I read the Kafka,' I blurt out, 'and it was fantastic. The Jew stuff's really put this whole thing into perspective for me.'

Another pause.

'I just wanted to say Thank You,' I gush.

'You do realise,' she says carefully, 'that my entire diatribe the other night was simply for effect.'

Longer pause.

'You *don't* realise that,' she says eventually. 'Oh dear.'

'Effect?' I eventually mutter. '*What* effect?'

'To piss Solomon off,' she sighs. 'To out-*sauce* the

King of Sass. To out-smart the Infernal Smart-Arse. To out-*Jabb*er the damn *Hut*.'

(Was Jabba especially *talkative*? I don't remember the narrative featuring a sub-plot about how extortionate his phone bills were.)

Before I can really respond to this bombshell, she adds, 'Of course I have no concrete reasons for even believing that Blaine *is* a Jew.'

Wha?

'Yeah. *Very* funny,' I mumble.

'Well why should he be?' she demands.

'Because he *must*.'

'But if he's *Jewish*,' she muses, 'then why does he have a huge tattoo of a crucified *Christ* on his back?'

'As a *homage* to Dali's original painting,' I say. 'He admires Dali's *work*.'

'That's just silly, Adair,' she snorts, 'and you know it.'

'He's a *Jew*!'

'Why?'

I'm clutching my head, derangedly. 'Because that's what makes *sense*. That's how it all adds up. Because I *like* him Jewish. I understand him better as a Jew, *and* the hostility he's generating.'

'Well that's your problem,' she snaps.

'My problem,' I hiss, 'was spending five and a half hours, in mortal turmoil, reading Primo bloody Levi, on *your* instigation . . .'

'*God*, you're a lightweight,' she says. 'Shame on you. You have all the moral fibre of a feather.'

I grab the Blaine book. 'But you were *right* about the Kafka,' I witter: 'And here's another thing . . . On the back page of his autobiography there's this small black-and-white photograph of Blaine, in a short-sleeved shirt, and on the soft flesh inside of his left arm are a series of numbers...'

I inspect the photograph again. '174517. Six digits. A tattoo. Like the ones they were given in Auschwitz.'

I lean over and grab the Levi and start flipping through it. My eye alights, rapidly, at the bottom of page 33. An italicised number.

'The exact-*same* tattoo Levi was given.' I gape, 'The *same* digits. I mean he wouldn't *dare* do that if he *wasn't* a Jew, would he?'

'Must be a direct reference to the Levi,' she begins to speculate, 'or some kind of clue...' (At last, at *last*, I've drawn her in), but then her subtle thought processes are interrupted by a persistent beeping on the line. '*Urgh*,' she mutters. 'Call Waiting...'

And cuts me off.

Thanks.
 Charmed.

Hang on. That was *my* phone. A message.

I play it back.

'It was *you*, wasn't it?' an unfamiliar female voice growls accusingly. 'I simply can't believe that you're doing this. It's obscene. It's so incredibly *wrong*. She's confused. She's not properly herself. She's vulnerable. She's *sick*. And if you have even an *inch* of decency you'll leave her the fuck *alone*.'

_Click.

The Vaselines, 'Jesus Don't Want Me For A Sunbeam'
   Classic eighties Indie shlock.
   God, I really, really love that track.

And it *is* a ridiculous name, now you actually come to mention it.

I replay the message to Solomon when he returns (extra-late) from some fantastic party at the Egyptian Embassy.

'She must be ill,' he says matter of factly, pulling off his jacket.

'Who?'

He rolls his eyes. 'Let's put all the *clues* together, shall we? Number One: the headaches.'

'Migraines,' I correct him.

'Number *Two*,' he persists, 'the fact that she's on first-name terms with a porter at Guys, when she doesn't actually *work* there . . .'

Ah yes. The hospital porter. Of *course*.

'Number Three: her diet. She's made healthy eating into an *art* form: low fat, low yeast *et cetera*.'

'But that's exactly what *Jalisa* said,' I interject.

Solomon scowls. 'You just spoke with Jalisa?'

'The other *evening*,' I counter deftly. 'And you utterly ridiculed her for it.'

He merely shrugs. 'Number Four: she's plainly psychotic. She sits alone on a wall all night, surrounded by Tupperware, her eyes pinned, unswervingly, on to the recumbent torso of an International Illusionist (when any *sensible* person would simply invest in cable). She sniffs strangers' shoes. She likes flashing her *pudenda* . . .' He pauses (as if saving the best until last). 'And she listens, voluntarily, to *Premier Christian Radio*.'

'In short . . .' He lets the dogs out into the backyard for a late-night piss. 'This nutcase is quite *spectacular* girlfriend material.'

Hmmn.

'You think I should cool things down a little?'

'No. I think you should set up *home* together. I hear the embankment's very congenial at this time of year.'

Ah.

'Drop her like a hot brick.' He opens the door and whistles. 'Avoid the magician. Date that dumpy girl from work instead. The ginger girl with a silly name. She's infinitely more suitable . . .' He pauses. 'More at your level.'

My level?

The dogs.
One
Two
Three
– trot demurely back inside again.

My level?

What's he actually *mean* by that?

Two a.m. I'm frenziedly tapping away on my keyboard, surfing the www.

Maybe he's right. Maybe she's ill. Maybe she's *very* ill. The headaches. The constant hospital visits. The porter. The wildly overprotective 'sister' figure . . .

Kidney failure.

Must be.

She's on dialysis.

I key frantically into Google.

D i a l y s i s . . .

Ping!

The Kidney *Dialysis* Foundation. *Now* we're talking . . .

So it transpires that the kidneys are a pair of bean-shaped organs located to the rear of the abdomen (6cm wide, 11cm long, 3cm thick, weighing in at 160 grams). They're made up of one million nephrons (and the nephrons are made up of a million *other* things. But let's not get into all that, *eh*?).

The kidney's main *function* is to remove toxins, waste and excess water from the body, but it also maintains the balance of salts and releases a variety of hormones . . . (Perhaps *this* could explain the mood swings?).

Symptoms of a kidney disorder . . .

Uh . . . A burning sensation passing water (Right. *Okay*). Blood in the urine (Yeah. *Whatever*). Puffy eyes

(Her eyes *are* sometimes puffy, actually). Swelling of the hands, feet and abdomen . . .

   What?!

   (No *wonder* the boots didn't fit. No *wonder* she felt 'confined'. No wonder her waist's so thick . . .)

   . . . and, breathlessness.

   (*Breathlessness*! The *panic* attack!)

   I read – at some length – about special diets (yup, yup, yup). Then about how regular dialysis can involve a patient visiting hospital for, on average, three hours approximately every four days.

That's it.

   Enough.

   The girl's a goner.

   Her *kidneys* are fucked.

Thank *God* I found this out now.

That poor, *sick* creature. So brave. So alone. So proud.
So beautiful. So mixed-up. So *bloated*.

I lie in bed and plan how I'm going to dedicate every
available *minute* from here on in to researching her
condition, raising awareness, being helpful and encour-
aging and gentle and *indispensable*.

I even consider donating a kidney of my own . . . play
this fantastic little film backwards and forwards in my
head for a while – the white hospital robe, the brave
smile, the hospital trolley, the incredibly sexy nurse, the
powerful anaesthetic . . .

Drive the pigs to market.
  Wake up with the birds, unbelievably refreshed.
  Think about that sexy nurse for a few minutes.
  Then get up, get dressed, go out and buy an i-Pod.

This is *serious*.

It takes me a whole *ten* days to transfer the most vital constituents of my record and CD collections on to this marvellous piece of 'cutting edge' technology.

I mean to have it *all*, right there, at your fingertips, *whenever* you want it.

Hoo-wee.

On the tenth day, Bly drops by.

'It's been two weeks,' she says, holding her bag nervously in both hands as she stands behind the kitchen table and stares at the dogs (who are sitting in a neat row on the other side, and staring straight back at her).

My level, he said. *My* level.

'In dog psychology,' I tell her, 'the stare is generally associated with aggressive behaviour. Try and blink a little.'

She stops staring.

'There's subterranean rumblings at the office,' she says, gazing up at the ceiling (like Damon Albarn at the peak of his Britpop mania), 'about giving you the old heave-ho.'

'But I've had the *flu*,' I whine.

'I know. That's what *I* said. But the flu isn't really in vogue right now – for the flu to work, conceptually, *everyone* needs to be catching it – and two weeks is . . . *well* . . . two *weeks*.'

She pulls out a chair.

'Make yourself at home,' I say.

'Thanks.'

She sits down. She tucks a tuft of flaming hair behind a small, white ear. She clears her throat. 'So . . .' she says, then pauses, worriedly. 'Why on *earth* are you looking at me like that?'

'You're actually quite a show-stopper,' I murmur (Well, underneath all that defensive blubber).

She blushes, 'Don't be *stupid*', and starts messing around with the pepper dispenser.

'Pretty *face*,' I qualify.

Her eyes tighten. 'What's *that* supposed to mean?'

'That you've got a pretty face, I guess.'

'You think I'm overweight? Is that it?'

'No. I just think you've got a pretty *face*.'

(Jesus Christ. What's it take to make a compliment *work* in this town?)

She rolls her eyes.

'But how heavy *are* you?'

'Why?'

'I just wondered.'

'I'm a size fourteen. That's an average size.'

'Yeah. Of *course*. In the West.'

Her brows shoot up (Nice brows. Personality-ful. Brows like Julianne Moore's after a month in the wilderness sans tweezers).

'What d'you mean, "In the *West*?"'

'I mean that it wouldn't be your "average" size in, say, Algeria.'

'In Algeria my size would be an irrelevance,' she snipes, 'because I'd be dressed head-to-toe in bloody purdah.'

I choose not to argue this point with her, but merely smile, sympathetically.

'You're actually quite *skinny*,' she snaps, 'for a man.'

Then she pauses. '*And* short.'

Then she pauses again. 'And your *hair*...'

But she runs out of steam at this point.

('High styled', springs to mind, 'beautifully coiffured', perhaps, 'brave', even.)

'Five foot nine *is* average,' I murmur.

She shrugs.

'Why the shrug?'

'In this country, maybe, but in – say – *Ethiopia*...'

She sighs. 'It's all relative, I guess.'

'Well, this is nice,' I mutter.

Silence.

'Blaine's actually looking a whole lot thinner now,' she observes.

I merely grimace.

'Why the face?' she asks.

'This is *my* face,' I say (a delicate combination of haughty and apologetic).

'So after weeks of analysing him into the damn ground,' she muses, 'suddenly Blaine is *persona non grata*?'

I wave my hand, airily. 'It's a crazy old life, *eh*!'

'What?' she snorts. 'Skiving off work? Downloading your record collection on to an i-Pod?'

I shrug.

'That's not being *busy*,' she sneers. 'That's just point-less *duplication*.'

I shrug again (Is this girl *entirely* oblivious to all basic forms of body language?).

'It's just *reformatting*,' she gradually builds up speed (Yup. *Now* we're for it), 'I mean how could Capitalism possibly *survive* without inventing a hundred different ways of doing the exact same thing?'

'Interesting point,' I demur.

'It's like life is a can of *Coke*,' she points at an empty can on the table, 'and instead of just *drinking* it we spend all this time and this *effort* deciding whether to have it in a glass or sip it through a *straw*.'

I nod.

'But it's the *liquid* that matters, Adie, not how you consume it.'

'Straight from the can, in my case,' I aver (angling – unashamedly – after the purist vote).

'I think you just missed my point,' she mutters.

'Well, if there isn't a *can*,' I say, 'how the heck do you expect to hold all the contents in?'

'I swear to God,' she says (effortlessly sidestepping my fine, philosophical barb), 'that you've only lost interest in Blaine lately because you're scared he's a gentile, and that'll mean all your exciting little conspiracy theories won't actually add up.'

'*Terrified*,' I scoff.

She smirks at me.

'I was never *that* interested anyway,' I obstinately persist, 'just momentarily *diverted*.'

'But does it really matter *what* Blaine's background is?' she battles on. 'Surely the important thing is what he chooses – consciously or otherwise – to "represent", and how people respond to it?'

'Of *course* what you are matters,' I scowl: 'You have to be legitimate at *some* level. Otherwise it's all just bullshit. You have to walk the walk to talk the talk. *Everybody* knows that.'

'So let me get this straight,' she murmurs. 'You were offended by Blaine's use of *Christian* iconography, to begin with. Then you found out that he was a Jew, and because people were throwing eggs at him, that was just dandy . . .' She pauses, frowning. 'Although in *my* book, if he *is* a Jew, then using the Christian stuff in such an unapologetically self-aggrandising way strikes me as perhaps a little dodgy . . .'

'Oh *Great*,' I sneer. '*Now* you get all sniffy about it. But when *I* was getting upset about the Christian angle, I was apparently just "overreacting" . . .'

She flaps her hand at this (like my words are just gnats). 'You're too literal,' she says, 'and that's your problem. This is Art. It's not about the person so much as the statement they're making. It doesn't really matter what his racial origins are . . .'

'Try telling that to the people throwing *eggs* at him,' I squeak.

'That's exactly *my* point,' she jumps in, cackling exuberantly.

It is?

It *is*?

I frown, confused.

'The way I'm seeing it, there are two things that Blaine is obsessed by,' she holds up a couple of fingers, 'suffering and *mystery*. Fortunately (for him) *all* religions, all nationalities, all cultures can relate to those things in some way or other. His work has a universal application. It's not about any particular *denomination*, but about the trials of humanity.' (*Work*? Who does she think he is? *Picasso*?)

I say nothing.

'You're just sulking,' she says. 'You were hoping to take the moral high ground over this whole Jew farrago, but the water's suddenly risen and now you've found yourself stranded on some rocky little promontory, feeling like a complete *dick*. But the truth is, you can swim. You're a *good* swimmer. So why not just *jump in*?'

She leans back on her chair, plainly delighted with herself.

The chair creaks.

'You've simply *got* to include all that *fabulous* "inundation" imagery,' I gasp (camping it up a little), 'in the DVD extras for your motivational video.'

She completely ignores this, simply laying both hands flat on to the table-top, delivering me a brilliant smile and proudly announcing: 'Black Sabbath, Volume IV. "Under The Sun".'

Three seconds pass us.

'*Urgh*, been there,' I finally grouch, '*done* that.'

Didn't have her down for a heavy rocker, somehow.

You think I was a little harsh?

You *do*?

Well, on *Monday* she texted 'The Thrills, "Don't Steal Our Sun".'

Tuesday: 'Donovan, "I'll Try For The Sun".'

Wednesday: 'The Libertines, "Don't Look Back Into The Sun".'

211

Talk about grabbing a baton and *running* with it.

Then catching you up and beating you *senseless* with the damn thing.

Again and again and again.

And *again*.

My level?

Twelve

Okay. I confess. I *did* go twice. *Three* times. But that's all.

And it was always completely spontaneous (a totally last-minute decision). And late. Always late. And I stayed on the bridge – well back, virtually invisible (just a few feet, literally, beyond the halfway point).

From this considerable distance she was just a blob, a blur. But I could tell it was Aphra (It's all in the posture, see? The tilt of the head, the jut of the chin . . .).

One night it rained – a steady rain – but she stayed on. She'd brought an umbrella with her (that particularly childish, *transparent* kind), and she put it up and just sat there. It would've made an amazing photograph (the light, the transparency, *his* transparency beyond her). But I hadn't brought my camera along.

Missed opportunity, *eh*?

I got wet that night; stood in the lee of the second gate and it almost sheltered me, although on a couple of occasions (but not this one) bridge officials moved me on.

Four times. I went four times. The fourth time I bumped into Punk's Not. Or he bumped into me. He was carrying six steaming cartons of hot coffee over the bridge in a specially adapted plastic tray.

'It's three fifty-seven on a Thursday morning,' he blared, tapping me on my shoulder, quite unexpectedly, 'What the hell are you doing here?'

(Almost having a *heart* attack, you *fucker*. Don't just *tap* me like that.)

'Late shift at work,' I say airily, 'just heading home.'

(Then I turn and face the other way, like I'm right in the middle of my *very important* journey.)

'What?' he scoffs. 'The mayor really needed some pencils sharpening and simply couldn't wait until dawn?'

'Backlog,' I sniff, 'I've had flu, as it happens.'

'Hilary too,' he says.

'How *hilar*ious,' I quip smugly.

(Ah, *vengeance*.)

'So fucking funny he *shat* himself,' Punk's Not muses.

'Yeah,' I nod, '*I* had that symptom.'

He offers me a cup of coffee.

'Oh, *Thanks*,' I say, and take one.

'i-Pod.'

Punk's Not points enviously towards my new technology.

'I mean that man's really the *tick* sucking on the pock-eaten *arse* of Performance Art,' I harp on, bilefully, nodding (meanwhile: Yup. This *is* the i-Pod, this *is* my baby) as I pull off the lid.

'Apparently they really compress the sound,' he says.

'*What*?' I glance up.

He draws his finger and thumb together (to demonstrate), 'They compress the sound. To save space. Rendering the music a little . . .' he muses, 'tinny.'

(The *bitch*)

'Anyway,' he continues, 'I've seen him *on*.'

'Who?'

(*Tinny*? Is he serious?)

'Hilary.'

'*On*?'

He nods.

(I quickly deduce that this is Magic Speak.)

'Really?'

'Yup.'

I balance the lid on the bridge's thick handrail and take a quick sip.

Urgh. Tea. And with *sugar*.

'He once told a colleague of mine,' I say, wincing slightly, 'that a close relative of hers would lose a limb . . .'

Punk's Not smirks. 'Yeah, *Bly*. I know all about that . . .'

'And then he did,' (I ignore him), 'in an accident.'

'Ever happen to *meet* her dad?' Punk's Not asks (a single brow raised, satirically).

I shake my head. 'You?'

He shakes his, too. 'Nope. But Hilary knew all about him from Bly's idle chat in the office. A hopeless alcoholic, apparently. Works . . .' He pauses, for effect. 'On a *threshing* machine.'

'*Fuck*.' I nearly snort tea all over him.

He grins. 'I mean credit where credit's due, *eh*?'

I take another sip of tea. The tea is good, in actual fact.

'Never waves,' Punk's Not muses. 'Not a waver.'

'Hilary?'

He nods.

'Probably frightened his scarf might topple off.'

'You neither,' he observes.

Huh?

'That's true,' I say eventually.

'Nor Aphra,' he continues. 'She never waves.'

This news surprises me.

'I generally find that the people most *committed* to the spectacle,' he says, 'who feel a real *part* of it, are the ones who rarely wave.'

I frown.

'How about you?'

He shakes his head. 'But then I'm *working*, aren't I?'

I pause, mid-sip.

'And I feel sorry for the guy,' Punk's Not continues. 'He's waving all bloody day. It's like people come and they wave. But there's thousands of them. And they all want something from him. That contact. That moment of intimacy. It's a complex exchange. And I think it probably takes its toll on him, psychologically.'

'But he *likes* to wave,' I say. 'And he *likes* to have a toll taken,' I add.

'I read somewhere that Blaine's most satisfying moment when he was buried alive for that week in New York,' Punk's Not says, 'was when he finally learned the art of pissing and waving at the same time. When he overcame all his inhibitions and could do both, without thinking.'

'Where'd you read that?'

'Don't remember. But isn't that so *magicianly?*' he chuckles. 'You know, just finding that special little knack, that tiny, vaguely socially unacceptable trick, then diligently perfecting it.'

'I suppose it is,' I say.

(*Magicianly*, eh?)

'And apparently his catheter wasn't the right size on that stunt, so he found himself pissing down on to his sheets all week.'

He grins. 'I mean can you imagine how much that coffin *stank* when he actually came out of it?'

'I've observed before,' I say (keen not to be left behind), 'how incredibly ill-prepared he sometimes seems. In the Ice Challenge he simply "forgot", at the last minute, to put his knee-pads on. And this was after *months* of training himself to sleep standing up, which he couldn't actually *do* without wearing the pads in case he stuck to the ice and couldn't get off.'

'There's a really *classic* story from that *Frozen in Time* thing,' Punk's Not sniggers (I note how he's memorised all the official titles and secretly despise him). 'They apparently had this kid out the back hoovering up all the melted ice as the glacier defrosted, and at one point he wasn't paying proper attention and he hoovered up this long transparent *tube* . . .'

'What was it?'

(I'm drawn in.)

'It was the tube for Blaine's urine. It was actually *glued*, by the cold, to the end of his penis. When that kid hoovered it up, you could apparently hear his screams reverberating all over Times Square.'

'*Ouch*.'

He nods. 'And the ice was four feet thick.'

We both glance over – grimacing sympathetically – towards the box.

'His girlfriend at the time probably felt like having a small yank on it herself,' I speculate.

'*Josie*?' he looks surprised. 'Wasn't she very supportive throughout?'

Oh.

'So where d'you work?' I divert.

'St Botolphs. The shelter. But I'm actually doing a stint of outreach while Blaine's here.'

(*What*? Punk's Not a *charity* worker? A paid up member of the God Squad?)

'It's been really great for Hilary, though,' he says, pulling the lid off another carton and taking a sip himself, 'to be able to return – without too much fuss and fanfare – to a place where people knew him from before . . .'
Silence.

'Knew him from before *what*?' I eventually murmur.
(*Oh Christ. Don't answer.*)

'The breakdown.'
Another silence.

'You should see him at the shelter, though,' he continues (as if the silence wasn't painful at all), 'just *reading* people. He's got it down to a fine art now. Every time there's a new face in the place, he bides his time for a few nights, keeps his eyes and his ears peeled, then just *totally* shits them up. Basically tells them all this stuff that they didn't even know about themselves. Astonishing details. Amazing predictions. Of course he plays it down a lot. Just says it's "kind of *mathematical*" . . .'

He shrugs. 'I wouldn't know about that, but it's certainly an impressive *knack* . . .'

He pushes the lid carefully back on to the cup.

I clear my throat, painfully.

'Is he over his flu yet?' I ask.

Punk's Not nods, benignly. 'I think we've pretty much got him through the worst of it,' he says, 'although it can be pretty dicey with street people. For some reason

they're especially prone to developing long-term prob-
lems with their lungs.'

I balance my cup, gingerly, on the handrail. Then once
it's obviously balanced, I pick it up again.

'Well, I'd better get these down there,' he says, tapping
the top of a carton, 'before they grow cold.'

He turns to go, then he pauses. 'Should I mention that
I just saw you to Aphra?' he asks.

I try – for a moment – to look blank. Then I give up.
'Better not,' I mutter.

He tips his head, in gentle acknowledgement. 'We're
all just doing our *best* for the girl, *eh*?' he says.

I nod.

He pauses. 'And if you ever feel like you need someone
to *talk* to . . .'

He smiles.

I try (I *try*) and smile back (but fail). Then he waves
and strolls off.

Shit, man.

I shove the lid back on my carton and march furiously (determinedly) in the opposite direction.

In fact I'm halfway up The Highway before it actually strikes me:

Punk's Not was wearing CATs. I swear to God. And
in *tan*.

Bloody *Aphra*.

Tinny?
Did he *actually*, really say that?

Tinny?

A second message comes. It arrives, without fanfare, while I'm lounging at the bar in our local pub on Sunday, ordering a third round and keeping half an eye on the *Live Match*, on Sky.

'If *I* was a man,' she says calmly, 'I would *beat you*

up. I really would. And I'd enjoy it. I'd take an *active* pleasure in it. Once was wrong, see? But it was *manageable*. Now it's every night. *Every* night. It's *madness*. And it won't last, trust me. It *can't* last. And if it does, by some miracle, then she'll blame *you*, ultimately. When everything falls apart, she'll blame *you* ..! Her voice cracks and she begins to cry. 'And so will I.'

Click.

For some reason I don't share this one with Solomon.

I mean what did I do that was so damn *bad*?

God.

Oh *God*.

The i-Pod's utterly filled up. It's crammed. It's choc-a-bloc. It's *complete*.

Now what?

It's no good. I'm too weak. I just *have* to take a look (a quick *peek*), to find out if I was actually right or not. (Josie. The girlfriend. Did my eyes deceive me when I watched the TV programme? Or did Punk's Not fuck up and get it all completely wrong?)

The Blaine book (shoved idly under my bed for the last week) is rapidly dragged out, and I'm heading diligently for the *Frozen in Time* chapter when my eye is drawn inexorably back . . .

Wow.

Nice *art*work. Great layout. Brilliant photos (author's own).

And it's extremely well written (it *is*). And very *dry*. And revealing. And intelligent. And self-aware (within reason). And actually . . . curiously . . . quite *beguilingly* charming. The *tone*. It's *spot on*. I can almost hear him speaking in that deep, slow, measured, slightly ironic-sounding drawl of his.

When I check out the acknowledgements I see it was co-written with this guy called Ratso who also wrote *On the Road with Bob Dylan*. And apart from 'Blaine's Challenge' (which is entertaining enough) there's also loads of information on how to perform various tricks (and pull various *scams*). I actually learn – there and then – how to relight a candle without holding the match to the wick, try it, at once, then dash upstairs and show off my achievement to a bemused-seeming Solomon.

Tons of science stuff. And history stuff (it's virtually a magician's *lexicon*). Blaine actually pinpoints his various magical heroes and influences, and if you read closely, it's possible to see what he's cherry-picked, why and where from: Alexander Herrmann; the *street* magician; Robert-Houdin, with his role as international envoy and '*peace*-bringer'; Houdini, with his amazing knack for *publicity*; Xavier Chabert, who really risked his *life* for his feats; Orson Welles – a keen amateur magician – gets a plug, for *duping* dumb America with his radio adaptation of H. G. Wells' *War of the Worlds* (So there's the *literary* angle neatly sorted, *eh?*). He even gives Fidel Castro a name-check for cunningly using trained white doves to bring this magical sense of 'legitimacy' and 'wonder' to his political machinations.

Here's another thing: there's tricks inside the text *itself*. Blaine claims, near the start, that his publishers (Pan) have agreed to print many different *versions* of the book, which means (*Wha?* You think we were born *yesterday?*) that *each* copy is somehow particular to the person who's bought it. That it's actually 'magical' in some way. At one point the casual narrative is suddenly interrupted by a *mind-reading* section, where Blaine whispers into the reader's ear *directly*, saying stuff like, 'You're easily hurt. You like to travel . . .'

Hell yeah. This is brain-fucking at an *executive* level.

I finally get to investigate the whole *Jewish* angle. *Man*, the autobiographical content is utterly *fascinating*. There's no mention at all of Blaine being Jewish himself (there's a general impression that he was raised in a nurturing, free-thinking, 1970s New Age style environment – I mean there's hard times and austerity, no TV and plenty of reading, but single-parent wages are carefully scrimped and saved for Montessori schooling).

It becomes increasingly apparent how important Jews have been to Blaine from the start. His hero – Houdini – was the *son* of a rabbi. Blaine's first big break? Being booked to do magic at a bar mitzvah when he was eighteen, and meeting the hugely wealthy and influential Steiner family who whisk him away to St-Tropez for the summer and teach him everything he could ever possibly want to know about money. And socialising. And *glamour* (he totally changes his *image*, at this stage, shaves his head, grows the goatee, dresses in black...I guess you could say it was a 'Jewish look'.)

To show *need*, he soon learns, is never a good thing.

But he kind of knew this, already. When he worked at a restaurant (this macrobiotic joint he went to in order to try and learn how to cook healthy food for his – by then – very sick mother) he used to perform tricks for all the customers there, and if they gave him a big tip, he'd often hand it straight back. He wasn't doing it for the cash, see? He was doing it to 'bring mystification', because people are at their most *beautiful* when they're at their most *vulnerable*, apparently.

He actually said that.

I'm reading the book backwards, Chinese-style, and it's when I get to the beginning that I finally hit gold. It's then that I see the photographs. Two photographs. In quick succession.

The first is of Houdini, Blaine's hero. Blaine says (underneath) how it was as a direct consequence of seeing this particular photo (in the library, when he was five) that all his subsequent interest in magic was spurred.

I inspect the photo very closely.

It's scary.

Houdini is straitjacketed and his legs are tied. He is balanced, precariously, on the edge of a high rooftop (or perhaps a bridge), and he seems to be holding on to that ledge only by dint of his *chin*, which is hooked (resolutely) around a metal strut.

Blaine says it was the eyes that initially fascinated him. The eyes are desperate. Staring. *Frantic* (in fact so mesmerised was Blaine by the look of Houdini's eyes in this particular photograph, that he actually had them *tattooed* on to his own arm when he grew up).

It's an exciting image. Melodramatic. *Kinky*, even.

I try to enter the mind of the 5-year-old Blaine. A father dead, a doting but hardworking mother, a sharp intelligence (Aged three he developed a passion for chess. His mother took him to the local parks where he challenged all the old geezers at the game), and this powerful, this overriding sense of physical precariousness.

They moved around a lot. One of his abiding memories of childhood, he says, was of staring backwards over his mother's shoulder as he was hurried away from a burning apartment block. 'For some strange reason,' he says, 'the buildings we were living in always burned down.'

(Yup. I know what you're thinking. '*Eeeek*! Shades of *The Omen*.')

And the second image? The *second* photograph? It's an early family shot. Nineteen seventy-five. A 3-year-old Blaine and his mother posing on a New York street together.

She's glamorous. Like a model. But smart-seeming, too. For the benefit of the photo she has hauled the baby

Blaine on to one of those New York newspaper dispensers. She is staring at him (mouth slightly ajar from the effort of lifting him up there, head still tipped back as she struggles to sit him *still*).

And Blaine? Looking confidently towards the camera. Holding his mother's knitted hat (with such delicacy and *precision*) between two tiny hands. Rotating it. Getting to grips with it. One hand flattened, as if he might – if he chooses (and definitely not, otherwise) – draw a small bird, or a pack of cards, or a bunch of those crazy arti-ficial flowers which magicians used to favour so heartily in the seventies from the pale fabric of that most-esteemed piece of woolly head-apparel.

Now here's the shocking thing: Blaine has the *exact* same eyes as Houdini on the rooftop. *Fact.* Even then, aged *three* (I flip back and forth. *Yup*).

It's as if Uri Geller was here, playing one of those mind-games where he tells his victim to draw 'anything you want' on to a piece of paper, and then, five minutes later, when the secret image is finally revealed, he opens his *own* piece of paper and has drawn precisely the same thing (Then he goes one step further and holds them together – front to back – and you can see through the paper that they are *exactly* the same size. The propor-tions are identical. *That's* how similar they are).

Houdini's eyes are full of fear, but those baby eyes? Haughty. With just a whiff of hostility (who's taking this picture? His father? A new friend? A relative? Does it matter? Because the tiny boy Blaine is fiercely protec-tive of his mother. This is *her hat*, his expression says, and she's *my* mother, so who the hell are *you, eh*?').

Tiny nostrils flared. Chin lifted.

I smile at his boyish defiance.

It's then – and only then (when my eye is idly inspecting the newspaper dispenser – that I notice his little legs, and the small, supportive, metal and elastic harness there. The left leg relaxed. The right leg kicked out slightly, under the stress of the wire.

Mystery and suffering. Mystery and *suffering*.

Bly's words rush back to me.

I really need to share. I *do*. But I don't dare phone Jalisa. And Bly will say I Told You So. And Solomon will just scoff and sneer . . .

Aphra's in a *towering* rage (we're talking 30 storey) when she finally gets around to answering her buzzer ('*What*?! *Who*?! Oh for *Christ's sake*. Just *come up*'), and she hasn't calmed down much by the time I've staggered up there. Her front door has been wedged open with a phonebook and she's in her tiny kitchen, throwing stuff around and cursing.

'What's wrong?' I ask, peering tentatively in (she's dressed in a beige, rough linen, deep-pocketed miniskirt, an expensive-seeming red V-neck sweater – and some antique red Scholl sandals with thick, flat wooden heels. Her hair's pulled back into a chaotic bun. Hairpins shoved in everywhere).

'The bloody . . .' she kicks the cooker and her sandal flies off. '*Fuck*. Something's *blown*. A wire. A *fuse*. I don't know. But I'm halfway through making dinner . . .' (or several dinners – from what I can tell – since all the worktops in that tiny space are literally crammed with bowls and boards and mixers).

She tries to bully me into fixing it.

'How many wires can there *be*?' she asks indignantly (when I try to tell her that this electrical lark isn't really my forte). 'I mean there's just a big, fat one at the back. How complicated is *that*?'

'I could get you a takeaway,' I offer.

She turns and looks at me, furiously. 'What do *you* know . . .' she splutters, and then suddenly, the stress in her face simply falls away and she just *grins*.

'Adair Graham Mac*Kenny*,' she says, holding out her arms (as though expecting me to jump into them, like an enthusistatic young *pup*). 'Long time no see, *eh*?'

She kisses me, with tender ceremony, on either cheek. (No hard feelings about the other night, then?)

Even through the immaculate veneer of her sudden cheerfulness I can tell that she's exhausted. It's only been a week or so, but she looks thinner. And the whites of her eyes are pinky-red. She seems a little high. Medication? Stress? Exhaustion?

'But what will I *do*?' she asks, pointing towards the chaos on the counter.

'I have an oven,' I say, 'at home. We could jump into a cab and hightail it on over there.'

'How far?' she asks.

'Five minutes, tops.'

'Good,' she says. 'Okay. Let's.'

Part of me thinks she might be upset by it. She might be *sensitive* (invalids can sometimes be funny like that), but she isn't. Not remotely. She's fine. In fact she's *beatific*.

We've dumped three bags of provisions (and one of Tupperware) on to the kitchen table, she's growled at the dogs (and they've fled) and she's followed me downstairs, quite willingly, into my lair.

I put N*e*r*d on the stereo – 'In Search Of . . .'

First thing she does is open a window.

'Air,' she gasps, then glances up towards street level.

'How lovely for you,' she murmurs, 'to see everyone's *shoes* . . .' She pauses, 'And up everyone's *skirts*, too.'

Then she sits down on my bed and I show her the pictures.

'The *eyes*,' I say (the way Blaine does in the text), flipping between the two images.

'Good gracious me. I get your *point*,' she murmurs.

'The way I see it,' I say, my own eyes drawn inexorably towards her shapely bare thigh, 'Houdini's like Blaine's inspirational *father*-figure.'

She tips her head slightly. '*Okay . . .*' she says, tentatively.

'We know nothing about his relationship with his *actual* dad,' I continue, 'except that he died when Blaine was young. It's entirely conceivable that he might've been obliged to watch him *suffer*, as a boy, and magic – this strange and mysterious world of wands and tarot – was an *escape* for him. A release.'

Aphra says nothing.

'At one point in the book he talks – at some length – about this recurring dream he has as a child. In the dream he suddenly finds himself standing inside this amazing room crammed with countless magical devices and huge, ornate glass display cases. He says that the room made him feel inexpressibly happy. It was a refuge. He would enter this and he would feel magic all around him. In fact he would enter this room and he *was* magic.'

I pause. 'These two worlds were probably entirely separate at first. But then one day, in the library, the 5-year-old Blaine accidentally happens across this extraordinary image of the great Houdini. And it's when his eyes connect with Houdini's eyes that those two initially disparate sides of his life suddenly forge together. Houdini was the unifier, see? When he saw Houdini's eyes, maybe – at some fundamental level – he recognised his *own* eyes (and through them, by extension, his own dead *father's* eyes). Through the terrified gaze of this master magician, Blaine suddenly experiences this powerful sense of a *unity of suffering*. And *magic* was the facilitator. *Magic* brought everything into relief. *Magic* brought his father *and* his suffering back to him. But through a filter. In an accessible way, a distanced way, a *controllable* way.'

Aphra stays quiet, presumably digesting my diatribe. I quietly indicate towards the little straps and bolts on the baby Blaine's leg.

'God bless him,' she gasps, and leans down to kiss the picture. 'God *bless* him.'

'But what about his *mother*?' I murmur. 'His mother always supported him, he says, no matter what. She was his rock. But part of me can't help thinking that maybe she supported him too much. And maybe that's because he'd lost his dad, but maybe it was *also* because he was actually sick himself, and she really needed to nurture him. He was in *pain*, so she indulged him.'

Aphra has fallen down off the bed on to her knees. She has crawled forward slightly and is inspecting a line of my shoes by the wall as she listens. Her skirt just about trims the back of her buttocks.

'He says at one point, when he was in his teens,' I blabber on, trying not to stare too much (but still staring), 'that he locked himself into his bedroom cupboard for two entire days. He can't remember why. But she didn't object, she just brought him all his food in on trays. And at another point he says how he slept on his hard bedroom floor for a whole *year* because he became obsessed by the idea of *mites* in his bed linen.'

She picks up my yellow trainers and sniffs them.

'You *love* black olives,' she says.

'He was very obsessive, very compulsive,' I continue, 'he used to challenge himself to do things – like climb a tree or cross a road, and as he grew older the challenges became more risky, more dangerous, but he convinced himself that if he didn't do them straight away then something bad would happen . . .'

'We've all done that,' Aphra mutters.

'*I* didn't.'

'Well *you're* the exception, then,' she says, grabbing an old pair of Patrick Cox's and inspecting them quizzically. 'Adair Graham MacKenny,' she sighs, '*so* well adjusted. A shining example to us *all*.'

A quick sniff later she murmurs, 'Mints. *Terrible* for male fertility.'

I simply gaze at her.

'Didn't anyone ever *tell* you that?'

She crawls over the floor towards me on her hands and knees (I can see her breasts, hanging down, through the V in her sweater, partially confined by some kind of bizarre, crocheted bright pink bra top). She reaches my legs, pushes them open and shoves herself between them. She stares into my face.

'Hello,' she whispers, then starts adjusting the collar on my shirt and tucking my hair behind my ears (in an irritating way, in a *false* way, like I'm some scruffy kid she's preparing for his first day of school, or an ancient *invalid* uncle). I grab her hands and restrain them. Then I kiss her. She bends back on her knees under the pressure. The harder I push, the more she gives. Eventually I've moved a foot forward and she's arched into a lithe, girlie Z. I feel her teeth against my lips and tongue. I open my eyes.

'What's so funny?' I ask.

'Everything,' she says. '*You*.'

I grab her shoulders, yank her forward and kiss her again.

'*Ow*,' she says afterwards, falling back on to her heels, touching her bottom lip, scowling, 'that *hurt*.' Three long seconds pass. Then she looks up, sees my concern and laughs.

She's vicious. Careless. Wildly provoking.

I let go of her shoulders (What to do next? How to *contain* this mischief?), and in that same moment she puts her hands down to her sweater, grabs the fabric at the waist and pulls it over her head.

Wow. She suddenly looks like a cover shot from one of those slightly sordid *Summer In Ibiza* albums. Very pale. Slightly dirty. Several pins drop from her head on to the wooden floor. Scraps of hair fall loose.

Slowly she rises up again and leans her weight in against me. Her hands are behind her back. I can see her fingers twisting lithely together as her chin rests on my shoulder. Then she turns her head and kisses my neck. I start to move my hands and she stops. I stop moving my hands and she starts again.

Her lips are soon at my ear. 'Remember that bit,' she murmurs, grabbing my lobe between her teeth and pulling slightly, 'when they're trying to dig up that old *tree* stump – Shane and the kid's father . . ?'

Her hands are on my knees, moving up slowly towards my thighs.

I nod, my breathing irregular.

'And they're just chopping into it, *hacking* into it, one after the other?'

She draws a deep breath, tickles my ear with her nose, moves her hands up past my hips, under my shirt and on to my stomach.

'But it's *incredibly* hard work, and *hot*,' she sighs, 'and they're just *dripping* with sweat . . .' She pushes me back, flat, on to the bed, lifts my shirt up, and slowly slithers the top half of her body over my groin and my stomach . . .

'Do you remember that?' she whispers.

I nod again.

She tweaks a nipple. 'If you *must* know . . .'

She suddenly sits bolt upright and her voice returns to normal. 'I actually found the writing throughout that entire section incredibly *laboured*.'

I open my eyes. She's gazing down at me, grinning. A hairclip falls on to my neck.

That's *it*. I grab her and toss her down on to the bed. She doesn't protest. She's just laughing, really loudly, as I sit astride her.

'Stop laughing,' I command roughly.

'I *can't*,' she pants. 'Your *face*. It's just so . . . so *funny*.'

Her arms are over her head. I half-look for marks there (the kind of marks I saw in the diagrams on the internet) but I don't see anything, so I push my hand firmly under her crochet.

Astonishing *nipples*.

Her back kinks at my touch and she laughs even louder.

I push the other hand down between her thighs where the skirt has ridden up. She whoops.

At the sound of her whooping two of the dogs shove their way through the dividing door from the kitchen (Oh *great*) and come careering down the stairs. Jax and Ivor. Jax begins barking when he espies me astride her.

She's laughing so loudly now I think she might be sick.

'Oh *God*,' she roars. 'No more weight on my stomach. It's killing me. I think I might be going to *vomit*.'

I climb off. I try and force the dogs back upstairs. But Ivor has grabbed one of my trainers and is shaking it around in an orgy of furious sexual hysteria.

'That's my best fucking *trainer*,' I bellow, above the cacophony.

Five flights with an *erection*. I finally retrieve the trainer in the bathroom, covered in saliva, with at least three – *count* them – serious puncture holes in the fabric around the toe area.

When I return downstairs again she's hard at work in the kitchen, chatting away, animatedly (skirt, sandals, crocheted bra top) with a delighted-looking Solomon. They're getting on like a *house* on fire.

Oh.

So apparently they have this *wonderful* acquaintance in common. Some queer silver designer called Tin-Tin who has a holiday home in Alaska which they've *both* actually visited over Christmas before ('I was ninety-nine, when were you?', 'Didn't Yasmin Le Bon go that year?'). Tin-Tin is a source of *unbelievable* fascination to them . . .

'Thinks he's the new Leigh Bowery . .'

'Lost two stone in one *hour* . .'

'Oh my *God*. The guest-room *linen*! It's antique. He got it at this fantastic house sale in Turin.'

'But did you notice how his eyebrows have grown back *ginger*?'

'What do you think about his new lover? *Total* cunt? Me too.'

'Wasn't all the stuff with Jennifer Lopez just utterly fucked up?'

'I know. It's absolutely inescapable. Cardamom is quite literally the base scent of *everything*.'

'Don't you fry the onions off first? *What*?! But *why* not?'

'Love the *Scholls*. Seriously. Screw those tight-arsed pricks at Birkenstock.'

'Jagger? The mystery ingredient? Gives it that *musky* quality? *Really*?'

Blah blah blah blah *blah*.

Hello? *Hello*?

Anyone here actually *remember* me?

So she cooks and they gabble away, non-stop, for over an hour. Then she fills Solomon a plate, piles the rest of the food into Tupperware and spirits herself out of there.

I follow behind, dragging my shoes on, bleating something about her jumper.

Thirteen

Prepare yourselves.
  (Oil your brakes, check your pads.)
  The gradient gets pretty *steep* from here.

I'm chasing Aphra up the road (*remember?*), and she's trying to flag down a cab. But it's after eleven on a Sunday evening and her chances of catching one now aren't looking too spectacular. So she decides to walk. I'm staggering along behind her, stopping, every so often (to try and tie my laces), but whenever I do, she dashes determinedly onwards.

  I eventually draw level. She's put her jumper back on (Thank God) and she's making great time. She's obviously in a hurry (Heaven forbid she should be late for Mr *Blaine*, huh?).

I try and grab a couple of the bags off her, but she knocks me back. 'Go *home*,' she says irritably. 'It's *late*. I'll be *fine*...'

The Highway is still busy (don't get me wrong), but it's not really the *ideal* kind of place for an attractive woman (*attractive*? Did *I* say that?) to take a late-night stroll in Scholls and a miniskirt.

'Let me at least stay with you until the Tower,' I wheedle. 'The way's much better lit from there.'

'You're a damn *pest*,' she scowls, finally (and very regretfully) passing two of the heavier bags across.

'So what a *coincidence*,' I murmur jealously (the crisis duly averted), 'You and Solomon having that friend of yours in common –'

'It's sad, don't you think?' she cuts in. 'That he took all those risks as a kid, supposedly to guard against anything *bad* happening, and then his mother's diagnosed with cancer?'

It takes me a second or two to catch on.

'Oh. Yes. *Yes*. I suppose it was.'

'Life's a bitch,' she whispers.

We cross The Highway together.

'He had a very crazy time of it in his mid-teens,' I say. 'Did you ever see the film *Saturday Night Fever*?'

'I *love* that film.' She grins.

'Well remember the bit when John Travolta's character...'

'Tony,' she sighs.

(*Wow*. She *does* love that film.)

'Yeah, Tony. Remember when he drives to the Brooklyn Bridge with his gang of friends and they climb up on it and fuck about, and basically almost *kill* themselves just pissing around and showing off?'

She rolls her eyes. 'Boys will be boys, *eh*?'

'And there's the sad one with the bad shoes and the silly afro . . ?'

She frowns.

'The *little* one, who everyone despises, who gets his girlfriend pregnant and doesn't know what to do about it?'

She finally catches on. 'Oh, you mean the *little* one . . .'

(Didn't I just *say* that?)

'Exactly. And if I remember correctly he's the nervous kid in the group, and he never usually joins in when they climb, but towards the end of the film, when he's especially desperate, he clambers up on to the bridge himself. He wants everyone to look at him – just this *once* – because he feels so bad and lonely and ignored. Then his foot slips, and he falls.'

'Bloody platform *heels*,' she growls.

(Uh, *yeah* . . .)

'Well Blaine used to do that.'

She turns to look at me. '*Really*?'

'Yup. But not the *falling* part, obviously.'

We walk a little further.

'Don't know which bridge it was,' I say. 'Somewhere in New Jersey, I guess. That's where they moved when his mother remarried. I get the feeling he doesn't look back on those times especially fondly . . .'

I pause. 'But he used to pull the same stunt. He'd just stroll over these crossbars on a bridge, hundreds of feet up, with all the cars below honking their horns in total panic. He was *wild*. And like they used to say in those nike ads, he'd "just *do* it". He didn't care.'

She shakes her head, slightly shocked. 'Always *hated* those ads,' she mutters.

'In fact one time he was pulling a similar kind of stunt

on a cliff-top. He was right on the edge of this precipice and he slipped, lost his footing, and just went hurtling down this dead drop . . .'

'*Then* what?'

'That's the weird thing. He thought he'd had it. He thought he was going to *die*. But by some bizarre miracle – which, to this day, he still doesn't entirely understand – he survived. A huge fall, and barely a scratch on him. After that all his friends used to call him, "the cat".'

'Nine lives . . .' Aphra's frowning. 'Well that hardly sets the greatest precedent, *does* it?'

'Why?'

'Because he thinks he's immortal. But of course he's not. Nobody is.'

I shrug. 'I suppose we could say that he lives a "charmed life".' Well . . . charmed in *some* ways, but definitely not in others. He's seen everyone he truly loves slowly die around him, but he's survived. Part of him, I'm certain, wants to punish himself for living on. And another part – a *Messianic* part – probably believes that he's pretty much indestructible.'

We're standing and talking by the Tower, now.

'I've gotta go,' she says, and takes the two bags from me.

'I had a *happy* time tonight.' She smiles. 'Thank you.'

Then she kisses me, softly, on the cheek, turns and heads off into the light.

I follow her.

Obviously.

I mean, wouldn't *you*?

She doesn't know I'm behind her. She never looks back (Nope. Not *once*), not even when she first takes her leave of me (when most normal people actually might). And maybe part of me thinks (to *begin* with, at least) that she will, and if she does, then I'll be able to turn resignedly around again (tongue-lashed and scalded), head off home, have a quick nip of Jim Beam, fall into a warm bath, a soft bed . . .

But she doesn't look back.

She crosses the bridge.

(How I *love* this damn bridge at night . . . Although I love it best at dawn; the sky tender and blushing like some uptight, Victorian virgin on the morning of her deflowering, the clouds crazily spiralling, the random puffs of vapour from the city's air conditioning, the tug horns blaring, a thousand lights on the riverside blazing, then gradually growing dimmer and more ineffectual in the shimmering glare of the rising sun.)

She stands at the far end of the bridge and watches Blaine for a while. Then she checks herself (I can tell – even from where I'm standing – that it takes some effort of will) and strolls on. She walks *on*. She's not heading for the nightwatch. And she's certainly not heading home again. So *where's* she going?

My following gets more furtive now (I mean if she catches me behind her at *this* stage it's gonna look pretty dodgy, *eh?*). She walks on briskly for a further five minutes, then she stops. I, peer up at the large, grey building towering above her.

But of course. Of *course*. Guys. The bloody *hospital*.

I shouldn't (don't even waste your breath), I *know* I shouldn't, but I still keep on following. And it's not like I'm saying that the hospital security is a bunch of *shit* or anything (wouldn't fucking *dare*), but I pursue her, unchallenged, down a labyrinth of corridors, through a dozen swing-doors, up a series of stairs . . .

Eventually she reaches her destination; enters a brightly-lit ward and marches up to the nurses' station.

I'm peering in at her through the wire-meshed glass in the heavy, white, hospital regulation swing-doors. She's talking with a nurse. A blonde nurse. The nurse is listening, then frowning, then responding quite emphatically. Aphra says something else, then dumps a bag of food on to the desk. The nurse grabs it, lifts it up, holds it out to her, gesticulating. Aphra turns on her heel. The nurse calls after her . . .

Jesus wept, she's heading back!

Fuck.

I sprint down the corridor and turn a sharp left.

She's still coming. I zip into a private room (dimly lit. Some poor plugged-up geezer beep-beeping it on a heart monitoring machine). *Still* I hear her footsteps approaching (How unlucky is *that*?). I shove my back against the wall, in the lee of the door, holding my breath.

I feel her – I *feel* her – peering in through the glass (the light from the hallway cuts out as her head blocks the gap).

I count to ten. Then to twenty.

She sneezes, loudly (the bloke on the bed stirs. His breathing quickens, his *heart* rate) . . .

And then she goes.

She *does*.

I count to five, put my hand on to the doorhandle, twist it, *pull* . . . Am *just* about to take my chance and scarper, when I detect a further – rather sharp – exchange underway in the hallway (between Aphra and the nurse), so I pause, push the door to, and glance anxiously around the room.

Wow. It's *nice* in here. *Very* nice. Homely. Swanky. Flower displays everywhere (forget the *bunch*. *Fuck* the bunch. The bunch is *so* passé), a strongly scented candle

– Jasmine? Lavender? – a veritable *stall* of fruit, and a whole host of well-framed family photographs all crammed together on a side table in a fashionably congenial bohemian mish-mash.

A piece of sculpture. A small, bronze *minotaur*. Looks old. And important.

Paintings on the walls. Huge fuckers. This *amazing* Ben Nicholson (swear to God, it's the real deal – I touch the paint with my thumb); something brilliant and abstract which just *must* be by Howard Hodgkin; and some very strange but rather magnificent work by the Chapman Brothers (which I saw – or something very like it – I'm pretty certain) at a recent exhibition.

Along from those, on a beautiful, dark-wood sideboard (ebony? Swathed in carved birds and ivy – *Man*, this just *can't* be hospital issue) are literally *dozens* of Get Well Soon cards (*someone* – or someones – certainly loves this sick-o). At the front of the pack is a scruffy, hand-drawn cartoon, which looks like the work – if I'm not *very* much mistaken – of no less an individual than serial Brit-Art sex-kitten, Tracy Emin.

An Apple laptop (of *course*. The last word in modern). A fantastic crystal ashtray (spotless).

And he's wearing a watch (this sick geezer, keeping *time*? Crazy, huh?), which the dull light catches. Solid gold. Flecks of ice. Looks like something which even 50 Cent might consider a little too blingin' *obvious*.

Bedside table is stacked with magazines and books (this is some *cultured* ill-mother-fucker). I cock my head towards the door, holding my breath. The argument continues.

At the sound of raised voices, the sick geezer (no word of a lie, he has this fabulous silk counterpane, hand-embroidered and beaded with this sumptuous – but manly – geometric pattern in black and silver) starts moving around and grunting slightly.

Has he seen me?

Oh *God*.

I take a step closer. I don't want to intimidate him – or to come over like some kind of crazy interloper (which – let's face it, I effectively *am*).

'Hello . . .'

In my keenness to introduce myself I knock into his books – quickly snake out my hand to stop the pile from falling (I mean is this *any* kind of an arrangement for a very sick person?) And guess what?

No. Seriously. *Guess* . . .

Top of the pile (I say *top* of the pile), *Shane* by Jack Schaefer.

Shit.

The door opens. It's the blonde nurse.

'Who are you?' she asks (she has a soft Irish accent, but her voice is tight and defensive, and her cheeks are still flushed from the argument she's just had).

'Adair Graham MacKenny,' I say calmly. 'I came along with Aphra.'

'Oh.'

The nurse scowls.

'This is *my* book,' I say, grabbing the *Shane*, opening it to the frontispiece and showing her my name printed there (Yup. I *know* it's a childish habit, but it's helping me out of *this* embarrassing predicament, isn't it?).

'You wrote that?'

(She looks momentarily impressed.)

'Don't be *ridiculous*,' I cluck. 'Jack *Schaefer*.'

The nurse continues to weight me up. 'So she brought you along to take her place?'

'Yes.' (If in doubt, agree. That's my philosophy.)

She glares at me for a moment, obviously quite disgusted (I check my fly), 'And you know Mr Leyland *well*?'

I shake my head. 'No. I couldn't honestly admit to that...'

'So is she *paying* you?'

I draw myself up to my full five foot eight (Oh come *on*, what's an inch between friends, *eh*?). 'Absolutely *not*.'

She turns and inspects a timetable on the wall.

'Taking the damn *piss*,' she mutters (in that lovely, musical, *nurse* way, just underneath her breath). 'Okay, *fine*,' she eventually grouches. 'Can I *get* you anything?'

(From her tone of voice I realise that my answer has to be 'No. Absolutely not.')

'Like what?' I ask.

'I dunno. Tea? Coffee?'

'Coffee. That'd be good. Milk, one sugar. Thanks.'

'Take a chair,' she scowls, and points.

I take the chair.

Wow. Nice chair. Philippe Starck.

She leaves.

I stare over – a little anxiously – towards my unsuspecting ward. He's in his late forties. Well upholstered. Not bad looking (like James Spader with an MA and less hair).

But ill. Very ill.

He tries to say something through his oxygen mask. I lean in closer.

'Vacant,' he says.

'Pardon?'

'*Vacant.*'

'Vacant?' I quiz him. 'Who is?'

He clumsily knocks the mask off. 'You *cunt.*'

Ah. Good. *Right* . . .

'She's a *nurse*,' he groans, 'not a fucking *tea* hostess.'

'Yes. Of course.' I clear my throat, nervously. 'Sorry.'

'Well don't apologise to *me*,' he pants.

(Is that an American accent? Australian? Canadian?)

He's silent for a while, struggling to breathe, his left hand shaking, uncontrollably.

'*Lovely* room,' I say.

No response.

'Certainly looks like you've been in here a while . . .'

Blanked.

'Made yourself *quite* at home, *eh*?'

'I'm fucking *dying*,' he snaps.

(Funny, isn't it, how these death's door types lose all sense of propriety?)

He turns and attempts to push his face back inside his mask. I jump up and help him. He brusquely nods his acknowledgement.

(Australian. I'm almost certain now. And sharp as a damn kumquat).

I slowly sit down again (I mean should I just *leave*? Or will things pan out better for me – legally speaking – if I stay a short while longer and prove myself *obliging*?).

'Fantastic chair,' I say.

'Can't take it with you . . .' he gasps (Vader *style-ee*).

'Of course not,' I say (chastened). 'Wouldn't *dream* of it.'

'No.' He rolls his eyes and points weakly to his chest. '*I* can't.'

For some reason, the image of a dying man struggling

to carry a Philippe Starck chair into the afterlife strikes me as rather droll.

'The Ben Nicholson's a better bet,' I opine, 'less bulky.'

He snorts (and I'm not sure whether it's actually with amusement), then he's quiet for a while, his breathing laboured, as if he's slowly gathering his resources together. 'Aphra?' he eventually asks. There's definitely an edge to his voice (Christ knows *I've* been there).

'Fine,' I say immediately.

Silence.

'She was gonna come in,' I continue, 'but I think the scented candle might've scared her.'

'Fucking thing,' he murmurs, continuing to fix me with a demanding glare.

'The oven in her flat broke down,' I burble on, shifting uncomfortably, 'so she came over to my place to cook . . .'

'Food?' he asks, almost excitedly.

'Of *course*,' I say (I mean what *else*?).

'For you?' he asks.

'Are you kidding?' I bleat pathetically. 'She brought it all over *here*, packed up in Tupperware.'

He's smiling. He seems to've been immeasurably heartened by this news.

'Where?' he eventually gasps.

'She gave it to the nurse.'

He slits his eyes.

'Bring it,' he says, and motions his hand clumsily towards the door.

I don't move.

'Maybe later, *eh*? Once nurse is off her war path –'

'Good cook,' he butts in.

'Oh *yeah*,' I heartily concur. 'I mean the way that girl handles a *leek* . . .'

He chuckles, dirtily (giving final confirmation – if any were necessary – of the indelible link between sex and the sickening).

'It may well interest you to know,' I say, 'that she prepared the entire meal in a short skirt and knitted bra. My unsuspecting flatmate almost had a *seizure* . . .'

He laughs even harder.

The nurse marches back in bearing a plastic cup of lukewarm instant coffee (holding it haughtily aloft like it's some manner of precious, ancient, papist artefact – perhaps St Paul the Apostle's *index* finger). She frowns when she sees him laughing.

'Don't make him laugh,' she says, 'it *hurts* him. His stomach muscles are extremely fragile.'

'What?' I tease her (she seems quite teasable). 'He can't laugh at *all*?'

She gives me a stern look.

'Not even the odd *giggle*?'

She sucks on her tongue.

'A small snigger?'

(His chest starts to move again.) She hisses.

'A tiny *snort*?'

Now he's really shaking. The beep from the heart monitor speeds up slightly.

She kicks me (like a vicious little Shetland), adjusts something on his arm (there's a tube entering there, and a bag of fluid hung up above the bed), straightens his oxygen mask, and tells him, '*Please* press the button if you're in serious pain, *okay*?'

He nods.

She turns back to face me again. 'So did Aphra send you here tonight with the *express* purpose of knocking him off?' she enquires.

251

I slowly shake my head.

'Then read him the *book*,' she says, tapping the cover with an aggressive finger, 'and less of the *other* stuff.'

She heads for the door.

'Bitch,' he murmurs.

'I *heard* that, you cheeky *sod*,' she rebuffs (quite some *lip* on her for a nursing professional).

His chest shakes a little more (he's pretty, bloody *genial* for a man with more wires in him than a computer terminal).

I open *Shane*, flip through it, discover the point at which the corner of the page has been turned over as a marker (Doesn't that girl have even the vaguest *idea* of how to treat a book respectfully?): chapter 6 (*Hmmn. Much as I suspected*), then start to read him the section about Sam Grafton's general store . . .

Before I've completed more than a couple of sentences, though, he puts out his hand.

'No,' he says. '*She's* reading that.'

Ah.

I grab the next book down from the pile: *The Future of Nostalgia* by Svetlana Boym (She's given the first chapter the nifty title 'Hypochondria of the Heart: Nostalgia, History and Memory'. Yo-ho! Well isn't *this* going to be a rip-roaring half-hour?).

As I begin to read (a little shakily at first) I see his hand snake out towards a small, custom-built table which he yanks around to face him. There's a notebook affixed to it – the pages held in place with strips of elastic – a pencil and a tiny reading light. He clicks the light on and grabs the pencil between his shaky fingers.

'*Slower*,' he barks, then proceeds to take a series of the world's most detailed and laborious notes.

In longhand.

With page references.

He's an Athlete of Pain. An *Olympian*. In the hours that follow I watch him vault and parry a thousand *searing* hurdles. But I don't stop. I don't comment (he clearly doesn't want that). I simply read on.

I see him grit his teeth, *gnash* them. I see the top-half of his torso jerk – uncontrollably – towards the bottom in a series of random, horrible, *pitiless* spasms. I see beads of sweat forming on his brow as his free hand clenches, then unclenches, then clenches again (but the working hand *still* diligently continues writing).

Sometimes there's a sudden, hog-like *grunt* – as the pain shoots from the back of his neck, to the back of his throat, up into his nose – and a small spray of mucus blasts out. His feet, under that eiderdown, are in constant motion, dancing an endless, joyless *jig* of torment.

The knees pull up, then flatten down, then pull up again. His shoulders lift, then rotate, then drop. He gasps. He pants . . .

Hard not to remember S'omogyi, the Hungarian Chemist, in the Primo Levi, and how difficult it was for *him* to give up the mortal coil. Almost three days of struggle, punctuated, only, by the awful, repetitive murmuring of 'Jawohl.'

'I never understood so clearly as at that moment,' Levi whispers, 'how laborious is the death of a man.'

Jawohl.
Jawohl.

Jesus Christ I *wish* he'd press that button.
  Kill the pain.
  Press the button.
  Go on.
  Press it.
  You know you want to.
  It'll make things better.
  It will.
  It *will*.
  Go on.
  That's what it's *there* for.
  Go on.
  Go *on*.
  Just press the damn thing!

But he doesn't. He won't. He *can't.*

I replace his notebook with a fresh one on two separate occasions. It's then that I discover (to my palpable *horror*) that he has a huge *pile* of the bastards in a suitcase by the wall. In fact there are *two* cases: one containing the notebooks he's already filled (numbering approximately seven to eight *dozen*), the other holding the empty ones (numbering approximately twenty-odd).

I'm literally *gagging* for a piss by around 4 a.m. (fine for *him*, he has a catheter). We're halfway through *St Peters-*

burg, the Cosmopolitan Province (page 124, chapter 9) when I grind to a halt, uncross my legs and beg a short intermission.

'Ever *been* to Russia?' he croaks agonisedly as I stand up.

'Never.'

'Pity,' he hisses, through pain-gritted teeth, '*I* have.'

I bump into a nurse, outside, in the corridor. A different nurse. A night-nurse.

'Is Brandy *still* up?' she asks (in a thick but confident Eastern Bloc accent).

'Afraid so,' I say.

'In agony?' she enquires.

I nod grimly.

'Only damn thing keeping him going,' she phlegmatically opines.

Then she pauses for a moment and smiles. 'Same as the rest of us, *huh*?'

It's 4 a.m. I've been clumsily articulating Russian place names for over five hours. For once in my life I'm not entirely certain how to respond.

'Admire your stamina,' this kindly philosopher-nurse murmurs (conserving my breath for me), then she pats me firmly on the shoulder and points straight down the corridor, 'Toilet's *that* way, okay?'

I am awoken at 8.15 by the book falling. It clatters off my lap and down on to the linoleum.

What?!

(How long've I been sleeping? One hour? Two hours?)

Brandy Leyland is flat out (Face battered and pocked like the head of an antique hammer. Skin like silver birch bark. Breath coming, then going, in racking bursts. Hands still clenched so hard his knuckles glimmer like alabaster).

I lean down and pick the book up. A young man enters. He seems surprised – and not entirely delighted, either – to see me there.

'Hi,' He holds out his hand. 'Punch Leyland. Don't believe I've had the pleasure?'

Punch?

I clamber to my feet. 'Adair Graham MacKenny,' I say, refusing to elucidate any further (If in doubt, clam up. That's my philosophy).

We shake (How *old* is this punk, anyway? Seventeen? Eighteen?).

'So Aphra didn't bother turning up again?' he asks (with more than a hint of I-told-you-so in his voice).

His father awakens, with an awful cough.

The nurse enters. The good nurse. She goes over to his side, removes his mask, wipes his mouth, props him up.

'So Aphra's a no-show again?' he repeats (like this is an itch he simply *must* scratch).

'She just *left*, actually,' I suddenly find myself muttering (hoping the nurse doesn't try to contradict me).

Brandy Leyland blinks his sickly affirmation.

The good nurse glances up and smiles. 'Surprised you didn't pass Mrs Leyland in the corridor,' she says briskly.

'*Second* Mrs Leyland,' the posh boy snipes.

?!

I am tired. *Fucking* tired. I head straight into work – avoiding Blaine, travelling there the back way – then sit hunched over my desk all morning, drinking black coffee, blinking and yawning (things aren't really feeling like they're quite 'hanging together' properly. I'm like a flat-pack cupboard with five of my screws missing).

Bly hunts me down at lunchtime (So who suddenly made *this* ginger filly my very best mucker, *eh*?).

'Good party, was it?' she asks, shaking my shoulder. I leap up with a holler (I was just resting my damn *eyes* for a second there, *okay*?).

'Fuckin' *riot*,' I mutter.

We leave the building together.

God I need *air*. I stand out front and *inhale*. I twist

my head around, throw my shoulders back, stretch my arms up . . .

Whoo. That's better.

It's then I spy Aphra.

Approaching from the left. Destination Blaine. And I am here – right *here* – standing slap bang in the middle of her simple trajectory (A cruel *twist* of fate you say? How about a compound *fracture*?).

Should/could/might/*must* get the hell out of her way. *Uh* . . .

Can't turn on my tail and dash back inside again (too obvious a manoeuvre, even for *me*), can't sprint down towards Blaine (she'll just call out and follow) . . .

My only viable option?

The *river*.

'Ever been on the *Belfast*?' I ask an unsuspecting Bly.

'What?'

'The *Belfast*? HMS *Belfast*?'

(Quick clue: it's huge, battleship grey, and permanently docked on the water just in front of you.)

'*Uh* . .!' she starts.

'But you *should*,' I say, grabbing her arm and steering her forward. 'You *must*. There's so much to *see*, and a fantastic café. Let's go. Come *on*. It'll be *fun* . .!'

She starts to pull her arm away. I tighten my grip, considerably. '*Fuck* it, Bly,' I growl, almost lifting her feet off the marble as we hurtle towards it, '*I'll* pay.'

Hate you to get the impression I was *tight* or anything.

Although there's nothing wrong in a modern man knowing the value of a *pound*, eh?

Fourteen

'*Love* this warship. Absolutely *love* it. Visited it – twice – as a boy. Bought the book, the craft model, three pencils, two pens, a balloon and an eraser. Bought the whole damn *experience* and the morello cherry on top.

Great kids' excursion – great *any*-person excursion. The best, hands down, in this part of London. Nothing else comes even *close* to it. Not the Tower, not the Tate Modern, not the stupid, fricken' *Wheel* . . .

Uh-*uh*.'

I spin Bly in through the entrance gate, buy us some tickets at the desk, belt through the shop, negotiate the gangplank – and the slightly ominous sailor-geezer stationed at its far end who wants to make us fill out a form to allow the price of our tickets to be eligible for some kind of charitable *tax* relief . . . (*Woah*. Hold *on*. We're not even on *board* your damn ship yet).

Then off we sail.

The experience has been leavened significantly (you might actually be interested to know) by the advent of the interactive video. But it's the same lovely old dust-bucket it ever was. Creaking. Sombre. Grizzled. Utterly monumental.

The big guns (rendered all the more delightful – in our eyes – for being focused pitilessly on our current place of work), the *huge* anchor (size of a small house), the portholes, the fore-deck, the aft-deck (okay, so if it's the *technical* stuff you're after then send a quick email to Ellen *fuckin'* MacArthur).

Bly is entertained (within reason – I mean my sell *was* quite a big one) by all the above-board activity, but she gets *really* excited when we head downstairs; backwards, grunting slightly, balanced precariously on a series of perilous, metal ladders (the kind of thing you might get – if you were a *very* lucky birdy – in a ramshackle aviary).

Down here (*mind* your head) we get to snoop around the infirmary (couple of macabre masked waxwork figures hacking away morosely at the guts of an injured sailor), the pharmacy, the stores, the *tuck* shop . . .

It's hot. Stuffy. Confined. And there's this constant, all-pervasive *drone* (the air-conditioning, I presume), which makes you feel as if you're staggering around aimlessly inside the ululating throat of a beatific pussy.

And talking of felines – Bly squeals with pleasure when she enters the sleeping quarters and espies the ship's cat (stuffed), sitting smugly in its tiny bed alongside a charming coterie of waxwork sailors (in various stages of dress and undress) falling in and out (most *companionably*) of their serried ranks of hammocks.

At *this* stage a helpful guide approaches and escorts her to the lock-up (not *literally*, but to see two, scary little steel-grey cells where the naughtiest sailors might sometimes be left to moulder).

Bly – and all credit to her for taking to this new experience (after her initial disquiet) with such *untrammelled* enthusiasm – then wants to go right down into the belly of this beast (the guts, the bowels), to the ammunition store, where the guide is now telling her that they used to manufacture all the shells etc. in readiness for combat . . .

Uh . . .

Yes.

It's at *this* precise point – when I turn my head slightly – that I behold a nonchalant Aphra (I know. I *know*. *I* thought she was claustrophobic too) leaning provocatively over the tuck-shop counter (wearing the same clothes as yesterday. Remember the skirt? The short *skirt*?) and reaching out her hand towards a waxwork storesman in a serious attempt to half-inch his cap.

One stretch.

Two stretches . . .

Phew!

And she finally manages it.

She applies the cap to her head (at a jaunty angle), *jinks* the brim down briefly in *my* direction (*Ay ay Captain*), then turns sharply on her heel and minces off.

Bly and the guide are making their way over towards the ladder which leads down on to a lower deck, still full of chat. Bly clambers down first (she's a lady, apparently) and the guide cheerfully indicates that I might like to follow, but I say, – 'Uh. *No*. I just want to finish watching this *fascinating* documentary about the *Belfast*'s *sister* ships . . .' So he shrugs and heads on down after her.

Right. Where *is* she?

I walk past the tuck shop, the infirmary, pause, cock my head, and listen carefully (this girl's wearing Scholls – that hefty wooden sole's a slap in the face to any kind of anonymity).

Clink-Clank, Clink-Clank . . .

Straight on.

Clink-Clank, Clink-Clank . . .

Left turn –

Clink-Clank, Clink-Clank . . .

How'd the *fuck* she climb that ladder?

Clink-Clank-Clank . . .

Yup. Inevitable. One sandal's fallen off –

Silence.

Bollocks. She's removed *both* of the buggers.

I'm back on the main deck, peering frantically about. I walk towards the prow, stand, turn, glance back, look higher . . .

A-*ha*!

She's up on the next level, perched on the captain's chair, lounging seductively over the wheel and gazing out (cap – *Lady and the Tramp*-style – yanked low over one eye). I promptly follow. More deck, *more* stairs . . .

Hmmn. Captain's chair now inhabited by a husky, pubescent American boy in Stars and Stripes trainers.

I head higher.

More guns. More gulls. I wait impatiently for a large family group to clamber down the stairs, then . . . *hup!* A final flight.

Phew.

I'm a little out of breath. Sweaty.

I peer around me, trying to find my bearings. There's an irregular *beeping* sound. *Ah*. We're in the ship's communications centre (heavily wood-lined; like a strangely incongruous Swiss-style chalet. Or a scruffy Swedish sauna. Take your pick). This 'space' is currently inhabited by a whole *host* of radio-style paraphernalia, a gruff waxwork wireless operator ('working' the Morse code) and Aphra.

263

The room is divided into two parts separated by a dark counter and a huge piece of glass. Aphra's standing on the non-technical side of the divide, holding her sandals – one in each hand – and reading a poster about the manifold innovations in communications technology during the first half of the twentieth century.

When I step into the room, she glances distractedly over her shoulder, then freezes, then spins around to look at me, with an expression of naive surprise.

'Oh,' she says sweetly: '*You* like warships *too*?'

The cap is cute.

The cap is very cute.

(And she knows it, *damn* her.)

I walk over and kiss her. She doesn't object. In fact when I pull back, she yanks off her cap and places it firmly on to *my* head. 'Hello Sailor,' she grins. I slide my hands under her skirt, bunch the fabric up, grab her, lift her up (she wraps her legs obligingly around my thighs), then stagger two steps to the side and prop her on to the handy, hip-level wooden counter, her back against the glass.

We kiss some more. Her kisses are salty. And wet.

She undoes my fly (and, but of *course*, she's wearing no underwear).

We fuck.

It's fantastic. Like the Queen has just smashed the most inconceivably *huge* and expensive bottle of Bollinger against the hard, smooth prow of this naughty, great hooker. The window shudders (God, glass manufacture from that epoch has been so *needlessly* derided in our times). My cap tips forward. She yanks it off (almost hitting me with a shoe). Throws her arm out. Bangs her elbow. Drops the cap. Brings her arm straight back.

Why do I open my eyes at this point?

Huh?

Was it all the cap stuff?

Was it the sound her elbow made hitting the glass?

Was it the fantastic way her legs twitched around me?

Who *cares* why?

I open my damn eyes.

They're blank at first; gazing, unfocusedly, through that plate-glass window. All those – *wow* – wires. All that – *ouch* – Bakelite – and even the – *Oooh, yes* – waxwork.

The – *keep going, please keep going* – wireless operator.

I mean the *detail*. The fucking *detail*! The hair. The suit. The hand. The finger.

Another hard, slippy kiss. *Uh*...I peek out, sideways.

Yes. The *finger*.

Just *bib-bib-bobbing* on that Morse code machine.

So he's not a model.

But you probably already realised that (Been on this ship *before*, have we?).

Okay.

So he probably feels more embarrassed about this than *I* do (This is the one helpful thing any *sensible* person might say under the circumstances in a desperate bid to try and keep his pecker up. And they may well be right. And all *credit* to them for that).

But *Jesus, John, Paul and Ringo* this is hideous. It's *excruciating*.

I mean the way he just keeps on tapping, *even* though he probably *knows* this might ultimately give him away, because (a) (Let's get inside his head for a moment) if he *stops*, then so will the beeping, and this may well alert us. (b) If he keeps *on* tapping, and we *do* notice his non-waxwork status, then at least it still looks like he's been keeping himself busy.

I am still thrusting.

Aphra is still grinding.

The wireless operator is still *tippy-tip-tip-tapping*.

Then Aphra comes. Then I come (How'd I *do* that?). Then she collapses over my shoulder and says, 'You smell of *death* . . .' pause, 'And *lavender*.'

Yeah. So how was it for *you*, Love?

No. Of *course* I don't tell her.

Now *this* is a good bit: once Aphra's got her breath back (pushed me off, jumped down and rearranged her skirt), she grabs the sailor's cap, bends over, sticks out first one leg, then the other, and delicately wipes the soft part of its old blue fabric from her inner ankle to her inner thigh.

'Young, numb and full of cum,' she sighs (I think – at this point – that the wireless guy might be in danger of suffering a coronary). Then she tosses the smeared historical artefact back at me.

'Take it down to the tuck shop, will you?' she asks sweetly. '*There's* a good boy.'

And off she trots.

I glance up at the ceiling (cap held firmly behind me). I wince. I check my fly. I whisper, '*Terribly* sorry', then glide out, inconspicuously.

Yes, I *know* she's fucking married.

But *viva* life, *huh*?

I finally catch up with Bly in the canteen (where else?). She's ordered me a cheese baguette, a blueberry muffin and a cup of tea. She tells me all about the ammunition store ('Those missiles. So *huge*. So well made. So amazingly *tactile* . . .'). I tell her that the top two decks are closed down for renovation.

'It *is* a shame. Yes. We *must* come back.'

We eat.

Bly takes a second to fill out the tax-concession thingummy (she's good like that). Then we leave.

I walk slightly stiffly. My dick's all crunchy.

Of *course* I put the cap back. Yes, it *was* slightly mottled and gooey.

But what amazingly *able* semen, *huh*?

Fifteen

Home. Bath. Bed.

Sleep like a damn *log*.

Am rudely awoken – *wah*? *eh*? *where the clock*? – at ten past eleven by an almighty commotion in the kitchen as Solomon manfully struggles to apply eye-drops to an unenthusiastic Jax (who has – he knows not *how* – recently contracted conjunctivitis), whilst simultaneously conducting a noisy argument with a strident, American female who sounds suspiciously like . . .

Who *else*?!

Jalisa!

I stagger upstairs and stand swaying in the doorway clutching my Blaine book (like I'm gonna ask her to *autograph* it for me) but no one looks over. No one even says 'Hi'.

'Your position is just so *riddled* with inconsistencies,' Jalisa's expostulating angrily, while a grim-faced Solomon locks Jax's head between his manly thighs, twizzles around frantically to try and reach the drops bottle, and then fails – signally – to do so.

'Pass me the stupid *drops*,' he demands.

But Jalisa's still talking.

'The allegations of illegal *gun* possession I can just about get my head around,' she says (Ah. So it's the tragic decline of South-West London UK Garage supremos So Solid Crew that they're discussing. Oh *ho*. Jalisa had better tread *very* carefully here. This ground is *decidedly* marshy). 'Although to threaten an innocent, African parking warden . . . How pathetic is that?'

'He never even took the gun out,' Solomon snarls. 'Now will you just *pass* me the medication?'

'He threatened him vocally. The gun was in his girlfriend's handbag. And the guy was being reasonable. He asked him to put some money in the meter or to move on. That was all.'

'The *drops*!' Solomon yells.

'I mean any normal warden would've ticketed him on the spot. And let's not forget,' she staunchly continues, 'that Asher D was actually a child actor before he graduated on to the dizzy heights of South-East London gangsta-dom. He was perfectly well raised. His mother runs the *Personnel* Department at Hackney Council. I mean give me a *break*. He starred in *Grange Hill* – or *The Bill*, I forget which – so it was hardly like the pressures of celebrity were an entirely new phenomenon to him . . .'

Solomon lunges for the drops. He manages to grab them, but the grip of his legs is temporarily weakened, and Jax – ever vigilant – snatches his chance to make a quick break for it and seeks brief refuge under the table (did ever a grown dog make so much *fuss* about a measly drop before?).

'*Damn* you!' Solomon bellows.

Jalisa's eyes fly wide open. 'Was that directed at *me* or at the dog?' she enquires icily.

Solomon falls to his knees (Yeah, that's *definitely* a question best ignored) and tries to grab Jax's collar. Jax's collar promptly slips off.

'So I can *accept* all the gun stuff,' Jalisa rants ever onward. 'All the trouble at the gigs. That poor kid getting stabbed and killed in Luton. The gun-fire in the Astoria. All the shit in Ayia Napa, all the hype and *posturing* even...'

'Come *here*,' Solomon instructs the dog, pointlessly shaking the collar at him.

'But it's the events in that hotel lobby in Cardiff that I struggle with...'

'How much *publicity*,' Solomon rocks back on to his heels, tossing the collar down (*Oops*. Now we're in trouble), 'do you remember there being when two individual members of the Crew were violently stabbed in *separate* nightclub attacks, *eh*?'

'Some,' she says, testily.

'Oh *really*?'

'Yes.'

'These people were living in fear of their *lives*. That was the *context*, Jalisa. That's why Asher D was carrying a gun. MC Romeo was stabbed for *no* reason. He was just randomly attacked. Even *you* must accept that he's a good guy. Wouldn't hurt a *fly*...'

'Well I don't know if I'd put it quite like *that*,' she demurs.

Jax, meanwhile, has clambered out from under the table and is now sitting calmly by the refrigerator, looking around him, quite obligingly (well, for a Doberman).

'*Gooood* boy.' Solomon edges his way slowly towards him. '*Goood* Jax. *Clever* Jax...'

He grabs hold of his head. Jax doesn't object (just looks a little hurt, perhaps, and surprised).

'*Right.*' Solomon prises Jax's head to the correct angle, pulls the eye wide with the fingers of one hand, then tips up the tiny bottle of eye-drops with his other. Nothing happens. The lid's still on.

'So Skat D, alias Darren Weir, enters a Cardiff hotel lobby ...' Jalisa starts up (with quite exquisitely bad timing).

'God, not *this* again...' Solomon groans, trying to pull the lid off with his teeth.

'He's standing around with all his So Solid posse. He sees a fifteen-year-old girl walking by. He makes a crude *pass* at her –'

'He just *spoke* to her,' Solomon interrupts weakly, 'he just *propositioned* her. He doesn't *grab* her or anything.'

'Are you *sure*?'

'Of *course* I ...'

Pop!

The lid flies off the tiny bottle. But Solomon's had to yank at it so ferociously that his hand flies back with an unexpected force and punches the refrigerator.

Jax barks and leaps up in panic. The bottle bursts out from between Solomon's fingers and rolls beneath the washing machine.

'You damn *bitch*,' he squeaks.

Jalisa, too, has sprung up, having presumed (she was facing the other way) that Solomon has just punched the refrigerator in order to add more colour (and defiance) to *his* side of the Skat D argument (and the 'bitch' comment certainly hasn't assisted matters).

'Taking a page from Skat D's book, *are* we?' she hisses.

'The girl hit him *first*,' Solomon's still down on his knees (Luckily. It's the only way he's coming out of this alive).

'She *slapped* him,' Jalisa gasps (as if the slap is some kind of fundamental legal and constitutional *right* of the female).

'*And*?'

'So he hits her back and he *breaks her jaw*!' Jalisa banshees.

'He went too far. . .' Solomon concedes, 'no one's actually denying that. But what about *Tupac*?'

Jalisa blinks.

Huh?

'What *about* Tupac?' she snarls.

Solomon shoves the flat of his hand under the washing machine and shuffles it about, violently. The bottle – and some onion peel – comes shooting out. The bottle rolls – at speed – in the general direction of the hallway.

'Jailed for statutory *rape*,' Solomon expounds, 'gets shot, dies, promptly becomes some kind of *folk* hero for radical American womanhood.'

Jalisa's jaw drops

Now he's gone too far.

I duck downstairs, grab some shoes, jeans, a jacket, the i-Pod, and head back up.

'What do you *mean* double standards?' Jalisa is bellowing.

'Double *standards*, you *hypocrite*,' Solomon yells defiantly, '*that's* what I mean. Because it's one of life's *many* cruel paradoxes that the more *fuckable* a man is, the less *culpable* his actions are . . .'

The air is sucked out of the room.

Silence.

I tiptoe – with the Blaine book – across the kitchen tiles. I place it down gently on to the table top. I fold it open. I point, tentatively. 'You were right about

Fitzcarraldo. Look. He's listed it under his eleven all-time favourite films. It comes in at number four.'

Jalisa glances down. 'I don't even *like* Tupac,' she murmurs, distractedly, then, 'Oh my *God*, he likes *Night of the Hunter* . . .'

I half-turn towards Solomon, touch my nose, warn-ingly, then hum five note-perfect bars from Norah Jones' 'Come Away With Me'.

He slits his eyes.

I pause (perhaps enjoying my pivotal peacemaking role slightly more than is completely healthy). 'Off the record,' I smugly confide, 'you're *completely* right about Tupac. All that sainthood shit's got *way* out of control if you ask me.'

I bow. I make a faultless exit.

Okay. So I tread on that tiny eye-medication bottle on my way out and smash it.

Fuck.

That pooch is now officially my friend for all eternity.

No. *No.* I can't quite believe that I'm doing this, either, but less than 35 minutes later I'm comfortably ensconced back in that Philippe Starck chair, up to my eye-balls in *The Future of Nostalgia* (Okay. So it's a great book, but why don't *you* try saying *tsyplenok zharenji** without the benefit of vodka?).

On my short walk over there I catch that brief (but so-necessary) glimpse of Aphra (from the bridge), sitting quietly on her wall; chin up and cheeks shining, carefully overseeing the rumpled Blaine at his nightly slumber.

Blaine (by the by) has been having a rather tough time of it lately (if Bly's detailed reports are to be taken seriously). On Saturday (Day 30), he apparently called

*The Soviet equivalent of Kentucky Fried.

out for food, banged on the walls of his box and began barking like a dog (he's hallucinating, has spells of dizziness, is short of breath, and his mouth tastes of pear drops).

Hmmm. Call me cynical (if you will), but doesn't it seem a mite *convenient* for this poignant little spectacle to've been timed for a *Saturday* – during his peak viewing period? We know the boy went to drama college, after all (and probably magicked himself a nice, neat, grade A there).

I experience some difficulty in gaining access this time (the *hospital*. Yup. The NHS *is* in safe hands after all), because my name isn't down on the list etc., but the man on reception is persuaded to phone up to the ward, and the Angry Blonde Nurse (her name, it transpires, is Lorna) comes stomping down and gives me the all-clear.

On our way back up, I ask if she's seen Aphra.

'An hour ago,' she puffs, 'dropped off a bag of food and then bolted.'

She pauses. 'I keep *telling* her he's off solids now – has been for weeks – but it just doesn't seem to sink *in*, somehow.'

She pulls a face.

'And how's *Mr* Leyland?'

'Bad,' she scowls, 'and considerably worse for not seeing her.'

She pauses. 'He just *dotes* on the woman. Although rumour has it she's been having an affair . . .'

'Really?'

'That's what the *real* family say. The first Mrs Leyland and Sherry Leyland, his unmarried sister.'

Sherry?

She clocks my expression. 'Famous family of *vintners*,' she explains, 'didn't you know that already?'

'Of *course*,' I scoff.

'Although Punch,' she continues dreamily, 'was named after his great-grandfather, who was a bare-knuckle fighter in Perth in the second half of the nineteenth century.'

(*My*. This girl certainly *has* swallowed the book of Leyland family history.)

I suddenly feel an uncommonly strong urge to say something *nice* about Aphra.

Uh . . . Yes.

Hmmn.

'She's a great cook,' I eventually murmur.

'He signed himself out for the night a couple of weeks ago,' she continues (refusing to commit on the culinary issue), 'he was slightly stronger then – but not nearly strong enough, if you want *my* opinion. . . They managed – I don't really know how – to keep it a secret from the others. Then apparently she just took him back to this cruddy little flat, tucked him up and deserted him. He was so distressed when he returned to the ward on the Monday morning that he had to be forcibly tranquillized. His sister sanctioned it. "For his own good," she said.'

She pauses.

'Lovely man. An amazing philanthropist. Hospital patron. Incredibly generous.'

'But *why* did she take him to the flat?' I ask (my mind, for some reason, still dwelling on that).

'Who?'

'Aphra.'

'Oh . . .'

She frowns.

'I don't know. Apparently he owns loads of real estate

in this area. They have a huge place on Regent Street, too, but since he's been officially *terminal*, lots of the Australian family have been staying there . . . *You* know, the kids, the first wife. Perhaps she just couldn't bear it any more. Or perhaps . . .'

She widens her eyes, meaningfully.

We're standing outside the door. I shrug, knock, and enter.

Must've been hard at it all day. He's ploughed his way through to chapter 17 – the conclusion. Only six pages to go (*Damn*. You know what this means? I'm to be denied the untold pleasures of Part 3: 'Exiles and Imagined Homelands: On Diasporic Intimacy').

Before I sit down (He's not going to make me go through that dense wodge of appendixes, is he?) I take a quick peek at the timetable.

Hmmn. Now let's see . . . Punch's been in (first thing. Of course), then the original Mrs Leyland (who – strangely enough – retains that same moniker i.e. Mrs L (1), then someone called Mordecai Roast (*classic* name, *eh*?), then Sister Leyland (riding under 'Sherry L'), who seems to stay longer than almost anybody else here, except for (last but not least) Aphra, who's due to start at ten and remain through to the morning (the most miserable shift by some margin, in my opinion).

He observes me scrutinising the timetable and grunts, 'Bad diabetic', by way of an explanation.

'Who is?'

He points to his chest, 'Me. Very bad. *Drinker* . .' He mimes taking a quick shot. 'Blood-sugar was erratic. She used to sit up at night and watch over me. The habit stuck.'

He closes his eyes.

'Johnny Walker, Black Label,' I say (it's a great knack of mine to guess a person's tipple. People are, after all, the brew they consume).

He snorts, derisively. Then he lifts his mask for a second and points at me.

'Jim Beam,' he says, 'with an inch of ginger wine.'

Jesus Christ.

He pauses. 'You have a powerful appetite for anything fortified.'

(*What*? So *which* of you bastards told him about my weakness for sherry?)

'Favourite artist . . .' he muses, 'Jackson Pollock.' He smirks: 'Because he "*lived*" it. But in your teens you worshipped Peter Blake, because of the *Sergeant Pepper* album cover . . .' He coughs for a while, then clears his throat. 'You thought it was "terribly clever".'

(So *wasn't* it? *Huh*?)

'Favourite *food* . . .' He frowns. 'White sliced, spread with ketchup, doubled over. Definitely no butter.'

'Good *God*.'

I lick my lips, anxiously (Reckon he might know how I shagged his wife this afternoon on HMS *Belfast* in the communications centre?).

'Wasted a lot of time sitting in bars with complete strangers over the years.' He shrugs. 'It's one of the few useful knacks I gleaned from the experience.'

(Fuck *him* anyway. It's brown sauce. And I can tolerate a smear – just a *smear* – of margarine on a good day).

I take a second pop.

'Maker's Mark.'

He smirks and jiggles his face mask at me.

'Chivas Regal.'

'Fucking *pathetic*,' he coughs, grabbing a hold of his pencil. 'Just read the damn book, will you?'

When Lorna's shift finishes, Brandy sends me off on a furtive little mission to discover (and retrieve) Aphra's food parcel. I don't have far to search, though. Good Nurse is standing in an adjacent kitchen, cheerfully devouring a summerfruit crêpe direct from the Tupperware.

'So Brandy wants to take a look at the food again, *huh*?' she asks, through her mouthful.

(Is this woman a *mind* reader?)

I nod.

She points to the bag. 'Tell him *not* to swallow, *only* to chew. That's the deal here, okay?'

I nod again.

She looks stern: '*Sure*?'

'Absolutely.' I grab the bag.

She touches my arm, confidingly. 'You know, when I was a *child*,' she whispers, 'I had one of those special dolls. Those *crying* dolls. You feed her water with a tiny, little bottle, then after a few seconds her *tears* start to flow, then you feel her nappy and of course she's *pissed* herself, so you change her.

But one day I decided to give her some *solids* along with the water. Proper food, yeah? Fed her some cabbage. Some chicken. I just pushed it right in . . .' She laboriously mimes this process. 'But it wouldn't go down properly. It just stuck there. Right behind the lips. Wouldn't flush out. And over the course of time, it started to *rot*,' she grimaces, 'and to *stink*.' She sighs at the memory, shakes her head, regretfully, then releases her grip and bustles off.

Who the hell *is* this woman, anyway? The reincarnated spirit of Nikolai Gogol?

Here's what she's prepared:
   A fresh green pesto served with home-fried potato crisps

A tiny, but perfect quail's egg florentine
Two fat poussins, oven-baked, with whole lemons
Stuffed baby aubergines with chilli and coconut
Mango and yoghurt chutney, date and orange chutney
(*To be served with six rye-flour chapattis*)
Stuffed baked apples
Half a summerfruit crêpe.

One cup of smooth guava lassi

He can't *swallow*, obviously. So I prop him up, he takes off his mask, coughs for a while, reaches some sort of equilibrium, and I pass him a tub. He closes his eyes and inhales ('*Ah . . .*'). Coughs some more (I wipe his mouth clean with a tissue), he requests a small forkful. I do the honours. He holds the food – dead still, on his tongue (mouth shut), for a minute or so, then he chews, winces, screws up his face in an agony of desire, inhales (to gain strength), and spits it back out (into a plastic cup).

He then cleans his palate with a rinse of water.

Kind of *messy*. And the entire process takes well over an hour.

Often his eyes fill with tears.

'Each taste,' he says afterwards, gasping for breath, 'each shape, each *texture*, crashes me into a whole new *wave* of memory . . .'

Then, '*Love* this fucking life,' he admonishes me.

I toss in Malibu and Coke, as a curve ball.

'That was my *very* favourite drink,' he simpers, 'as a teenage girl.'

Yeah. Might shelve the champagne cocktail for a while.

As if in joyful celebration of all our culinary endeavours, the next book we commence reading is Colin Spencer's thwacking-great *British Food: An Extraordinary Thousand Years of History*.

By 3 a.m. we've worked our way through 'Anglo-Saxon Gastronomy,' 'Norman Gourmets: 1100–1300', 'Anarchy and Haute Cuisine 1300–1500' and 'Tudor Wealth and Domesticity'.

I'm in the midst of a detailed description of how to prepare 'Cabbage Cream' (a sugary Tudor delight made out of individual 'sheets' or 'leaves' of skin, fished from off the top of a warm bowl of cream), when –

–

Oh *shit*

–

Brandy Leyland suddenly drops his pencil and collapses sideways. He vomits, copiously, into his oxygen mask – a lethal black-cherry coloured substance – and immediately commences choking on it. I jump up, curse, yank off the mask and ring for the nurse. She strides in.

'I swear to *God* he didn't swallow anything,' I tell her, watching, in horror, as the cherry substance drips down off the bedsheets and on to the floor tiles.

'Don't worry.' She arranges him firmly into the recovery position, cleans his nostrils out and he starts to scream. Piercing screams at first (*girl* screams), until his vocal cords give up (collapse? What do vocal cords *do*?) and he just peeps and squeaks like an inefficient dog whistle.

'Go home,' she says cheerfully, pushing her hand into his mouth and grappling with his tongue, 'come back tomorrow.'

I'm halfway down the stairs when I realise that I'm still clutching the Spencer book. But I'm too scared to take it back up. And the porter's gone temporarily AWOL (*Uh . . . Safe in whose hands was that?*). So I'm obliged to lug it home with me.

Could come in handy, though, on the off chance that I wake up at five, desperate to understand more about Jane Austen's passion for ox cheek.

When I walk past Blaine, I see that Aphra's temporarily abandoned her station –

Where she be?

– so I stand, and *I* watch for twenty minutes or so (perhaps secretly hoping that she might actually rematerialise).

He's restless tonight. Tossing and turning. On his back, then on his belly. Knees up, then down. Arms flung out, willy-nilly . . .

I imagine some no-nonsense Australian housewife watching this exact same image on Sky – with half an eye on her rampaging toddler – as she devours a haphazard afternoon tea.

And then I remember something Blaine said about how he feels at his most honest, his most *pure*, when he's performing his Challenges, then something else, about how, when he was *Frozen in Time*, he coped with all the pain and all the anxiety by dint of simply *fantasising*.

A warm *bath* (you might be forgiven for thinking), a mug of *cocoa*, a Caribbean *holiday* . . .

Uh-*uh*. *Miles* off.

His fantasies weren't happy ones. Instead he imagined that he was a prisoner of *war*, or that he was suffering and dying from some horrendous *disease*. And these crazy thoughts sustained him, they made him rally, they kept him strong.

('Uh . . . *excuse* me, but there seems to be a badly-trained production assistant violently yanking at the small plastic *tube* which is currently glued to the tip of my *cock* . . . Would you actually just mind telling him to pull a little *harder* there?')

Here's another thing: Blaine got himself fit for *Vertigo* (standing on that pillar in New York) by walking around the city in a 65lb *chain mail suit* (A romantic image, certainly, but just *consider* – if he'd encountered a random rain storm on 24th Street, he'd've been rusted into *oblivion* by Broadway).

These masochistic feats all put me in mind, somehow, of that poor Archbishop of Canterbury (Thomas à Becket) who was murdered in his cathedral, and then, when his servants kindly stripped his body of all its bishoply regalia ('You take the cross, I'll take the rings'), they discovered, to their astonishment, that he was wearing a *hair shirt*, underneath, right next to the skin, which'd been itching him for *years* into an excruciating piety.

But he'd kept it together.

Like any true saint would.

Remember St Simeon – on whose bizarre example that particular Challenge was based? (Okay, so I didn't, either, before I read Blaine's book.) This was a man who spent 37 *years* on top of various pillars (circa AD 389 – his cable reception was much better up there), a man who, as a matter of *course*, went 40 days – the whole of *Lent* – without even the tiniest *morsel* of edible sustenance. And why?

Why? Because he was fucked up. *That's* why. He was a nut-case. A *fanatic*. Because – and this really *is* the bottom line – just like Blaine, he simply *loved* to do it.

Oh yeah (I nearly forgot), and because he used personal suffering 'as a vehicle for interpreting Christ's Teaching'.

What? You think Christ didn't go through enough *himself*?

I mean why the *hell* didn't he just go that extra *mile*, huh?

Glass in his *shoes*, perhaps.

You know, now I actually come to *think* about it, the quality of sound on the i-Pod *does* seem a little too compressed. Boxed up. Flattened out. *Smaller.*

Have *you* noticed that?

And here's another thing: now that I actually have all this choice, I find that I just keep on hankering after the *same* short selection. Time and again. *Ad infinitum.*

Which is terribly disappointing.

Ideologically speaking.

Home.

At *last*.

I quietly let myself into the house, tiptoe through to the kitchen, and am not a little surprised to discover Jalisa, sitting alone at the table – wrapped up in one of Solomon's Oriental robes (which is way too big for her), drinking a mint tea and reading the Blaine book.

'Don't you find that Blaine story quite amazing?' she says, not even glancing up (as if I've been standing there, all night, just *waiting* for her observations).

'Which one?'

'He's a six-year-old kid, travelling alone to school on the subway. It's a very straightforward journey, just two stops. And he's playing with this bunch of tarot cards, which he loves to perform tricks with...'

I suddenly remember.

'Yes,' I take over, 'and these two old women take an

interest in the cards, so he shows them a trick or two, but his hand slips at one point and he accidentally *drops* them –'

'The train *stops* suddenly,' she interrupts (the story fresher in her mind), 'and they fall on to the floor. But by the time they've gathered them all together, he's missed his stop.'

'So he panics.'

'But then the women get off the train with him at the next station, take him over to the other side, catch another train back, walk him to school, and explain to his teacher why he's late . . .'

She glances up at me, then down at the book again. 'He says that this experience taught him how much – even at such a young age – his magic *affected* people.'

She smiles. 'But what it *actually* taught him, was how magic was a useful device for making people *care* for him. Magic placed him in *jeopardy*, and then magic seemingly pulled him through again.'

She closes the book and puts a hand up to her eyes.

'I think I caught conjunctivitis off the dog.'

'*What*? That's ridiculous.'

She sighs. 'I caught it off a *cat* before . . .'

'Well in *that* case, maybe Jax caught it off *you*.'

She gives this possibility some serious thought.

I pick up the book myself and turn to an image towards the back.

'Did you see this?'

I point to a photo (a still, taken from a local woman's home video) of the top of Blaine's casket, which was taken during the *Buried Alive* stunt.

'What is it?' she asks.

'A black cross. The woman who took this says that

it appeared above the casket and just *hung* there, at all times, throughout the week that he was buried.'

Jalisa stares at it, her expression incredulous.

'He goes on to say,' I continue, 'in the *text*, how he planned to get buried on *Good Friday*, that his birthday fell on *Easter Sunday* that year, but then they finally decided to delay the whole thing until the religious holidays were over.'

She rolls her red eyes – they *are* very red, actually (*Hmmn.* Must remember what mug she's been drinking that tea from, and avoid it like the plague in the morning).

'I love the way,' she grins, 'that he never makes any kind of *overt* statement. He leaves those imaginative leaps to the reader – or the spectator. He just presents all this quasi-religious information as if it's by-the-by, pure coincidence, stuff that simply *happens* . . .'

'Because please let's not forget,' I lecture sternly, 'that Jesus Christ was a master magician; turning one loaf into a thousand loaves, the water into wine . . .'

She chuckles, 'And didn't Jesus also get slated in his time?'

'They crucified him in the press, apparently.'

'Ho ho,' she ho-hos.

I do a little curtsy.

'I was fascinated,' she continues, 'by all that stuff, early on, about the "magic room" he saw in his dreams.'

'Me too.'

'Blaine says the room stopped appearing to him when he got to an age where he realised that depending on the "props" of magic wasn't the way to go. That "real" magic wasn't about boxes with false bottoms in them, it was something more true, more "grown up", more powerful . . .'

293

She slowly shakes her head.

'You're not buying that?'

'No. Why? Are you?'

I shrug.

'He wants us to believe that all the magic he does now is *real*,' she says. 'But I find it difficult to accept that this "magic room" of his childhood wasn't actually a belief in *real* magic. Children are credulous. They're full of wonder. For a child, *anything* is possible. I can't help feeling like the adult Blaine has cleverly flipped the meaning of his dream inside out ...'

'So why did the magic room disappear from his dreams, then?' I ask the Oh Wise One.

'Isn't it obvious?' She throws out her hand, dismissively (accidentally loosening the folds of her robe). 'The room disappeared when this terrible realisation finally dawned on him that magic *was* an illusion. It disappeared when he realised that there was *no such thing* as *real* magic. Only a clever combination of cunning, luck and manipulation. I mean he openly states himself that the psychology of magic is the same as the psychology of a small-time con. Magic is just a combination of pre-planning, deception and a powerful ego.'

I ponder this for a while.

'You think he's in denial, at some level?'

'At *some* level, yes. He has to be. Otherwise it wouldn't work. I mean he makes a big deal in the book about how all the greatest magicians were people who "played the part" of someone with supernatural powers. But what does that actually really *mean*? Because anyone can play a *part*, but then it's still fundamentally just *play* ...'

She sighs. 'The fact is that it's this playful *gap* which Blaine is most interested in. It's what he exploits. It's where his power resides. His strength, as a performer, lies in this confusion. But he calls it "mystery" . . .'

She pauses, perhaps slightly confused herself, now. 'I mean he talks a great deal about "belief" in the book, as if a person having the innocent facility simply to *believe* without questioning is something magical, something wonderful, as if a person's at their very best when they're truly "open", truly "vulnerable", but I keep on wondering exactly *what* they're believing in. What *lives* in that gap between appearance and fact? You can call me cynical, but I'm not entirely convinced that it's necessarily a *good* thing . . .'

She glances up – for confirmation – observes my goofy smile, quickly glances down, bellows, 'You *shit*!' and frantically grapples with those loosened folds of fabric.

Now *that's* the kind of gap a man can believe in.

Of course I wouldn't *dream* of looking.

Far too much respect there.

Although, for the record: *very* dark nipples.
  And much *fuller* than you might initially imagine.

Okay. Let's all just forget I said that, *eh*?

Sixteen

Something strange and disturbing happens en route to work. I've just crossed Tower Bridge (on the left-hand side, with its view of the east and Canary Wharf), have jogged down that (now) infamous curving stairwell (the site of my first, late-night encounter with the green-hoofed Aphra), have turned a sharp right (in order to facilitate an early-morning trip to the Shad Thames Starbucks), when I espy *Hilary* (sans headcloth), crouched over (*hunched*), a few yards along from the embankment wall.

My instinct is to saunter on by, but then I remember Punk's Not's comments of the other evening and think better of it. I walk over. He glances up, sees it's me, but says nothing.

'What the hell're you doing?' I ask him.

'Moth,' he murmurs, pointing.

Eh?

I peer down. Good *God*. He's right. The most *spectacular* moth. About five inches in diameter, subtly coloured – but magnificently patterned – in a range of dark chocolate browns, subtle fawns and pale creams. Fluffy torso. Two fantastic, golden antennae.

But something's wrong. I pull in closer and see that

someone's cleverly stuck it on to a wodge of yellow bubblegum.

'Oh Christ. Who'd do *that*?'

Hilary shakes his head.

'It's quite exquisite,' he says, then adds (in case I was in any doubt), 'I really *love* moths.'

I take a step back. 'D'you know what kind it is?'

'Nope.'

'D'you reckon it's indigenous?'

He shrugs. 'Could've come in on a boat, I guess. One of the big cruise ships which travel around Europe and dock here at the Tower.'

He stares at it some more, plainly quite mesmerised.

'You stand guard,' I tell him, 'and I'll go and buy a bottle of water so we can try and wash some of that gunk off.'

He waits. I go to get the water (and two coffees. And two buns. *Aw*).

Then we commence our heroic battle to save the moth.

The moth is very obliging. And it's still quite gutsy (quite *lively*, too), which we both construe as a positive sign.

Hilary gently holds on to its abdomen and the tip of one large wing as I slowly pour some water on to the gum surrounding its leg area. Once a small pool of liquid has been created around it, Hilary gradually tries to pull it free.

The moth struggles, impressively, to kick its legs clear. But the gum is stuck thoroughly to its belly and to the pavement below.

At this critical point, Aphra turns up.

'What the hell're you doing?' she asks, placing her bag of Tupperware down on to the cobbles.

'Moth,' Hilary says.

I don't look up. I look sideways. I see that she's wearing

a ferocious pair of orange-patent-leather winkle-pickers which render her feet almost a third-again as long. She leans over.

'Yuk,' she says.

'Someone stuck it down on to the pavement with a piece of gum,' I murmur (in that blank yet heartfelt tone especially favoured by the doctors on *ER*).

Hilary, meanwhile, has trotted off to find some kind of pointed implement – an old nail, a *stick* – so that he can flip the gum away with it.

'Good night, was it?' I ask her, my voice slightly jaundiced-sounding (*why*, I'm not entirely sure).

'Have you ever noticed how terribly Hilary *stinks*?' she asks. 'Like old sweat and shit and Bovril?'

I flinch (I mean, is the poor bastard even out of earshot?).

I point to her shoes. 'Been auditioning for *pantomime*, have we?'

She snorts – almost a *guffaw* (now *that's* a result).

I glance up at her, half-smiling. She's inspecting the moth again. 'You know, that isn't *gum*,' she says, matter-of-factly, 'that's its guts.'

'*What*?'

Hilary returns bearing the dried stem of a dead flower.

'Aphra thinks that goo might be the moth's intestines,' I tell him.

He crouches down and begins to poke around.

'Oh *fuck*,' he says, his voiced hushed in horror, 'I think she's right. I think it *is*.'

We all recoil and then stare at the moth some more.

'But they're so *yellow*,' I say, 'and so *sticky*. And it still seems so *alive* . . .'

'There *is* something quite amazing . . .' Hilary begins. Then Aphra kicks out her winkle-pickered foot and slams it down on top of it. Once. Twice. She performs a small pirouette.

'Dead,' she says (with some satisfaction), casually inspecting the sole of her shoe which is now smattered in moth-goo. She grabs my bottle of water and splashes it over. She scrapes the shoe clean on the side of a nearby bench.

She inspects it again.

It's pristine.

She uses the remaining water to wash the side of the bench off (so *Public Spirited* of her), then hands me the empty bottle back.

Hilary stands up.

'*Well*,' he says, 'I suppose that's *that*, then.'

'Poor moth,' I say.

We both inspect the spot.

'Blaine had a restless night,' she informs us, 'and woke slightly *earlier* than usual this morning. But he seems in pretty good spirits, just the same.'

Then she chucks me, fondly, under the chin, nods towards Hilary, grabs her bag, and *Arabian Nights* it off down the cobbles, apparently without a care.

'So *compassionate*,' Hilary says thickly.

'I bought you some coffee,' I say, 'and a bun.'

'Thanks,' he says, staring down, once again, at the small stain where the moth used to be, 'that was nice of you. But I ate earlier.'

Earlier? When? At fucking *dawn*?

So I take them to Bly, at work, and pretend I bought them for *her*, instead.

She glugs down the coffee, then *inhales* the bun, after.
   (*Oops*. Quick burp.)
   The girl's *dependable* like that.

But is that obnoxious ginger *really* her natural hair colour?

In fact I'm so *relieved* by her cheerful straightforward-ness that I start telling her about what I perceive as being the shortcomings of i-Pod . . .

'"Holidays In The Sun"' she suddenly screams. 'The *Sex* Pistols!'

Okay.
   So just . . .
   You know.

Sitting at my desk.

Doing some work.

Suppressing my yawns.

Then at 10.17 my phone rings.

'Bring the book back,' a woman's voice demands.

'Pardon?'

'The Spencer. The *book*. Bring it back.'

It's *her*.

'But I'm at work.'

'I don't *care*. Brandy *needs* it. He wants it *now*. So bring it the hell *back*.'

Approximately twenty minutes later, and I'm standing in the hospital foyer trying to persuade a porter to spirit that troublesome tome upstairs for me, when that dark, pretty, older, *angry* woman from Aphra's flat rolls up and taps me on the shoulder.

I turn. I *start* –

Eh?

Oh *fuck*.

Ambuuuush!

She then grabs me by the arm (while the porter watches on, in astonishment) and drags me outside (Good. So now *he* has me down as some kind of child killer) on to the handy raised walkway which connects the hospital to the train station (Yup. *Just* what this situation lacked; that fascinating element of physical jeopardy).

'So try and explain *this* one,' she hisses, shoving me up roughly against a wrought-iron railing (Ow!)

'There *is* no explanation,' I answer (I mean can *you* think of one?).

'That just *won't do*,' she growls.

'Well it's gonna *have* to,' I say firmly (*Hey*. Where'd this impressive core of moral certainty suddenly spring up from?).

She just stares at me, in disgust.

'Who *are* you, anyway?' I ask (not a little indignant).

'His *First Wife*,' she snaps (with capital letters – like she's happily betrothed to the American President). 'And who the hell are *you*, for that matter?'

(*Huh*? Didn't I introduce myself to this bitch once before?)

'The prick,' I respond (with that *charming* streak of self-deprecation I'm now so legendary for), 'who was dumb enough to give you his *phone* number.'

'I'm very sorry,' she says haughtily, 'but I just don't *get* your sense of humour.'

'That's because I wasn't actually *being* funny,' I tell her. (If I *was*, though, it'd be an *entirely* different matter.)

'Now you're starting to *scare* me,' she says.

(Oh *God*, not *this* again).

'You scare easy,' I murmur.

'What do you *mean* by that?'

'You scare easy,' I say, but louder, this time.

'What *are* you?' she squeaks, jabbing her index finger into my shoulder. 'Some kind of *stalker*? A *weirdo*? What do you *want*? What's your *agenda*?'

'All I *want*,' I tell her calmly, 'is for you to leave me the *fuck* alone.'

(So it's only a Muji shirt, but I happen to be quite *fond* of it.)

'*What*?'

She looks incredulous.

'*One*,' I say, 'I think you're crazy. *Two*,' I add, 'I think you should stop phoning me. *Three*,' I continue swiftly, 'I haven't *warmed* to you particularly, so *four*,' I climax, 'I think we should *avoid* each other.'

'Then *stay away from my family*,' she bellows.

(Oh *lovely*. Just as a huddle of pretty nurses stroll by.)

'Nothing would please me more,' I snap back.

'Good,' she says (slightly put out by my compliance). We stare at each other.

'Let go of my arm,' I say.

'With *pleasure*,' she says.

She lets go.

I pass her the book. I start to walk.

'But what about *Aphra*?' she yells after me.

I don't look around. I just keep on walking

'I *know* she's not coming in. I *know* that you're covering for her,' she continues yelling. 'She just won't *speak* to anyone . . .'

It's then – very neatly, and with the minimum of fuss – that I lift my right hand high and show her the finger.

Come *on* . . .
   It was a *joke*.
   It was *funny*.

And what *about* Aphra, anyway?

Moth killer.

Hmmn. Talking of *funny*...

Now here's a *really* hilarious thing: I've suddenly noticed how when I'm passing the time of day in the general vicinity of Blaine lately – on my way to the shops, perhaps, or to the café, or on my walk home, maybe – *whatever* – and I'm just hanging out for a moment, soaking up the *atmosphere*, possibly having a quick chat with some passing stranger (some really *normal*, really *amicable*-seeming individual), that suddenly – out of the blue – they'll just turn and say something like, 'God, I just *wish* I'd brought those rotten *tomatoes* with me...' And they'll be staring up at Blaine with an expression of such pure, such condensed *hostility*. And I'll turn and glance up at him myself, struggling to see the thing they're seeing, struggling to remember that furious feeling *I* once felt, but all I'll see is a coffee-coloured, black-haired man, quietly *sitting* there, smiling, waving, doing nothing in particular.

Just a man.

And I'll look back at the person, and I'll realise that I can't tell. I just can't *tell* any more. I can't understand what's going on inside of them. I can't see what they're seeing. I can't comprehend where all that anger's coming from. And – worse still – I'm not sure where *mine's* gone (Where he *be*? *Eh*?).

Not knowing unsettles me. It *baffles* me. It's *disturbing*.

So do I *say* anything (you're probably wondering)? No. I say nothing. Do I walk away? No. Not at all, I stand my ground, I stay. I might even – for that matter – continue smiling and nodding and talking...

But inside – *inside* – something's happening. I'll be gradually closing off. I'll feel myself *withdrawing* (almost as if a hatch has fallen). And then I'll slowly feel myself

307

rising (*seriously*). Like a *bubble*. Floating up and away
. . . Bobbing around aimlessly on the river breeze, above
everything, perhaps touching a hard surface occasionally
– the edge of a wall or boat, or a random piece of masonry
– then just pushing off (not bursting, *never* bursting).
Just *pushing* off, and floating away again.

Kind of quiet. Kind of blank.

Just pushing off. Just floating.

Wow.
I mean that's pretty *funny*, don't you think?

Okay, so it's not bellyaching stuff.

(Did I actually suggest it *would* be?)

It's not tear-spilling, *gut*-clutching stuff.

It's not . . .

Whoops. There I go again ... Up, up, *up* ...

God. Where's my *head* at, lately?

Bly catches me, at four, fast asleep behind a voluminous office fictus.

'*Oi*,' she whispers. 'If you're actually *serious* about getting away with this, then perhaps you should be aware that your big *feet* are sticking out.'

'*Uh*?'

I sit up, yank my knees in.

'Shift over.'

She crawls behind the pot and joins me (although the hair – let's face it – must be a dead giveaway).

When she draws in closer she smells of apples.

'Granny Smiths,' I say, yawning.

'My shampoo,' she says.

'How *sweet*,' I say. 'Isn't that how nice girls' hair always smelled in the seventies?'

'Wouldn't know,' she says, 'I wasn't a nice girl then.' We sit.

'So what's happening?' she asks.

'Wha'd you mean?'

'You're sleeping behind a fictus,' she sighs, 'when everybody *knows* that the only sensible way to skive off properly in this place is by dozing on the toilet.'

(Oh. Do the *girls* do that too?)

'Are you interrogating me about this,' I ask suspiciously, 'in your Human Resources capacity?'

She smiles. 'Just try and think of it,' she says tenderly (gently removing a fictus leaf from the close vicinity of my right eye), 'simply as one evolved ape interacting with another.'

(Yeah. *That* works. Okay.)

'So what's wrong?' she asks.

I try and think of something *palpable* to respond with, but can't quite rise to the challenge.

'Can you see Blaine from this angle?' she finally wonders, craning her neck around to gaze through the darkened glass.

'I was having a nice little *chat*,' I say, 'with this father and daughter, earlier. Just normal people from Hammersmith. Came straight down here on the District Line. Girl eighteen or nineteen, intelligent, slightly punky-looking. Dad really affable. In his early fifties. And they're standing there together, staring up at Blaine, and we're chatting about how the weather's turned colder.

Then all of a sudden the girl starts formulating wildly about Blaine, about what a *fool* he is, and how much she *hates* him, and the dad's just standing by, nodding, smiling on...'

Bly's staring at me, rather strangely.

'And I'm just thinking "Why?"' I glance over at her, furiously. '"*Why*?" Then suddenly I'm *tired*. I'm *very* tired.'

Even as I speak I feel my eyelids drooping.

'The problem,' she says quietly, 'is surely that there *is* no real reason to hate him.'

I frown. 'How's that?'

She shrugs. 'Because he's a blank canvas. He's transparent. He's *clear*. So when people look up at him they don't hate what *he* is. They project everything they're feeling on to him. They *vent* their hatred – their conformity, their rage, their poverty, their fear, their confusion – on to him.'

She pauses. 'And it works in exactly the same way for the *positive* people. Blaine becomes everything that they aspire to, everything they admire. He's like a mirror in which people can see the very best and the very *worst* of themselves. That's the simple genius of what he's doing. That's the trick. That's the *magic*. See?'

Good *Lord*. Think she might actually *have* something there.

'*Loving* your work,' I say, then I squeeze her arm, warmly, and retreat to the toilet.

Seventeen

Got a great little system going with Good Nurse.

Here's how we do it:

As soon as Brandy's final visitors have said their fond farewells, she rings me on my mobile (I'm hanging around in the train station, trying to chat up the girl on the photographic counter of the all-night-chemist), she tells me the coast is clear, and I barge straight on up there.

'Pepper Schnapps?'

'Fuck off.'

We've finished the Spencer. In fact we've finished *A Corner of a Foreign Field: An Indian History of a British Sport*, by Ramachandra Guha (and I loved every second of it). Now we're on Erich Segal's *The Death of Comedy* (You currently find me miserably hacking through a dense maze of iambic pentameter in chapter Sixteen, 'Shakespeare: Errors and Eros').

I've observed – just in passing – how much more erratic Brandy's note-taking has become over the last few nights. More than once I've seen his pencil move on to the surface of the table below the notebook, but still continue writing there, or I've seen the point break, and watched him scribbling on – lead-free – for literally *pages*, with nothing but the flattened stump.

I mention as much to Good Nurse (Day 36, a Friday night) on my brief excursion to the toilet.

She gazes at me, in open astonishment.

'He's *blind*,' she says.

'*What*?'

'Since that night I sent you home. Didn't you *notice*?'

I shake my head.

'Did he not *mention* it to you?'

'No.'

My voice sounds hollow.

'Then say nothing.' She squeezes my arm. 'Just pretend.'

So that's what I do.

He's never asked why Aphra doesn't come. But he's asked about the food.

'Did she bring the food?' he'll gasp.

And I'll say, 'Of course she did.'

Then I'll open the containers and describe what she's prepared.

'So we're looking at a strange, hollow *green* thing, like a tiny courgette. Seeds in the middle . . .'

'Okra, you *tit*.'

'With whole red chillies . . .'

'Mustard seeds and coconut . . .' he takes over, grinning behind his mask, as he recollects.

'And in *here* . . . Uh . . . a strange kind of pink *slop* . . . Looks like . . .'

'Strawberry mousse,' he sighs. 'Try some.'

I dip my finger in.

'Describe,' he whispers.

And I'll describe it in the best way that I possibly can.

Sometimes I'll tell him exactly which shoes she was wearing when she made the delivery (If I got close enough, at any point, to take a proper look), and he'll smile and he'll nod.

Death is close upon him now. The room feels full of Death's strange, sweet breath. It vies with the scent of the perfumed candle. Death makes the bedsheets crackle. He makes the chair squeak on the lino. He knocks the cards over and forgets to pick them up again.

Death is here.

Even the nurses feel his tingle.

Let's not talk about the pain.

Let's not *think* about the pain.

Nothing to be gained by that, *eh*?

Look –

Here's a turn up: the table next to the bed is almost bare now (the books are all read). The suitcase by the window is completely empty (the little note books are all full). And no new cards have arrived, lately, with their uplifting little messages, insisting that he Get himself Well.

Yesterday, when he reached the last page of the notebook he was using, I took it from him, walked over to the case, opened it, fiddled around inside it for a while, then brought him back the exact-same one.

He took it from me, frowned (when he felt the rough texture of the pages with his thumb), then nodded, smiled, and continued writing.

'Absinthe?'

Long pause.

Long pause.

'Makes the heart grow fonder.'

I laugh. He laughs. Then he coughs (tears pouring down his cheeks. Feet curling up).

Was it then?

(I'm struggling to remember.)

Was it then that the lights went out?

I read for another hour.

I complete the chapter.

I close the book.

I stand.

Death pulls the chair back for me (very obligingly).

Death sighs, then taps his foot, then checks his watch, officiously.

It's time for the Family.

I grab *Shane* from the bedside table and stick it in my pocket. Then I take it out again and hide it under his pillow.

Good book for a journey, *eh*?

Eighteen

I find Aphra where I knew she'd be.

It's almost dawn. But not quite.

I sit on the wall, a few feet along from her.

'Houdini,' I murmur, 'was close to his mother.'

She says nothing.

'His father was a rabbi, but very traditional, and when they emigrated to America his views were considered a little old fashioned for the New World. So things got tough for the family. The father moved away to work. Houdini was only about twelve at the time, but his father made him *swear* to take care of his mother. And he did. From that point onwards he worked tirelessly – almost maniacally – with that single aim in mind.'

She says nothing.

'Blaine felt he never got that opportunity; to care for his mother in the ways he felt he should've. He believes that the only *real* love is the love between a mother and her child.'

She says nothing.

'But there's this strange *conflict* within him,' I say, 'because when Blaine first found his wings in the world of magic and performing, when everything finally came together for him – both creatively and ideologically – when he cut his hair and grew his goatee and started dressing in black; when he *became* 'David Blaine, Street Magician', basically; this transformation corresponded, almost exactly, with the death of the one person he loved most in all the world.'

Still nothing.

'He'd taken this trip to France, lived the high life in St Tropez for six months with the extremely wealthy Steiner family. When he came back, though, his mother was dying. He felt like he'd let her down – when she'd needed him the most – like he'd betrayed her.'

She finally turns to look at me.

'*Did* he?'

There's an unexpected urgency in her voice.

I can't answer.

'He says her last three words, before she died, were "*God is Love*".'

I clear my throat. It's tightened up, for some reason.

'But when he was standing on that ninety foot pole, in the middle of New York,' I continue, 'a whole *eight years* later – *Vertigo*, May 2002 – he had this strangely powerful revelation in which he suddenly realised that life was just a series of sunrises and sunsets. Nothing more.'

'Does he *still* think that?' she interrupts.

'Maybe. I don't know. But what I *am* sure of, is that at some level he believes that magic took his mother from him. Magic is his life's other great love, see? But it seems destined to be a tragic one.'

She shakes her head. 'No. *Now* you're just being ridiculous. *This* . . .' She points. 'This is all about *living*. The closer to death he draws, the more *alive* he becomes.'

I shrug.

'His friends apparently despair of him,' I say, 'they get furious with him when he pulls these stunts. They do everything they possibly can to try and stop him. But once his mind's made up, there's literally *nothing* anybody can do to make him change it. And it's only a grim awareness of this fact which finally makes them supportive. Blaine might be in *physical* danger, but he holds the people who love him *emotionally* captive. That's a very cruel transaction which he seems perfectly at ease with.'

She frowns.

'Imagine that,' I say, smiling, 'having the whole *world* standing by, utterly helpless, in the thrall of your self-destructiveness.'

She kicks out a leg. She's wearing a crazy pair of Greek-style sandals in pale grey leather, the laces of which criss-cross up her shins to the hinge of her knee, concluding there in a loose, leather bow.

'*Like* them?'

I give this question some serious consideration.

(*What*? Absolutely *not*. They make her look like some kind of low-rent, Roman *serving* boy.)

'Yes,' I answer, 'I think they're lovely.'

She gives me a straight look then turns away.

'Barely worth all the *chafing*, really,' she says, with a sigh.

That's probably the last time I'll ever see her.

There are some things you just *know*, huh?

But I stand on the bridge and watch the sunrise that morning.

And it's a perfectly adequate one. Nothing too spectac-ular.

I walk home. I make myself some toast. I have a shave. I take the dogs to the park. I watch some kids' TV. I fall asleep. And when I awaken, it's early evening. The TV's still on. It's an ad-break. There's an advert for shampoo, then one for car insurance, then an image of Blaine flashes on to the screen.

Blaine.

In his box.

From the front – from the side – from the front again.

'Staying *in* this autumn?' the voiceover enquires coyly, then proceeds to reel off a choice selection of programmes from the channel's autumn schedules.

But I'm not listening. I'm staring at Blaine. Blaine on *TV*. I fall off the sofa and draw closer to the screen. Must be old footage. Because he's so much *fatter*. And I'm seeing all the buildings around him, *locating* him, between the trees, and the sky and the river.

I'm feeling the bridge (I am), I'm *feeling* it – that huge, overmediated landmark, that monolith . . .

And suddenly it just . . . it just *resonates*.

It *does*.

It *sings* to me.

Because it's not great or old or grand or historical any more. It's just . . . just *there*. It's *real*. It's *dimensional*. And I *own* it. I've landed. I've taken *hold*.

I'm shaking all over, my eyes are tearing up, I'm gasping and laughing . . .

And in the *heart* of all this leaf, this sky, this masonry?

Slap bang in the *middle* of them? One man, one ridiculous man, so *transformed*.

I reach out my hand to the screen and feel the stiff buzz of static there. And suddenly I'm crying. Weeping uncontrollably. Because I've fucking *arrived*. I understand. I'm *there*.

Then Solomon walks in and finds me.

Hand on the screen, weeping, the whole sordid *deal*. Oh *yeah*.

'Adair?'

This is worse than when he caught me wanking over a muted-out Judge Judy.

The *gavel*.

And at least she was *female*.

He pours me a stiff bourbon. He runs me a bath. He makes me dinner. He hires *Amores Perreros* on video and makes me watch it with him.

Sunday, I get a text from *Jalisa* of all people.

'*Read his Dream Manifesto,*' it says, '*esp. no. 13.*'

I haul the Blaine book out again.

The Manifesto . . . It's right at the back. *Here* we go:

Okay . . . *blah blah* . . . Don't overindulge, respect all life, take a trip to the *sea*, love yourself, read more, listen more, learn from your mistakes . . .

All very obvious, very sensible, very straightforward stuff.

Then my eye drops to no. 13, the last of the bunch:

'Don't create a robot that's superior to human beings or it will wipe out the human race.'

O-kay.

Let's move right on, *shall* we?

Monday. While I'm out at work, we receive a delivery. I find it blocking up the hallway when I get back that evening.

The Chair. And *Shane*. And a message (stuck to the seat, on that so-familiar notepaper, in that so-familiar hand) which says:

'Bols, you cunt.

And this is a fucking Mies van der Rohe –

Don't you (or your skinny arse) know *anything*?'

Skinny arse?

Skinny *arse*?

So did I ever even *hint* that Furniture Design was my forte?

Did I?

And here's another thing: to consciously *choose* to abuse the very booze you were *christened* in?
  No bloody *wonder* that arty-farty SOB didn't want to let on.

Bols?!

What's wrong with Remy Martin?

The next day, on the dawning of Day 40, I bump into Hilary. He's standing on the park steps, by the wire, casually perusing a poster of Leonardo Di Caprio (which some imbecile has hung up there), his Fortune Reading sign tucked under one arm, that infernal headscarf tossed around his neck. And he's clutching two cups of coffee in a plastic holder. One bun. He's obviously waiting for somebody. I clamber up and join him.

'Quiet, isn't it?' I say, glancing around (nobody about but a couple of guards, and the usual straggle of suited city-folk scurrying to work).

'Yup.'

Blaine is still asleep.

We both stare up at him. We're the only two people around (strange, eh? That an event can be so huge in one moment, yet so very intimate the next?).

'Got some bad news for you,' he says, clearing his throat.

'Oh yeah?'

(For a moment I think it's going to be something about Aphra. But it's not. What am I even *thinking*? Of *course* it won't be.)

'You're gonna get the sack. Tomorrow.'

He turns and offers me a coffee.

'I got you this,' he says. 'Sorry.'

And he smiles.

So what can I *do*? I take the cup.

'Could only afford one bun,' he says.

(*Hmmn.* Now *here's* an interesting social dilemma . . .)

It's during this small, almost *domestic* interlude that Blaine suddenly awakens. One second he's fast asleep, lying flat, totally *comatose*. The next, he's rocketed up. With an awful gasp. His eyes staring. His mouth hanging open.

(The fluidity of *movement*. The *momentum*. The *panic*.)

Then he turns – in that brief instant – he *turns*, still jolted, and he stares straight at me.

One

Two

Three

Then, 'Oh. It's *you*,' his face seems to say, and it *relaxes* (his expression relieved yet *irritable*, like I'm some sickly, needy *dog* who happens to've wandered into view). A weak smile. He lifts up his hand, automatically.

David Blaine – *the* David Blaine – waves at me.

Without prompting.

Good *God*.

(Do I wave *back*, you're wondering. Of *course* I don't. I *can't*. I'm holding the damn *coffee* carton in one hand, see? And in the other I'm holding the bloody *bun* Hilary gave me.)

He turns and grabs his notebook (like Aphra said he would, *just* like she said) and he scratches his curly head with the end of his pencil. He calms himself down. He slowly realigns his celebrity mantle (a little to the left. *Okay*. Now a little to the right . . . I'm actually a multi-*multi*millionaire. Did you happen to *know* that?). Then he sighs and he begins to write . . .

I blink. I hide my confusion by sipping the coffee. It's almost cold. 'Coffee's almost cold,' I gripe.

Wednesday, I get the *sack*.

Hey! Mayor Ken Livingstone? You can suck my fat *cock*.

Thursday, Bly pops around to see me and casually lets slip how Hilary got his job back.

But in *my* department.

Did the fucking interview *Monday*.

Yup. *That's* how they get'cha.

(*Aw.* And there was you idly thinking how there was gonna be some kind of life-affirming *romance* between Bly and me once that dirty hussy Aphra was out of the picture . . .

That bitch got me *fired*.

So pull your damn *horns* in.)

Three days and counting . . .

Everything speeds up.
  And everything slows down.
  Concurrently.
  Funny how life can do that.

Bly and I actually stroll down there together – *companionably*, if you *must* know – that last Thursday night. And its *packed* with mums and with dads, with teens and with kids. And there's this twenty-four-hour homeless *singing* marathon (A bunch of students determined to use their charitable instincts to drive the poor bastard round the bend again). A blonde cockney girl with a grating voice is banging relentlessly on her tambourine and hollering. And Blaine's there, exhausted-seeming – lying on his side – his hood pulled up, like a bemused King of Siam, welcoming a hotch-potch of eccentric foreigners to his wayward fiefdom.

But later – after we go – there must've been a riot. The following morning the entire pavement is a skating rink of yellow yolk and albumen. The atmosphere is leaden. And there are schoolboys on the bridge, hurling onions at him. A local woman walks by, with her dogs, she stands and stares at them. 'Shame on you,' she keeps saying. '*Shame* on you.'

But the boys keep on throwing, their eyes glazed over, like they can't even see her, like they can't even see him.

The cockney girl is still there, still hollering, still banging on her tambourine. And she seems to be singing straight *at* them. She's plum in the firing line of all those onions (remember that deal with the angle of the bridge and everything?) but she seems actively intent on provoking them further. And I don't know why. I'm not sure whose *side* she's on. And I'm not honestly sure if *she* knows, either.

It's been so long.

Soon the fences come down.
    They erect a huge screen.

The last day. A Sunday. By early afternoon, gangs of people are starting to line the bridge already. And there are dense crowds on the embankment, including huge Asian families from the East End who are wandering around cheerfully, secure – for *once* – in the knowledge that they won't be the people having the fruit thrown at them.
    The stairs are jammed. The T-shirts are selling. Strange

music is playing over the loudspeaker (dippy, shitty, modern, *hippie* stuff with a female singer). The angle of the box has been readjusted, to give a larger crowd a much better view of it, and on the massive screen a static image of Blaine is being projected, an unflattering shot, which looks like it might possibly be the passport photo of a down-at-heel worker from the Algerian Embassy.

There is an ambulance.

Blaine has his back to the crowd. He's talking – through a hatch – to the people in the disabled access / viewing area behind him. It's a long conversation. But the crowds don't care. They're so full of happy anticipation. Sometimes he lifts up his mattress and peaks out through the glass bottom and interacts with the people directly below him.

He looks wan, and so thin, now. His hair is flattened down over his forehead. And every so often he pulls at the beard on his chin, neurotically, as if he longs to yank the bristle clear out of the skin. But he's holding it together. In fact he's *finding* himself again. Little by little that necessary transition is taking place – from sitting-duck to superstar, from total access to none.

Bly says she'll come, and even *Solomon* says he might drop by (you believe *that*? Then you'll believe anything). Twenty minutes till lift-off, though, and I'm here all alone, slightly surprised that the bridge isn't busier.

. At the far end – apart from the roasted chestnut stall and the hot-dog seller – it's still relatively negotiable. Way off in the distance you can see the box – hanging, luminescent – but a tree obscures the big screen where a documentary is being played (this is presumably Korine's big moment) in which Blaine appears to be pulling out his own heart on a quiet London street, in front of a bemused-looking woman who plainly just wishes he'd shut up and fuck off.

There's shots of city pigeons, creepy, glockenspiel music, simpletons gazing confusedly at the camera, nudists, red balloons, all subtly intercut with ardent fans making speeches about how Blaine has taught us all something unforgettable about the human spirit.

I walk on, past the ticket kiosk (by the first of the two main towers), squeeze around the corner – things are getting pretty *tight* here – and see a woman climbing up on to some thick, hazardous-looking grey railings. I follow her lead and clamber up on to the other end. We balance precariously together there.

People of all colours are rushing by. Hasidic Jews in abundance with their hats, their ornate ringlets and their crazy silk attire. Kurds, Turks, Africans, hard-core Muslims, hooded gangs of city urchins. People with prams. *Toddlers*. An old Indian guy – like an ancient *mystic* of some kind – with his hair caught up into a bright blue turban, being pushed along in a wheelchair.

And the Pool of London is full of boats (to the foreground of the *Belfast*, which is lit from below, generating a mess of funnels and geometric shadows, like some

kind of lovely, moist, mad-angled Stanley Spencer);
they're mainly police launches (this thing could potentially be a logistical *disaster*), there's the fire-rescue
launch, and the harbour master . . .

Has this bridge *ever* been so full of laughter and bustle?

But we can't see him (not from here, not with the
naked eye), because the TV lights reflect off the box, so
he's just this hunched black shadow, like a fly swatted
against the glass, a smear. Only very rarely does the huge
screen project live images of him. And when it does, he
offers such a strange and violent contrast to the carnival
around him. Like one of those videotaped *kidnap* victims,
cruelly manipulated by terrorists to pull his home
nation's heartstrings.

Time passes. The party continues. But tonight we're
ALL to be held to ransom by the TV executives. Forty-
four days – to the minute, to the *second* – comes and
goes without incident, and *still* he remains suspended.
Some people are getting emotional, are shouting, '*Let
him down! Let him go!*' A nervous voice over an intercom
system tells us that there's only *one* more commercial
break, and then . . .

And then finally – *finally* – it's time. There's not a
countdown, there's not a drum roll, just a green crane
lowering a perspex box, a smattering of applause, and
when it lands, with a thump, he doesn't climb straight
out. He stays in. He seems almost *afraid* to leave
(remember Kafka? 'The Hunger Artist?'). He's changed
his clothes; still in his trademark black, but wearing a
loose robe and a scarf. And there's something so formal,
so poignant, so *dressed-up* about him.

He's posing for photographs. The stretcher is there,
the ambulancemen in their fluorescent yellow jackets.

Some scales. They take off his coat, his scarf, and weigh him. *Weigh him?*

He's lost four stone, they announce.

(So what're *we* meant to do now? Cheer? Like he's Weight-watcher of the Year?)

He seems – it's hard to tell – quiet? Overwhelmed? Bemused? He suddenly starts shaking. They wrap him up in a blanket. They ask him some questions. He begins to say something, and just as he opens his mouth, a terrible cacophony – or a magnificent one, depending how you look at things – roars out over the river.

Eh?

I spin about on my railings, craning my neck, but can't see anything. I jump down into the crowd. My T-shirt gets caught and I'm left momentarily dangling. I tear it free, push my way through to the edge of the bridge and peer over.

Ten thousand people have just turned, en masse, to see a tiny, hired boat, crammed to the *gills* with groovers and Brothers, and on the roof? Three shady figures, one with a mike. In the water around them, a still tinier craft in which a film-maker holds a camera.

It's Dizzee Rascal, this year's Mercury Prize Winner! He's singing his new single. '*Just a Rascal, Dizzee Rascal … Just a Rascal, Dizzee Rascal.*'

He's making himself a video – using the lights, using the crowds, using the atmosphere …

Wha?!

Can it be *possible*? That this scraggy, opportunistic East-End scrap is planning to steal the initiative – the limelight – from the world's greatest illusionist?

If I look closer I can make something else out. *Solomon*

(no word of a lie). He's waving from the back. He's beaming, ear to ear.

'DIZZEE!' I find myself screaming, when the song reaches its climax and then cuts out.

'*DIZZEE!*'

And as one, the people on that boat turn, look up at the bridge, and they *cheer*.

So what's the deal with Rasket? Has he come to push everyone's faces in it?

This sprig of young cum – this cocky afterthought – this shock of vitality?

And Blaine? What would *he* make of it? Does he notice? Would he *care*? Is he furious? Is he *beyond* all that?

I don't know. But I'm beaming. And the Rasket starts singing again, and the Brothers start dancing, and the boat takes a couple of reckless swerves, and the sound system is blasting back the nets on all those million pound riverside pads and flats . . .

First the nearly-Jew, starving?

Then the raucous *black* kid?

What the hell's *happening* to this neighbourhood?!

That night I watch the news and Blaine barely figures. The PM's had heart murmurs. Three soldiers are shot in Iraq. At about eleven I see a short report. They're saying it was all an anticlimax. They show Blaine, close-up, and it's a different Blaine from the one I saw on the bridge. It's a tragic Blaine. He's choked with emotion. And he's saying, 'I just want to thank . . .' and then this cry comes out of him. Like the squeal of a baby fox. A bleat. Then they carry him off.

It's only TV. But I swear to God, in that moment, my heart nearly stops.

Hang on a minute, though . . .

Listen. Listen *closely* . . .

In the background I hear *Rasket*; the relentless thud of his distinctive bass-line, the jackdaw cackle of his rebellious lyric. It's *him*. Yet nobody *mentions* Rasket's coup . . .

Sure, they want him in their colour supplements, and on their cutting-edge radio shows. But they need to squeeze him out of here. He won't *fit* here. He *just won't do*.

But guess what? *Fuck* them. *Yeah*. Fuck the deriders and the egg-throwers and the opinion formers.

Fuck them all!

Because he *came*, see? And he *sang*, and he *took*.

Hmmn. Wonder where he might've got *that* idea from.

So what happened after?

They took Blaine to hospital? They put him on a drip for seven days? They fussed over his electrolyte balance? They waited to see if he'd done himself 'any permanent damage'? They bid millions for his diaries?

On the BBC radio news, in the morning, they say, 'Illusionist David Blaine has left his perspex box after forty-four days and nights with apparently no food of any kind.'

Apparently.

Couldn't even give him *that*.

Isn't it all about *boxes*, huh? He arrived an illusionist but he came out something else. He changed (I *need* to believe it). But the world says you can't change. You pulled the wool over our eyes *once*, kid, you played tricks on us *before*. You made us feel all confused and stupid, and you could do it again, at *any* moment. We just can't – we *won't* – take you from one neat box and put you into another. No way. Uh-*uh*.

The following morning, a Monday, I return for the last time to the scene of the crime. And when I get to the point on the bridge where I caught my first glint of him – that initial sighting, that seductive perspex glimmer – there's just this huge *hole* in the sky. Even the crane has gone. And when I get to the far end, where all the cars used to honk their horns at him, I see every driver, turning and staring. I see their heads turn, one after the other. And all they see now are clouds and the tops of trees. And seagulls. But their heads *still* turn, and they

344

look. Car after car after car. And it's a ballet of I Miss You David.

A Symphony of He's Gone.

I got the words wrong. No kidding. The opening words. *Shane*. I said 'barely as tall as our perimeter fence' (Remember?), but when I looked – when I *checked* – I saw that it was actually 'barely topping the backboard of father's old chuck-wagon'. Which is better, *much* better, *eh*?

'I guess that's all there is to tell . .

Chapter 16. It's the shortest chapter you could ever imagine. And it ends:

'He was the man who rode into our little valley out of the heart of our great glowing west and when his work was done rode back whence he had come and he was Shane.'

Observe the total lack of punctuation.

(Jesus H. How'd he ever get away with that stuff?)

Not even a comma after 'whence he had come'? Or a *dash*?

Man.

Is Jack Schaefer some fuck-you, balls-out writer or *what*?